Eagle, Kathleen

ONCE UPON A WEDDING

DATE DUE

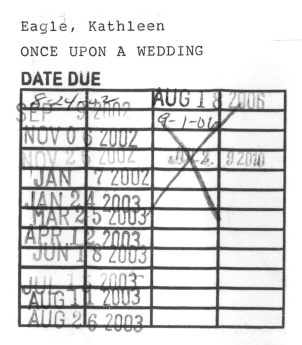

8-24-02	AUG 18 2006	
SEP 9 2002	9-1-06	
NOV 06 2002		
NOV 25 2002	JUL 2 9 2010	
JAN 7 2002		
JAN 24 2003		
MAR 25 2003		
APR 12 2003		
JUN 18 2003		
JUL 15 2003		
AUG 11 2003		
AUG 26 2003		

Once Upon a Wedding

Once Upon a Wedding

Kathleen Eagle

WILLIAM MORROW | *AN IMPRINT OF* HARPERCOLLINS*PUBLISHERS*

HarperCollins books may be purchased for educational, business,
or sales promotional use. For information please write:
Special Markets Department, HarperCollins Publishers Inc.,
10 East 53rd Street, New York, NY 10022.

FIRST EDITION

DESIGNED BY MICHAEL MENDELSOHN

Printed on acid-free paper

Library of Congress Cataloging-in-Publication Data

Eagle, Kathleen.
  Once upon a wedding / by Kathleen Eagle.—1st ed.
    p.   cm.
  ISBN 0-06-621472-6
  1. Mothers and daughters—Fiction.   2. Divorced women—
Fiction.   3. Weddings—Fiction.   I. Title.

PS3555.A385 I8   2002

                                        2001059631
  02 03 04 05 06 RRD/WBC 10 9 8 7 6 5 4 3 2 1

To Elizabeth and John,
from the Mother of the Princess Bride.
May September 30, 2000, be the first day
of happily ever after.

Acknowledgments

My thanks to the special women who inspired so much of the spirit of this book by showing me how a circle of women armed with needle and thread can work miracles by morning. Kay, Lillian, Donna, and Kelly, you are Elizabeth's fairy godmothers and my heroines.

Chapter 1

*I*n all four chambers of her practical heart, Camille Delonga believed that one of the surest ways of blowing a considerable pile of money was to hitch a girl's dream onto the six-foot train of a woman's wedding dress. The proof of her sentiment, in all its floral-scented glory, lay before her as she and her mother waited to be ushered to their seats in church. There the children of her friend for life, Bridget Mayfield, had been baptized.

Camille had dutifully been there for both babies. The first one had yowled like a tomcat on the make, and Camille recalled wondering how Bridget could live with that noise. The second, who would soon be walking down the aisle in a different sort of white dress from the one she'd worn over twenty years ago, had taken to her christening spotlight like a Christmas cherub. By then babies were looking downright darling to Camille, as were her own beach-ball belly and the bad boy who'd promised to be her mate for life. Soon the belly had deflated. Later the promise. But the beginnings had been glorious, filled, in the way of beginnings, with soft colors, summer flowers, and much music. Way too much music.

In the last year Camille had heard more about the details and the worries and the changes in the plans for Lauren's wedding than she cared to remember. But today, like the day of Lauren's first name-giving, all was right with the world. Bridget and Camille had seen each other through some thickheaded and thin-skinned times, and they were still friends. Bridget was the one who enjoyed playing in money. Camille preferred to put it to work, but she enjoyed seeing how Bridget's spending played out. Bridget called Camille a vicarious shopper, but neither saw anything wrong with that. They balanced, often beautifully.

Mother of the bride had been Bridget's best role ever. Every phone call began with a wedding update. She offered a wedding monologue every time they had lunch with Ellie Terrell, the third leg of their girlfriend tripod. Bridget would be soaring over some great wedding find one week and suffering over some perceived loss the next. "In for a penny, in for a pound" had become Bridget's mantra. *In for a pile of bills,* Camille thought, and she'd said as much, because they were friends.

Not that her opinion on this particular matter counted with Bridget, but thank God it counted with Jordan. "You don't need to be the princess bride," Camille had told her daughter a time or ten. "When your turn comes, have a small, tasteful ceremony, a party for close family and friends, and put the money you save toward a house."

Jordan always agreed, if tacitly. After all, no objection was as good as an agreement. Jordan could be quite sensible when she put her mind to it, which she often did these days. True, she hadn't stuck it out in college, but she had a good head on her shoulders. She could be anything she wanted to be, just as soon as she decided what that was. Camille had no reservations about putting all her pennies and pounds into her daughter's education, even when Jordan had dropped out. Education was never a waste.

"Mrs. Burke, Mrs. Delonga, you both look beautiful." Usher James Mayfield greeted them with a killer smile. "I've saved you two ladies the best seats in the house."

Camille tried to remember how long it had been since the bride's older brother had left home. He had known her as Mrs. Burke when he was growing up, but she'd reclaimed her maiden name after her divorce. James must have been in college by then. Bridget's kids had always been such good manner-minders, which somehow irritated Camille enough to want to correct James's error on the spot. But she beat down the urge. Both of Bridget's children had finished college. Ever-polite college graduates. Your basic *other people's kids.*

"You look like a million bucks in that tux, young man," said Rosemary Delonga as she took James's arm. "I suppose you've noticed how nicely my granddaughter has filled out."

Over the top of Rosemary's new platinum blond wig, James sent Camille a sweet, sheepish look. "Yes, ma'am, I surely have."

Camille smiled as they walked down the aisle to the strains of a string quartet. "How long will you be home?"

"Indefinitely," James whispered. "I'm moving back to the Cities. How's this?"

Seats on the aisle. Perfect. Camille went in first so that her mother would have the best view. "How're you doing, Mama? Feeling okay?"

"This is one of my favorite concertos. The musicians are good."

"They ought to be. They belong to the St. Paul Chamber Orchestra."

"Bridget has good taste." Rosemary settled back in the oak pew and opened the vellum program. "I just love weddings."

Since when? Camille wondered. She could count the weddings she'd attended with her mother on half a hand. The last that came to mind was her brother Matt's wedding. She'd been newly married herself then, but Creed had been on the road with his band and she'd attended without him. Camille had spent most of the reception with Mama and her friends, pretending she didn't notice that they were pretending not to wonder whether she had any regrets yet.

But before Matt's wedding, the Delongas had rarely proclaimed themselves the marrying kind. Mama had taken Camille to an older cousin's wedding when she was about ten or twelve. She remembered being the only kid among the few family members in attendance. Most of them had cried through the whole thing. When she'd asked what was wrong, Mama had whispered, "Nothing." Then she'd blown her nose, wiped, wiped again, and muttered, "Yet."

Later Camille remembered sitting in a green brocade chair in the ladies' room watching her mother repair a side seam in the weepy bride's dress and listening to Aunt Carol remind her daughter that she should have known the dress was going to be too tight by the time her wedding day rolled around.

That particular marriage had lasted two years, but the couple had managed to produce three children.

"I didn't know Ellie was going to sing," Rosemary whispered, her nose buried in the program.

"Bridget hired a professional soloist, but she backed out, so Ellie came to the rescue."

"Should've asked her in the first place. Nobody sings better than Ellie. Not *this* kind of music anyway." Rosemary offered her daughter the flying eyebrow, which always alluded to a supposedly obvious unmentionable.

Generally, the unmentionable was Camille's former husband, and the point, ironically, usually had to do with the virtues Rosemary had recently begun to attribute to him. Camille shook her head, chuckling. Creed's absence had made his ex-mother-in-law's heart grow decidedly fonder.

"Ellie's pretty nervous, what with all Bridget's fussing around over professional musicians. It was really short notice." Even so, Camille wasn't surprised when she found Ellie's name on her program. "But I see she managed to get these reprinted. No flaws allowed."

"Might as well do it right." Rosemary continued to scan the program, noting, "A pastor and a minister. Mixed marriage."

Camille gave a soundless laugh. The many recipes for marriage created the possibility of so much adventure. There were so many colorful mixes, complete with collaborative risks. It was enough to scare a mother spitless. Camille understood all that now. Recalling Mama's dire warnings, she swore she'd never utter them herself even if she were bursting at the seams with them. Still, fitting into her mother's shoes was not as unthinkable as it had been twenty-three years ago.

She couldn't imagine a man worthy of the dark-haired beauty who glided past her now, leading the wedding procession.

Somehow Jordan made the fluffy peach bridesmaid's dress look regal. "No, please, no bow on the butt," she'd begged, but Lauren had already made her selection. One by one the big satin bows passed Camille's pew. Plump maid of honor Marion Moony looked like a prize pumpkin, poor girl.

Catty, catty, two-by-four. The old chant echoed in Camille's head, clashing with the wedding march. She smiled at a nameless woman across the aisle, as though they were thinking the same thing, sharing in the wickedness the way she would have with Bridget and Ellie years ago. They'd done their share of critiquing fashions from the sidelines, until one of the three chided the others to restore order. "Catty, catty," was the call for charity. *Noblesse Oblige.* They'd believed in the natural superiority of the buff and beautiful. It had been easy back then. They'd had nothing else to go on.

The music changed. Throughout the church, feet shuffled, knees cracked, and people whispered, one to another. "Here she comes. Oh, look, here she comes."

Not one of Bridget's detailed descriptions had done justice to the designer gown's form-fitting, beaded silk bodice or to its voluminous skirt. Layer after layer of airy white tulle lapped the polished maple floor like sea foam and lent a dancer's grace to the bride's solemn stride. Beneath the silken veil, the girl's face was radiant. Her eyes sparkled. This was her moment.

With his daughter on his perfectly tailored arm, Timothy May-field had never looked more handsome. His summer tan seemed to add substance to his thinning brown hair, and his smile seemed remarkably effortless. Camille had felt vaguely prickly around Tim lately. She couldn't put her finger on what it was. But she was glad to see him smiling like a man who had something of value in his life rather than in his possession.

Camille tried to imagine Creed walking his daughter down the aisle. They would make quite a picture together, father and daughter. She liked the image, traditional as it was. For better, for worse, and for all the other double-sided pieces of change in the marriage bag, Creed had always cherished his daughter.

Most possessions, however, had not been terribly important to her former husband, including the wedding ring he'd seldom worn. He'd said jewelry bothered him when he played his guitar. Watches bothered him, too, and maybe it was because he never wore one that the passage of time did not. Camille hadn't heard from him in at least a year.

Has it been that long? he would say the next time they spoke, and he would sound genuinely surprised. Creed Burke could not keep track of time for love or money, which was one reason he'd lost out on both. He would *want* to walk his daughter down the aisle. He would have sterling intentions, and he would promise to be there, but whether it would be safe to put his name on the program was another matter.

Oh, but wouldn't father and daughter look beautiful walking down the aisle together?

"Where's the flower girl?" Rosemary whispered.

"Bridget said she didn't want any kid scenes."

Rosemary shook her head, taking in the peach-colored line of ladies happily waiting, flanked by the men in black who stood uncomfortably at attention like a row of pickets. "I'm surprised she left anything out."

Camille glanced at her mother, detecting fatigue in her voice. "If it gets too long, we don't have to stay."

"I'm fine. Wouldn't be here if I wasn't."

Camille had learned of late to take her mother at her word. She wasn't fine, but she was coping remarkably well with whatever she meant by "fine." It had taken her a while, but Rosemary had become a trouper. Now that she was living with Camille and Jordan, she could afford to be.

Or maybe she'd always had an inner strength that she'd never been called on to use. Her illness had brought out a capacity for tolerance that nobody had suspected she possessed. Unquiet music, unusual movies, unsunny days, and *very* unlikely people were all just fine with Mama these days.

But then she was on some very fine drugs.

Ellie's solo rendition of "Morning Has Broken" was beautiful. The bride and groom's personal vows—which Bridget had proposed to edit, but her friends had successfully restrained her—fell short of good poetry but were certainly sweet. The exchange of rings prompted more than a few of the witnessing couples to clasp hands. The kiss was timeless, the applause heartfelt, and the recession joyous.

And then came the wait.

"We're not going to stand in that line, Mama." Camille eyed the crowded aisle and then scanned the far corners of the church for a side exit. "Are you sure you're up for the reception?"

"I wouldn't miss it. Bridget's not one to skimp on the goodies." Rosemary waved at someone behind Camille. "Ellie, you little Swedish nightingale, you did us proud."

"You see there, honey?" From behind his wife, Stan Terrell put his slight hands on her sturdy shoulders and gave an affectionate squeeze.

"You were great, but don't take my word for it. You've got all kinds of compliments coming."

"Can I collapse now?" She tipped her head to the side, gave at the knees, and sank to the level of Stan's shoulder. "I'm going to take you two at your word, but I think that was my swan song. I was so nervous." On a quick breath, Ellie inflated herself back to her full height. "I think Bridget expected a little more . . . I don't know . . . oomph."

"What are you, a tuba?" Camille laughed as she reached for Ellie's hand. "Bridget's in a complete tizzy, but she had to love your song. It was beautiful, and it was you. Ellie Oomph."

"Oomph city," Stan added. "My golden-throated tuba tubby. The pink one."

Camille would have elbowed him in the paunch, but Ellie gave him an affectionate squeeze.

"Tubby the Tuba," Rosemary corrected.

"Wrong era, Mama. And I don't see any tubbies here."

"Your daughter's not fifty yet," Ellie reminded Rosemary. "Still floatin' in de Nile."

"That's right. I'm the baby." Camille smiled just enough to form her single dimple. She had almost another year. "How many dances can you spare me tonight, Stan?"

. . .

James Mayfield's silky smile still affected Jordan the way it had when she was fourteen. A surefire trigger for the flippin' fuzzies. Deep down inside her the chrysalises were silently splitting open, one by one, tickling the walls of her stomach even before the sound of his voice set the butterfly wings aflutter.

"If the limo is crowded," he offered, "I have room for you in my car."

Richard Frazier beat her to the punch.

"Yeah, we'll jump in with you," Jordan's assigned groomsman said eagerly. With a glance he dismissed the two white luxury cars parked next to the curb. "I hate crawling over all those—"

James took Jordan's arm. "Actually—Richard, is it? Actually, the backseat of my car is full of stuff. I just moved."

Jordan looked up at James, sufficiently dumbfounded by his proprietary move that she couldn't think of one for herself. She had resigned herself to being marionette for a day, being placed according to Lauren's master plan and enduring any hardships her role as lead bridesmaid might entail—including her old friend's boring new brother-in-law—like a true woman. Was liberation now at hand?

"Oh." The younger man rocked back on his heels, befuddled. "Yeah. But we're kinda paired up, and Mrs. Mayfield wants us all—"

"The rest of them are all loaded up, and Mrs. Mayfield is nowhere in sight." James touched Jordan's bare back and directed her toward the blue car in the parking lot. "I'm thinking one less dress in that boat to get crushed."

"Okay, well . . ." Richard didn't seem to realize that he had nothing to say about the decision. He glanced at Jordan as he took a couple of backward steps toward the limo. "See you at the hotel?"

She gave a quick nod and a perfunctory smile, which disappeared the moment Richard decided to turn and walk forward.

"I'm going to drown your sister in the punch bowl for sticking me with that *dweeb*," she said under her breath.

James laughed.

Jordan wished to God she had chosen a different word.

"I thought I detected a little ill will in the front line," he said as he opened the car door for her. "Slim pickin's among the penguins is what it looks like, although Tony's roommate seems like a good guy."

She glanced at him as she gathered up her skirt. He smiled, obviously unaware that it felt weird to have him open a door for her, never mind standing there holding it open until she'd reeled in all her drapery. Giving his sister and her friends rides had never been his favorite assignment, but as a young girl, Jordan could ride for days on the cachet of simply being seen getting in and out of James Mayfield's car.

"There's a reason the roommate gets to be the best man and the brother gets relegated to fifth groomsman," she told him when he slid into the driver's seat. "He's just *so* obnoxious."

"How so is just so?"

"He's been hitting on me for two days, and he's pitifully devoid of hitting skills." She leaned back against the headrest and watched the changing view of green leaves, sunshine, and shadows through the sunroof. "I don't think he's brushed his teeth in a month."

"Same old Jordan." James chuckled. "That's why I thought I'd step in."

She turned to him, astonished. "To rescue me?"

"No, him. Spare the poor boy's ego."

"Spare the toothbrush, sacrifice the ego," she quipped.

"Cold but fair. A real Minnesota forecast from a Minnesota girl."

"I'll give you my chicken breast if you head him off whenever he leans in my direction. I'll even throw in my cake."

"There'll be no cake throwing at this shindig, young lady. Besides, I still have problems with the knee you kicked the last time I tried to take your cake."

"Lauren's birthday party," she recalled. Oh, God, she'd hated him that day. She'd come into the kitchen after doing cartwheels in the backyard with the other girls, and he'd told her she was wearing nice pink underpants. She'd kicked him more for the humiliation than the attempted cake theft, kicked him so hard that Bridget had had to put an ice pack on his knee. Jordan remembered the angry look she'd gotten from Bridget.

"Don't call me 'young lady' unless you want me to mistake you for my mother, which would ruin your fun and my prospects for salvation. Did I ever apologize for that?"

He shrugged. "Not in so many words. How do you know I'm not already spoken for tonight?"

"I asked Lauren. You're not spoken for at all. And I've seen you dance, so I know your feet are screwed on straight. I promise to watch out for your bum knee."

"You always were a bossy brat. I was hoping you'd outgrown that."

"You had no hopes with regard to me, James Mayfield."

"Maybe I do now."

Jordan wouldn't bet on it, but it would amuse her to spend an evening speculating. If she could remember that not every comment required a clever rejoinder, she could surely hold her own for a few hours with James the Genius, as his mother had dubbed him. Let him do a little speculating, too. She pulled down the visor, checking the mirror, more for reassurance than lipstick.

He laughed. "Or maybe I will by the time the night's over."

· · ·

In her stunning pewter Vera Wang, Bridget should have been in her glory. Her daughter's wedding was the best party she'd ever put together. The hotel ballroom, already rich in gilt and glass, had been made lush with the fragrance of flowers and food, the soothing trickle of fountains, the opulence of added fabric and finery, all carefully arranged under Bridget's watchful eye and according to her precise plan. Like Camille, she had only one daughter, and that daughter would have only one wedding. Mayfield marriages were designed to last a lifetime. Lauren's wedding was to be Bridget's signature achievement. The guests stood in awe.

But Bridget herself seemed let down. From her station at "the odd-couple" table, Camille watched her old roomie drift from group to group, table to table, her smile less than inspired. Maybe she was nervous about the cake cutting, or maybe a few guests had neglected to RSVP but had turned up anyway. Perhaps the kitchen had run out of free-range capon with wild rice.

Camille had suggested she choose Rock Cornish game hen instead of capon to head off the inevitable dispute over whether a castrated cock could ever truly range free and whether such a meal was appropriate for a wedding feast, even if it was a specialty of the house. She was frankly surprised to see the capon make the final cut.

She didn't realize she'd commented aloud on the menu until Rosemary's laugh compounded her surprise.

"Chicken is chicken, honey, and it's something you've never been, except in situations like this." Rosemary patted her daughter's hand. "I'm sorry, but I'm just not up to leading the way anymore. You'll have to mingle cold turkey."

"I'd rather read the menu with my mother and watch the pretty people on parade," she said. "Unless you're not up to any of it."

"Are you kidding? I'm hungry." Rosemary perused the elegant menu card. "Did I order chicken or beef?"

Camille was not a happy mingler, and she was grateful to her mother for providing her with a reason not to take her usual feeble stab at it. They would be like two dowagers. Let the company come to them, one or two at a time. Ellie, whose social skills were more like Camille's than Bridget's, found refuge at the odd-couple table after two widowed aunts had gone in search of punch and a bachelor co-worker of Tim's had gone off, too, undoubtedly glad the women had turned down his offer to bring them something from the bar.

"Can you believe Stan ran into somebody he knows in this crowd?"

"Of course I can believe it," Camille said. "Stan could go to the Arctic Circle and run into somebody he knows."

When Ellie had met Stan Terrell, he'd been a chef in a hotel restaurant. Ellie had been a teaching colleague of Camille's, but once she got married, she quit teaching to help Stan open his own small restaurant and catering business. Camille didn't teach any longer either, but the friends shared memories of those days and still had the "once-a-teacher" identity. They also traded the worries and pleasures of being entrepreneurs. And Stan and Camille shared a love of Ellie. It was all they needed in common to appreciate each other—no foursome necessary.

Her friendship with Bridget didn't quite work that way. If she and Bridget hadn't gone so far back, Camille's divorce might have done their friendship in. It wasn't so much the odd number for dinner, although to Bridget that could be as awkward as the loss of a table leg, but the odd sense she had that her single status made somebody—in this case Bridget—uncomfortable.

"She's not herself tonight, is she?" Ellie noted.

"Well, who would be?" Rosemary said.

"Bridget," Camille insisted. She was counting on her, in fact, and she wasn't sure why. "If anybody could pull this off and enjoy it, too, it would be Bridget. So why is she avoiding us?"

"We're not going to let her," Ellie determined as she waved the mother of the bride over to their table. From several feet away, Bridget tried to escape with a one-finger promise of a momentary return.

Camille discovered that her butt wasn't stuck to her chair.

"You're going to sit with us for a minute so we can persuade you that everything is going just beautifully." She dragged Bridget to their table and sat her down in the white-damask-draped chair between true-blue friends. "This thing has a life of its own now, Bridge, and it's the high-off-the-hog variety. Time for you to relax and enjoy yourself. How did the pictures go?"

"Fine, I think," Bridget said distractedly. "We'll see how happy we all are when we get the proofs." She gave a nervous laugh, checked her watch. "Dinner in twenty minutes. Wait till you hear the band. You'll stay, won't you?"

"Is there some sort of circle dance on the program? Because I'm not doing any animal imitations."

"No Funky Chicken?" Ellie teased, flapping her elbows.

"I'll never be that old. And I'm way past the Bunny Hop. The only partnerless dance I'll take part in is a traditional circle. I like the symbolism."

"What about the holding hands with strangers? She wouldn't shake hands when she was little because it meant holding hands with strangers."

Camille shot her mother a warning look. *No little Camille stories, please.*

"We hired an excellent dance band," Bridget said. "And there are plenty of unattached men here."

"I've seen one who looks old enough to be interesting and two who look young enough to be desirable." Camille lifted one shoulder, folded her arms. "All I have to do is decide which feature I can do without."

"Wouldn't it be easier to approach it the other way?" Ellie proposed.

"What other way?" Camille laughed. "Oh, that. Easier to begin with, maybe."

"And more fun. Accentuate the positive and you can go by instinct. Mood." Ellie mugged with delight. "By feel."

"Good idea. When the lights go down, I'll walk around and pick a partner by feel." Camille tried to get Bridget involved. "How long are you hosting the bar?"

"All night, for those who behave themselves."

"We're taking our business elsewhere, Mama," Camille said across the table, then turned back to Bridget. "You didn't tell me that James had moved back home."

Bridget jumped on the change of subject. "I'm hoping he'll go back to graduate school and do what he was meant to do. He's so gifted."

"What was his major? History?"

Bridget measured an inch between professionally manicured fingernails. "He's this close to his master's in archaeology, and he works for a bank. It's such a waste."

"Not if it pays the bills," Rosemary said.

"He's going in circles, though. Once they get sidetracked by a paycheck, it's hard to get them to see beyond that." Bridget glanced at the empty middle chairs at the head table. "But Lauren and Anthony are going to be just fine. I've seen the last of her tuition bills, and Anthony's father is bringing him into his firm. She'll be fine. He comes from a fine family." She turned to Ellie. "Did you meet the Fraziers?"

"We did. Nice folks."

"Folks," Bridget said with a flighty titter. "Lauren has two sets of 'folks' now. Can you imagine?" She glanced at Camille. "Is Jordan ready to go back to school yet?"

"I'll let you know when she is, Bridge." Sore subject. For the moment the fun was over, and it had nothing to do with the fact that the woman Bridget had hired to move people around was headed toward them. "Your director summons, dear. Is it time for your close-up?"

Bridget hopped up as though she'd been bitten in the butt. "They must be here! I have to make sure the trumpeter is in place, and the carpet, and that everyone has . . ."

They watched her hurry away muttering. Ellie went to locate Stan, and Camille helped Rosemary find a shortcut around the crowd as they sifted like fine hourglass sand through the ballroom's double doors and poured into the lobby, where tuxedoed waiters passed trays of champagne for a proper greeting of the wedding party.

"Are you getting tired, Mama?"

"I'll let you know," Rosemary snapped. She caught herself and repeated gently, "I'll let you know, Cammy. I want to soak it all in as long as I can."

Camille gave a tight smile. "We don't know most of these people."

"But they're celebrating Lauren's wedding, and we watched Lauren grow up."

And now they watched the beautiful young people claim the limelight as they were trumpeted, toasted, applauded. What had long struck Camille as extravagance suddenly seemed right—especially when James Mayfield ushered Jordan into the lobby, both of them laughing at only they knew what. They were together in a way that struck Camille with an all-over sense of knowing. It wasn't clairvoyance. It was *care*voyance. She'd always hated it when her own mother had known about her business before she'd had a right to, but she'd come to understand that the right to know wasn't an issue with motherhood. The *issue* was the issue. Knowing simply came, not with the territory but with the womb.

And there it was, written in her daughter's smile as only a mother could read it. James Mayfield.

"We watched him grow up, too," Rosemary said quietly. "A rare comfort, that."

"Meaning?"

"Meaning I see what you see, but not the same way."

"Meaning?"

"Meaning I've been there, Cammy." She offered that welcome, if infuriating, knowing smile. "And in spite of all that, you're still my daughter."

.   .   .

James kept his promise to monopolize Jordan. Not that he'd made that promise in so many words, but words didn't seem necessary. They were a couple, at least for the evening. If he helped himself to something, he offered her some. When she spoke with someone else, she included him. It all seemed to take a natural course. No one interfered. No one tried to separate them for dining or dancing or drinking. They wore couplehood well.

Because they'd been dancing like dreamers, it put her off balance when he lifted his cheek from hers to ask a mundane question.

"So you still live at home?"

"Well, yes. For the time being. My grandmother's been sick." She blinked against the light, which was annoying, if soft. "She's going to be fine now. She had surgery, but she seems to be recovering, getting her strength back."

"That's good."

"Yes, but it gave us a scare. I need to stick close by and help out."

"Hey, there's nothing wrong with living at home. I did it myself when I was a kid."

She gave him a reproving glance, one that might have passed between them often, had they been together the way it felt that they had—the way they fit together, flowed together, each filling all the spaces left by the other. God, it felt good. It all worked perfectly, as though they'd learned the steps together and had been together forever. But this was the first time.

She was usually quite self-conscious when she danced—how she looked and felt, what other dancers thought of her moves, her partner's moves. But she had none of those thoughts dancing with James. On a floor full of wedding dancers, only one pair mattered.

She didn't recognize the song the band was playing, but she recognized what her father called "domesticated" country music. *Country stock with the horns knocked off.* Or maybe it was just some old song you always felt as though you'd known in another life. She wasn't about to ask what it was and open herself up to another "kid" joke, but she wanted to know, to remember.

James smiled. "Reminds me of your dad's band."

It didn't surprise her that he could read her mind. It wouldn't shock her if he could predict her next thought. The fact that her father figured into all this was the only surprise.

"I used to think of excuses to go over to your house so I could listen to them practice," he explained.

"You liked country music?"

"I used to think Creed Burke was the model of cool."

"So did I, but I wouldn't have taken you for a country music fan."

"I was sorry to hear about them splitting up."

"The band?"

"Your parents."

"Oh." *The band* would have made more sense, but his sympathy touched her where she was unaccustomed to being touched. Hoping to pass the pity like a hot potato, she scanned the room for her mother, muttering, "I don't hear that very often."

Her mother hadn't budged from her table. She and Grandma had attracted some old couple to their table—probably related to Tony. They looked more like Frazier elders than Mayfields, who tended toward shabby chic even in their dress. She had to remember to steer clear of James's grandmother, Ramona, whose wedding gift to the bride and groom was undoubtedly a wet blanket. Thank God her grandmother hadn't lost her sense of humor. But as for her mother . . .

"You don't hear *what* very often?"

Jordan looked up, saw his concern, and thanked him with a smile. "That someone was sorry to hear about them splitting up. I thought it was just me. Everyone else seemed to see it coming."

"Do you see him much?"

"Not anymore. At first I did, but we both got busy with our lives." She bounced the disappointment off with a shrug. "Separate ways, separate lives. That's what happens to families these days."

"And look what happens to the kids." He teased her with his irresistible lopsided grin. "You turn your back for a few years, and they disappear."

"Not altogether."

"Close enough to please me without breaking any laws."

"Age is so relative. I mean, look at you. You were a young man when you went away."

"And now I'm over the hill."

"Not until October tenth, when you'll turn thirty." She could tell that her memory came as a pleasant surprise to him. "I can't help it. Trivia is my forte."

"Everybody needs at least one. Meanwhile, I'm trying to calculate whether you're old enough to drink."

"I'm the same age as your sister."

He laughed. "My sister will never be old enough to drink."

"Twenty-three, still living at home, college dropout, no longer a virgin. What else do you want to know?"

"Not the last part. Take that back."

"I was kidding," she said too quickly. "Okay, I was trying to be clever, and I haven't quite got the hang of it yet."

"Stick with me, baby. You will."

"Why, James Mayfield, I would never have guessed." She offered a saucy smile. "You're not very good at it either."

Chapter 2

The next morning Jordan swept into the sunny blue-and-white kitchen as though she were about to host a talk show. "Good morning, dear Mother," she chirped as she took a mug from a cup hook in the cupboard. "Dear Grandmother, good morning." Rosemary merited a passing peck on the cheek on the way to the coffeepot. "How are you feeling?"

"Not as good as you, obviously. Is it safe to assume you enjoyed the wedding?" Rosemary asked.

"The wedding *was* nice, wasn't it?" Jordan brought her coffee to the table.

"Ah, but the reception was even better, wasn't it? The beef, the cake . . ."

"Delectable, indeed."

"I thought you had the chicken," Camille said, nearly deadpan.

"Was there food, too?"

Jordan's giggle reminded Camille of her daughter's boy-crazy days. Thank heaven she'd made it through that period relatively unscathed. Although Rosemary had been no help, talking up this one and teasing about that one. Beefcake *indeed*.

Even now it was to her grandmother that Jordan leaned to confide, "I got goose bumps every time he'd say anything to me when we were dancing."

"Silver-tongued devil, is he?" It was hard to believe Rosemary had needed help getting out of bed that morning, the way her eyes were dancing now.

"I don't know about his tongue yet, but his breath felt like gold dust trickling down the side of my neck."

"It's a little early in the morning for purple prose," Camille said flatly. "I thought you'd outgrown that old James Mayfield crush."

"What is it with the outgrowing? That's what he said." Jordan sat back in her chair, smiling. Mother and grandmother didn't have to hear the recorder in her head to know that it was replaying every word and nuance from the previous night. "No, he *hoped* I'd outgrown some nonsense or other. I kicked him in the knee one time, and he still remembers it. Can you believe it?"

"I can if he aches when it rains," Rosemary said.

Camille gave her daughter exactly the cautionary look she was expected to give. "As long as it's just his knee that aches."

"I hope . . ." Jordan's wicked chuckle sounded nothing like the giggle of a moment ago. "I hope he's aching all over this morning, head to toe."

"Do tell," Camille said. "Where did you kick him this time?"

"I laid neither foot nor hand nor any part of my person on the man."

"I hope he can say the same of you."

Jordan looked her mother in the eye and smiled. "But I think I made a lasting impression nevertheless."

"With what?"

"Cleverness. Not to mention the proximity of my nubile young body."

"Nice talk in front of your grandmother."

"I'm just wondering if I can still be nubile," Rosemary said. "Do you have to be young to be nubile?"

"See? Grandma's totally cool. You're the one who's getting that hint of indignation in her tone when you could be taking a cue from your own mother. God, Mom, mobilize your own nubility before it's too late."

Camille turned to Rosemary. "Did she just tell me to get a life?"

"I think so. And I'm telling you to get off her case so we get a few more details." Rosemary sighed. "It's too late for anything but vicarious nubility for this ol' gal."

"Well, I also hit him with my pheromones," Jordan said.

"You forgot to tell me about pheromones, Mama. I had mojo, but I didn't know anything about pheromones."

"They work like a charm," Jordan said. "I could tell he was blindsided. He didn't know where it was coming from or what it was, but the scent was irresistible."

"Who makes it?" Rosemary wanted to know. "Chanel?"

"I make it," Jordan claimed proudly. "Nobody else does, just me. I must not have had my own recipe when I was fourteen, but I do now."

"I'm worried about what his recipe does to you. He's still a little more . . ." The word "experienced" came to mind, but Camille knew better than to make that suggestion. "Well, the age difference hasn't changed."

"Of course it has. It's good that he caught up to me last night, because in another year or two I'd probably pass him up." Jordan braced her forearms on the edge of the table. Clearly it was all she could do to keep from hugging herself. "We had so much fun last night. Everything just clicked. What we said, what we did—everything. It felt so right, just the way we danced together. I mean . . ." She gave her mother and grandmother that look of frustration over the generational language barrier. "It's hard to describe."

"He seems like a nice boy." Rosemary turned to Camille. "What was it Bridget said he was going back to school for? History?"

"He didn't say anything about going back to school," Jordan reported, as though she would be the first to know. "It sounds like he's doing well at his job. His transfer came with a promotion. I'm sure he's all done with school."

"Maybe for now, but you never really know when you'll want more school," Camille reminded her. She couldn't resist, even though she knew she'd have a better chance of furthering her hopes if she kept quiet about them.

"School is not the answer to everybody's *every* need." Abruptly Jordan pushed up from the table, taking her half-full coffee mug with her to the sink. "I've been feeling the need for a little more independence lately. I'm thinking of looking for a place of my own."

Camille stiffened. "But there's so much room here, and your rent is so low."

"See, that's the thing." Jordan, who never did her dishes, was actually rinsing her cup. She smacked the faucet handle down. "I feel like I *should* be paying rent."

"Why? This is your home."

"I know." She turned to face her mother. "But it's not my own place. I just think it's time for me to give it another shot."

"School?"

"Being on my own," Jordan said quietly.

They hadn't talked about this for a while, not since Rosemary had come back home to stay. She had not sold her condo, which was the sensible thing to do, but they all knew that she would never leave again. And the condo was Rosemary's own place.

But the house had not been Mama's. It had been *Mama and Daddy's*. After Jack Delonga had died, Rosemary stayed in the house for two more years. Soon after Jordan was born, she had sold the house to Camille and Creed because Camille hadn't wanted to let it go. Rosemary had made it possible, even easy for them to buy the house. It was her official, if tacit, acceptance of the marriage she had opposed.

Camille had had no problem staying on there after the divorce. The house had always been her home. She understood Jordan's need for a place of her own, even though she flinched whenever Jordan used the phrase. But it wasn't time yet. The education, the preparation, the grooming of Jordan were still incomplete.

"I thought you were going to finish school first."

"What made you think that?" Jordan turned to the sink again, then glanced back at her coolly. "A round of concerted wishful thinking?"

"On the contrary, Miss Knows-All Woman, it's what *you're* thinking that makes me think you must be ready to go back to school and become a teacher instead of an aide. You want a place of your own on an aide's salary? In this town, honey, you might be able to afford one room in a neighborhood with bars on the windows."

"At least they'll be *my* bars and *my* windows."

Leave it at that, Camille told herself. She caught the same warning in Rosemary's eyes, but she'd already decided not to hold back.

"They'll be some absentee landlord's bars, and you'll get *one* window."

"I'm going to jail now for my shortcomings?" Jordan's laugh came surprisingly easily. "Grandma, have you noticed how little slack these successful people allow for us working stiffs?"

"All you need is a couple of semesters—" Camille persisted.

"And I'll get them," Jordan told her mother patiently. "I promise I'll do my time." She raised her palm, signaling for a yield. "Someday. And I believe Dad said I was *Daughter* of Knows-All Woman."

"It's just that you're so good with kids," Camille insisted, trying very hard to sound wise rather than whiny. She hated it when the tone in her head didn't match the one that came out of her mouth. "And you're worth so much more."

"Right now I'm worth what I'm worth." Jordan put her cup in the dishwasher. "And I'm not worth much when I lose half the morning. I've got things to do."

"I know I'm not worth much today," Rosemary put in. "After last night's revelry I'm pooped. That's as late as I've stayed up in more than a year."

"You kids must have reveled until the wee hours." Camille took her mother's cue instinctively, using her mother's old script. "I don't know what time it was, but I heard—"

Jordan cut her off with a glance. "You'd sleep better if I didn't live with you."

"My weird sleeping patterns have nothing to do with you," Camille said. "I just can't seem to sleep through the night anymore."

"You simply can't stop yourself from keeping track of my comings and goings, Mom. Be honest. We can't just be roommates."

"You and I can be roommates, Jordie." Rosemary said. "We'll let Knows-All Woman be the housemother."

"Oh, Grandma." Jordan tipped Rosemary's strawberry blond wig askew from behind as she slipped her arms around the old woman's neck and bussed her cheek. "If I ever need a roommate, you're the first person I'll call."

"You'll need one if you decide to move out," Camille grumbled, glancing away from the kiss as though she'd caught herself spying on lovers.

She felt almost jealous, which really was a ridiculous notion. Why would she be jealous of the wonderful relationship between grandmother and granddaughter?

The ensuing silence felt awkward. Camille stared into her coffee, worried that looking up would give away her confusion. Jordan was able to express herself easily, and Camille admired her for it. She was especially demonstrative with her grandmother, always had been. This was a good thing, a healthy—

"The wedding really turned out nice, didn't it?" Jordan said quietly.

Camille looked up. All eyes were on her. She smiled and nodded.

"But those *dresses*." In her crisp blouse and slacks, Jordan assumed a prissy arms-out, hands-up pose, batted her eyelashes and pursed her lips. "Five dollies on the shelf."

"They weren't that bad," Camille said. "You looked beautiful, honey."

"Nobody's ever going to wear them again," Jordan said. "I think you should try to choose something that looks nice on everyone. But on the whole it all turned out really well. Lauren and Tony were on cloud nine."

She sat down at the table again, apparently changing her mind about being on her way before Sunday morning turned to afternoon. "So give it to me straight," she began, folding her hands, looking from one woman's face to the other like the teacher her mother thought she should be. "Do you think marriages last longer when you make a big production of the wedding?"

Her question surprised them both.

"Well, I mean, isn't it like you're making a statement, or maybe an investment? It seems like people need to stand up in front of everybody they know and publicly commit so they can't back out so easily later on."

So easily? Camille knew exactly where the prissy finger was pointed now. And now she *did* need more coffee. Preferably spiked.

"What was your wedding like, Grandma? I know you had a beautiful dress. Did you have bridesmaids?"

"I had one. My best friend, Regina. She was my best friend all though school, and we stood up for each other when we got married. Then she moved to Texas, and we didn't see each other much after that. I got a nice note from her daughter after she died last year." She paid her respects with a pause, then offered Jordan a wan smile. "But she was my attendant, and I made both our dresses."

"Of course." Jordan nodded, undoubtedly assuming that everyone made their clothes back in the forties. "Where is it? I've only seen the one picture."

"The dress got lost in the great flood. It wouldn't have fit either of you anyway, and as it turned out . . ." Rosemary glanced at Camille. "Well, those were the days when I was the one waiting up on your mother, among other things. So she went off and got married in a plain brown wrapper."

"And it cost us all of twenty-four dollars," Camille said.

"Maybe that's why it didn't really take," Jordan said.

"You're here, aren't you? As far as I'm concerned, I got my money's worth."

"Isn't that what the Anglos paid for Manhattan?" Jordan said with a slow smile. "I don't know about you, but the Indians definitely got screwed."

"You don't know about me?" Camille raised an eyebrow. "As I said, *you're here, aren't you?*"

"Mother!"

They were laughing now, but Camille didn't like the direction this was taking. Ordinarily, she could easily handle these two against her one. Bring on the sex, religion, or politics, and she'd debate until they surrendered or went away mad because they knew damn well she was right. But not weddings. Weddings were not fun, not for debate. Not when it turned personal.

And what was more personal than marriage?

Camille sighed. "It really *did* take, honey, at least for a while. Maybe we should have gotten a booster after so many years, like a vaccination against"—she lifted one shoulder—"irreconcilable differences."

"I never understood exactly what that meant," Jordan said quietly.

"It meant that, in the end, your grandmother was right. Your dad and I came from two different worlds, and that little intersection we

made between them just wasn't solid enough to build a marriage on."
With a glance at her mother, Camille admitted, "We're just too different, that's all."

"He's a man, and you're a woman," Rosemary said. "It doesn't get
any more different than that."

Jordan laughed. "You could have married Bridget. Or Ellie. Or
both!"

"Right." Camille rolled her eyes. "Your dad and I got married in a
fever, as Mama has pointed out to me many times. We went to the
courthouse, then rented a room at the hotel where he had a gig that
night. That was our honeymoon."

"I'll bet he dedicated a song to his new bride that night." And
because Camille couldn't keep the answer from showing in her eyes,
Jordan pressed, "What was it?"

"Something like 'I've Got Friends in Low Places.' "

"No way. That's too recent." Jordan touched her mother's hand.
"C'mon, tell me."

"I think it was 'Always.' "

She wasn't fooling either of them. She *knew* it was "Always." If she
listened inside her head, she could still hear Creed singing that song.
She'd even thought about asking him to tape it for her again. In a very
different kind of fever, she'd burned all his tapes. When Jordan had told
on her, he'd given his daughter her own set. The hell with her mother.

The tapes were all homemade. Creed had never had anything
professionally recorded—never even rented studio time to make a
demo, as far as Camille knew. Not that he doubted his talent so much,
but he insisted on avoiding success at all cost.

"What would you do differently if you could go back? One thing."
Jordan wouldn't let up. "Not marry him?"

"I can't say I wouldn't . . ." Camille glanced at Rosemary, whose face remained unreadable. No triumph of the truly all-knowing, no antipathy, not even a hint of pity. Camille shrugged. "I mean, you change one thing, and everything else—"

"No, don't think about me," Jordan insisted. "Think about you and him. Would you cut that part out of your life, just erase it?"

"And replace it with what?"

"Would he leave a hole even if he'd never been there? If you'd never had a fever, would you be healthier now?"

Camille laughed. She was healthy. She couldn't be healthier. "What a crazy question."

"What do you think, Grandma? Would she turn him down if she could do it over again?"

"The way I heard it, the marriage was as much your mom's idea as your dad's. I've asked myself would she have married him still if I hadn't been so dead set against it? And I think she would have. I *know* she would have." Rosemary adjusted her wig, pulling at a synthetic curl. "It didn't have anything to do with what I thought. It had to do with how they felt, and maybe that was the part I objected to most. So I had no part in it."

"I was bound and determined, but you were right all along," Camille recited.

"My sentiments come back to haunt me."

"Well, you were. Even though, I have to admit, somewhere along the way you did stop making that claim. But the truth is, there was no way the two of us were ever going to make it together."

"Like you said, you made Jordan together."

"But we didn't make a successful marriage together."

"What was sixteen years?" Rosemary challenged. "Weren't there good times as well as bad? Just because they're both still wearing their rings when one spouse buries the other, does that make it a successful marriage?"

Camille glanced at her mother's hands. She had always loved them, even though they weren't particularly pretty. According to Rosemary, who had stubby fingers and prunelike skin, Camille was lucky to have inherited her father's hands. But Rosemary had *used* her hands. She was the essence of the handywoman. She crafted and created, designed and stitched. They were comforting hands, clever hands. And the only jewelry she ever wore on them—still wore, no matter what anyone said—was her wedding band.

Her gold band reflected the morning sun. "I'm just not sure it's all or nothing," she mused.

Rosemary examined her left hand, turning it from pale palm to spotted back. She still chewed her fingernails like a child, but pretty things were still made by those plain hands.

"What do divorced people do with their wedding pictures?" Jordan wondered. "Every time I turned around yesterday, somebody was taking pictures. I'll bet they spent five thousand dollars or more on photographers and videographers, not to mention all the personal cameras. I was just thinking . . . What do you do? Divide them in half? Tear them in half?"

"I wouldn't know," Camille said.

"Wasn't that picture of the two of you standing by the fountain in the hotel lobby taken on your wedding day?"

"That's all there is," Camille said, remembering that she'd stuck it in a box and put the box in the bottom drawer of her dresser. "Hardly worth going to the trouble of dividing."

"What I would do is save them for my children," Rosemary said.

"Time passes, people move away, pass away, and you realize your history is slipping away with them. Then you start trying to track these things down. You don't think about keeping family history so much when you're young, when your tax records and bank statements become your personal paper trail." She slid her own daughter a reassuring glance. "Doesn't matter whether they're divorced. Your parents are your parents, and their parents are your grandparents, and so on up the tree. Family is still family."

"Which makes me think I haven't seen Dad's sisters in ages," Jordan said. "I should drive out to South Dakota and surprise them."

"They'd like that. They always made such a fuss over you." Camille smiled. "And I'd go with you. I didn't divorce the Burkes."

"Or the Little Moons? Or the Bad Hearts?"

"One of Creed's aunts told me that they were going to keep me and disown him for letting me go. Frankly, I don't think they see much of him anymore either."

Jordan plucked at the fringe on the blue place mat on the table. "James said he grew up thinking Dad was the coolest guy around. He used to dream of playing in a band, too."

Camille groaned. "Most boys go through that, but eventually they grow up."

"Dad must be doing okay. He has a house with more than one window."

"Back on the *reservation*," Camille said. She realized how patronizing she sounded, but she resisted the temptation to try to recant.

What was there to recant? He'd inherited a little house from his mother's brother, which gave him, he said, a place to put his stuff. And it *was* on the reservation.

"Anyway, I doubt that he spends any more time there than he did here."

"He was a musician when you married him," Jordan reminded her. "You should've known."

"That's right, he was, but I'd never known any musicians." She laid her hand over Jordan's. "It's nobody's fault, honey. It doesn't have to be anybody's fault. Sometimes things start breaking down, and you can't repair them. It might only be one or two parts that get corroded, but the marriage won't work without them."

"If it were my marriage, I'd work on it. I'd get new parts."

"Sometimes things have already gone too far, and there's no going back. You can't live with them the way they are, and you can't change them."

"So don't get married?"

"I'm not saying that."

"But something's bound to go wrong sooner or later," Jordan said. "You just have to work it out."

Camille knew exactly what her daughter was thinking. She remembered having the same thought. *I'll do better than my parents did.*

She smiled. "You'll do fine."

"Maybe I won't get married."

"You'll still do fine."

"Or maybe I'll get married in a big way. Big statement. Big hair, big dress, big party."

Camille groaned.

"What kind of a wedding did Bridget have?" Jordan wondered.

"Outdoors, by the lake, wildflowers in her hair, gauzy dress by Gunne Sak." Camille laughed, remembering her chic roommate as a seventies flower child. "Can you imagine?"

"The bride was barefoot and pregnant," Rosemary supplied.

"Mama!" Camille came to the defense. "They were seniors in college, had no money, and the wedding was lovely. And it *took*. They're still together."

"What about Ellie?" Jordan asked.

"They had a nice little church wedding. It wasn't fancy," Camille recalled. "It was the church part that was important to Ellie. I can see that. But I still don't know why anyone would have a big production."

"I'm not sure I do either," Jordan said.

"A quiet ceremony, close family and friends, and a tasteful dinner party. I can see that, too," Camille said. But she'd said it before, and it occurred to her that the suggestion had never quite lit any sort of fire in Jordan's eyes. She offered a mother's smile. "I can see you looking radiant. I can see me, getting all misty. And I can see your grandmother—"

"Who do you see giving me away?"

"Giving you away?" Camille remembered asking herself the same question as she'd watched Lauren Mayfield walk down the aisle on her father's arm.

Why did that have to be the kicker? Why, in this day and age, did it even come to mind?

"I can't see you letting anyone give you away. You're much too independent for that."

"That sounds pretty good." Jordan patted her mother's hand. "As reasons go."

Camille laughed. As unsentimental as the three of them generally were, it was just one of those days for hand patting.

Chapter 3

Camille had finally gotten over the guilt she felt when she went to work.

She found it hard to believe she could earn such a good living playing in wax and clay. There were countless artists who were far more talented than she who would starve without their day job, but she'd quit hers years ago in favor of play-for-pay. So much for fairness. But with all those artists starving in China and elsewhere, Camille was obligated to appreciate her good fortune, to meditate on its roots while her hands took all the creative pains. She'd never felt guilty about teaching, but making metal sculpture at home was a dream job come true.

Today's image had come from the wedding. Father and daughter walking down the aisle, father of the bride, fortunate daughter. Fortunate when the weather was fair if you were the daughter of a fair-weather father, as Jordan was and as Camille had been. Storms kept some fathers away. But such was the fortune that art was made of. The image became the vining stems and falling petals that would form the fire screen a client had commissioned as a gift for his newly married daughter.

Quite a gift it would be. An original Camille Delonga did not come cheap. She had thrown her frugal woman's caution to the wind when she discovered that the higher the price, the happier the client. Craft shoppers were customers, but art collectors were clients. Shoppers bought, while collectors invested, which was why money was no longer an object in Camille's business. She had learned to name the price her unfettered market would bear without hesitation. One man's wedding gift for his daughter might pay for someone else's daughter's entire wedding. But any feelings of guilt Camille might have felt over naming her price had gone the way of guilt over getting paid for playing in her father's workshop.

She glanced at the far corner of the sculpture studio where Jack Delonga's hand tools still hung on the pegs where he'd always kept them. He had been a man of his time, a man's man who had fathered his children the manly way; he had planted his seed. From conception through age five they were fragile and messy. They were go-to-Mama creatures. But the moment her brother, Matt, had picked up a baseball bat, their father had known exactly what to do with him. *Play ball.*

Camille had remained a cute little curiosity until she'd discovered that she could earn a small piece of her father's attention in the workshop. When Matt had lost interest in the little toolbox he'd received for his birthday, Camille had claimed it. At the age of five, her main interest in the box was adding related items to its compartments, arranging, and rearranging her finds. But she'd soon discovered that the toolbox and her attachment to it were her ticket to the workshop, where she could spend precious hours in Daddy's presence.

But the answer to *Where's Daddy?* was usually *Gone to work,* which meant that he wouldn't be around for days and days. Jack was a pilot—first in the Navy and then for an airline. Camille grew up thinking of *gone* as a place, just like Washington or New York, where her friends' fathers occasionally went for their work. During her back-yard show days she'd made up a song about him called "A Real Gone Daddy." She'd sung it for Creed a time or two, mercifully omitting the choreography.

Creed had never known her father. They would have liked each other, she thought now. She recalled telling Creed as much in the early days. "You're so much like my dad."

"Is that good or bad?" he'd ask her each time, as though the answer might have changed.

"It's good," she always quipped. "I loved my dad."

And he'd loved her, too, in his way. He'd allowed her to share his workshop. Whenever he was home—actually within the walls of the house—he disappeared regularly into the basement to work on some wood project that he would never quite finish. He had allocated a cor-ner to Camille. She'd started working with wood, then discovered Daddy's soldering iron, and moved into metals and eventually over-took him in terms of production. But she'd tried not to take up too much more space than he'd assigned her himself, even after she'd come to realize he wouldn't notice unless she neglected to put his tools away. So she'd been careful. She'd been good. She didn't want to drive him away.

When Rosemary decided to sell the house, Camille couldn't see it go to strangers. By that time, thanks to her care and feeding of the checkbook, she and Creed had a nest egg socked away. It was Creed who'd suggested buying the house from Rosemary. Camille had been a teacher then, and Creed's band was a regular fixture in the local nightspots. But it wasn't until Rosemary was ready to sell her home that Creed's attitude toward committing to a mortgage softened. Camille knew that it wasn't the debt that bothered him; it was being tied down. He liked to think he could pick up and move any time. It was in the blood, he'd say. Indian blood.

But her mother's house was a different story. Creed had enlarged the workshop to better accommodate Camille's metal sculpture, which was gradually transforming itself from hobby to lucrative business. He'd encouraged her to plunge into her art full time long before she was willing to call herself an artist. When her pieces began to command handsome prices, she was able to consider the prospect of starting a business. She taught art, and she gave a good deal of credence to the adage that those who can, do; those who can't, teach. She wasn't really an artist. A craftsman, maybe. She'd become a master of her craft. She squirmed when people called her an artist, but she didn't protest anymore. The term made good business sense.

Her father had built the workshop. Her husband had expanded it. They had both gone from her now, leaving it all to her—the shop and the work. They'd left it to her to make a home of the house she and her brother had grown up in, make a life with her mother and daughter in a house devoid of men, make use of the workshop she now called her studio, make a living by making beautiful things to sell to people who made so much money they had run out of practical ways to spend it.

Fortunately, she had the wherewithal, and she had done it all. She had, in the eyes of many people, *made it*. Some would even say that, making a good living and being able to do it at home, she had it made.

"I have to be there by eleven."

Camille jerked around on her stool, banging her knee on the table leg. "Yow! Mama, you scared the living . . ."

"So it *is* a fright wig." Rosemary stuck out her lower lip and blew at the strawberry blond bangs of another new hairpiece. "I thought that salesgirl said it was just the *right* wig."

"No, you look fine." Camille tapped pencil point to the paper taped to the drafting table. "I was just lost in this project."

"And I was just joking. Try to take the hint, honey. It'll make things easier." Rosemary touched Camille's shoulder. "I'm sorry to take you away when you're working. I'd drive myself, but I won't feel like driving home afterward."

"It's no problem, Mama. I wish you'd let me stay with you through the chemo treatment."

"Not a chance. All I want is a ride." Rosemary handed Camille her purse and her car keys. "Remember how bored you used to get when you had to wait for me at the beauty parlor? I don't need you to sit there and watch them fix on me. I like to be able to relax in the chair."

"I promise not to tear pictures out of the magazines." Camille felt around under the desk with her feet for her shoes.

"You're going out to lunch with your friends, and I'm going to the clinic. That's the plan."

"Does it hurt, getting those treatments?"

"Not if I don't think about it, which I'll do if you're standing there watching me."

"But you let Jordan—"

"But you let Matt do it," Rosemary mimicked, far more affectionately than she used to. Lately all memories got the same gentle treatment, along with a wistful smile or a laugh. "Jordan's an easygoing kid, honey. You're not."

"I . . ." She couldn't argue that particular point. "I'm willing to stay."

"What? You don't want people to think you'd just drop your poor old sick mother at the clinic and go off for lunch with your friends?"

"I don't want you to think I won't be there if you need me."

"I don't want to use up your goodwill before I really *do* need you." Rosemary's wistful smile was for more than a memory of her daughter this time. "I know I can depend on you. There's no question of that."

"Then what's the question?" Camille asked. Dependability wasn't something that warranted such a sweet smile.

"Can we go pretty soon? My appointment's at eleven."

· · ·

"Lunch" with Ellie and Bridget had never been by appointment, nor was it always at lunchtime. But there was always food and plenty of dish. The get-togethers had become more frequent since nobody had kids to worry about anymore. Back in the mommy days, spouses had occasionally been included, but there had been no couple outings since Camille's divorce. The men didn't miss it—they would never have crossed paths unless their wives had been friends, even though Creed and Stan had hit it off pretty well. But who could make sense out of the way men valued friendship?

Fortunately, Camille didn't have to think about that—or any other strange aspects of men's emotional behavior—anymore. All she had to worry about was her *own* friends, and whether there was such a thing as post-wedding blues.

Ellie, as always, read her mind.

"What are you going to do with yourself now that the wedding's over?" Ellie asked Bridget after they'd ordered their soups and salads.

"She's going to have to go back to work to pay for it," Camille teased.

"You can't pay for a wedding like that on a teacher's salary, which is all I've ever done," Bridget informed her without even cracking a smile. Apparently it took a while to recover the sense of humor as well. "I have been thinking about getting some sort of a job, though. I just don't know what would be suitable."

Suitable? Bridget hadn't had a job in twenty years.

"You could plan weddings," Ellie offered, at least half seriously.

"Only for love," Bridget said. "That's a stressful job, planning a wedding. I want low stress, high pay, maybe a little travel, but only to meet with interesting people in luxurious places." She tapped steepled fingers together, nail tips to nail tips, and glanced up at the chandelier that was the restaurant's centerpiece. "Let's see, what else? Full benefits, security, autonomy, a generous expense account—the sort of perks someone with my qualifications deserves."

Camille slid Ellie a grin. "Are they advertising for a new princess anywhere?"

"You have to marry an insufferable snob for that job," Ellie said. "And then you have to live with your mother-in-law."

"Oh, but think of the wedding that comes with it," said Camille as she leaned back for the delivery of the water and tea.

"You can't be divorced," Bridget averred. "And since Timothy isn't a prince, I'd have to divorce him first. Otherwise, it's not a bad idea. I think I'd be good at it." She reached for the white porcelain box of pink and blue sweetener packets. "You didn't think Lauren's dress was too frou-frou, did you? I wasn't happy with the way it looked all crushed after she rode in the limo. I should have taken a cue from poor Princess Di. All that fabric gets rumpled so quickly."

"That's part of the tradition, isn't it?" Camille sipped her tea while her friends looked to her to elaborate. "You know, of course, that the rumpled white dress betokens the rumpled white sheets soon to follow. It's all part of the symbolism. Abundance, lushness, the juxtaposition of innocence and fertility."

Bridget smiled. "And the wrinkles, representing life's myriad little wrinkles."

"Which, of course, can be ironed out with a little patience," Camille said.

"And a lot of collagen." Bridget toasted the product with her glass of tea.

"By the way, ladies, they have wonderful desserts here." Camille, the chocoholic, always checked the desserts before considering an entrée.

"Not for me. I lost some weight before the wedding, but I found it again." No more than the size of an end slice of melon, Bridget's belly would have gone unnoticed if she hadn't given it a pat. "Believe me, in this case, there is no joy when that which was lost is found."

"So you can relax now. You might as well share a Chocolate Volcano with me," Camille offered. "The eruption that relieves the pressure, the flavor that soothes the soul."

"You're going to start worrying about weight one of these days, Cam, and I'm going to tempt you the same way."

"Promises, promises. How about you, Ellie? A little chocolate on chocolate with a soupçon of mocha on the side?"

Ellie's eyes widened, then quickly narrowed. "Camille, you are so wicked."

"Actually, I have put on a few more pounds lately, but who's weighing us in? Remember when we worried about chocolate giving us zits instead of hips?"

"The babies gave us hips," Bridget said.

"And turned the tits into boobs," Camille said with a laugh. "Speaking of babies, you must be pleased to have James move back."

"She's not the only one." Ellie smiled. "Jordan seems to be quite pleased, too."

Bridget took Ellie to task with a cool look, as though she'd made an indecent suggestion. "They were just dancing together."

"They came to pick up a sofa I offered him for his apartment," Ellie reported. She sipped her tea, bouncing a quizzical glance from the face of one friend to the other.

"*They?*" Bridget challenged.

"And the electricity between those two . . ." Ellie set her glass down slowly. "Put it this way, they could sell the excess to the power company and still be setting off sparks."

"That's ridiculous. Jordan's way too young for James." Bridget turned to Camille and snapped, "She hasn't even finished college."

For Bridget it was tantamount to accusing Camille of being an unfit mother.

"I know. I keep hoping." Camille gave a tight smile. "She likes her job."

"As a teacher's aide? Nobody likes being a teacher's aide." Bridget sighed, backing off physically as well as verbally. "Just the way nobody likes being a loan officer, which is what I keep telling James. He should finish his graduate work. He's just so gifted. And Jordan's definitely not . . ."

While Bridget weighed her choices, Camille's pointed glance warned Ellie to let her finish.

"Old enough."

Wait over, weight lifted.

"He's like her big brother." Bridget had to wonder at her friends' relief. "The very idea seems almost incestuous, don't you think?"

"What idea?" Camille asked innocently.

"The two of them"—Bridget's long, iridescent nails gave flash to her undulating fingers—"making sparks."

"I don't know about incestuous, but he's certainly not the man for Jordan," Ellie put in.

Bridget's initial nod went down with a scowl. "Why not?"

"Well, for one thing, he's not tall enough."

"Not—"

Camille was laughing now, shaking her head at Ellie, who didn't care a whit about being taller than her husband. Never had.

But Bridget didn't quite get it, and never had, so she continued to sputter.

"They're not . . ."

"Of course not. She's . . ." Camille gestured, palm up.

"Well, yes, and he is, too."

"And neither one of them is . . ."

"Not by a long shot," Bridget agreed.

"I don't know what you two are talking about, but I know what I saw," Ellie said. "And it was just as sweet as could be."

Bridget's hands-down gesture put the very idea to rest. "Not to change the subject, but how's your mom, Cam?"

"She's doing well." Camille nodded firmly. "She's going to be fine. The chemo makes her tired, but otherwise she hasn't been sick. It's just"—she tugged at her thick, mostly brown hair, which she'd always worn in a classic bob—"you know how she is about her hair."

"It grows back thicker than ever." Bridget flashed an encouraging smile. "That's what I've heard."

"The things we have to put up with," Ellie complained. "As if hot flashes weren't indignity enough. A guy looks fine with his head shaved. Right in style."

"Those are just inconveniences, Ellie," Bridget said. "Hardly worth mentioning when you've got cancer to worry about."

"I know. I didn't mean—"

"No, it is worth mentioning," Camille said. "It's all of a piece."

A piece becoming pieces. She saw herself catching pieces of her mother to keep them from falling away and then standing there like an idiot, not knowing what to do with them. It was *just hair.* But when it had happened, Rosemary's brave front had been the most heartbreaking part. The comment about all the money she would save on those weekly beauty shop visits had undone Camille completely.

"You want to keep it whole," she said quietly. "Keep *her* whole."

"We know how to fuss over hair," Ellie said. "That's something we can handle. We've done it all our lives."

"Our mothers taught us how." Bridget chuckled. "For the longest time I thought straight hair was a birth defect."

"I liked the way you had it done for the wedding," Camille said, trying to remember how Bridget's hair had actually been done that day.

"It wasn't any different, really, just a little bigger. You know I've always coveted your hair, Camille."

"Mama's gift. I should show you a picture of her when she was

Jordan's age. Everyone thinks Jordan is the spitting image of Creed, but when you see that picture of Mama . . ."

"I have."

"You've brought it out a time or two, Cam," Ellie supplied. "I can see both you and Jordan in your mother's face, even without a picture."

"Jordan's far more striking, which, of course, is Creed's gift."

The mention of his name brought the conversation to a momentary standstill. *The errant one.* His death would have been a more acceptable departure than divorce. Death was less threatening. Everyone did it.

"Have you heard from him lately?" Bridget asked finally.

"Not for a while. I don't know whether Jordan has, but I . . ." Camille shrugged, gave her head a quick shake. "So is everything back to normal in the Mayfield house?"

"It'll never be normal without the kids," Bridget said.

"Of course it will. You'll redefine normal." Camille forced a cheerful tone. "An office apiece, another den, extra closets. It'll be you and Tim, sprawling out all over the house."

"Naked if you want."

"Why, Ellie Mae," Camille chided, using the nickname Ellie had inevitably been teased with in school. "Bridge, what do you say we go out to the farm some night and do a little window peeping?"

Bridget closed her eyes. "Omigod, I can see it now. The mind boggles."

"No boggling," Ellie commanded. "You boggle, I jiggle."

Heads turned at the other tables as their giggling got out of hand. Gestures replaced the words they couldn't get out for the laughter. The serving of salads went nearly unnoticed.

"I don't know about sprawling all over the house." Bridget composed herself with the delicate wiping of a tear along the side of her finger. "We still have tons of James's stuff in the basement."

"Don't let them leave their stuff in your basement," Ellie warned after a gulp of romaine. "Dear Abby says to give them six months to decide what they want to save and then call Goodwill."

"Who knows whether we'll want to keep such a big house? Maybe we'll move into a condo. Tim's tired of the upkeep. When he retires, I'm sure we'll be southbound."

"Why would you ever want to leave Minnesota?" Ellie was serious. She was the consummate Minnesota girl. "You've got your kids here now, your friends, Tim's mother."

"That's reason enough right there." Bridget pointed a finger over her fork handle. "Ramona the Grim."

"She'll follow you to Florida."

"All I said was 'south.' We're telling her south of the border. You know what happens if you die in a foreign country? They can hold your body indefinitely."

"So you could be late for your own funeral." Knowing Tim's mother, Camille could easily guess the line of reasoning. Ramona had been dying for twenty years.

"Worse," Bridget said. "Parts of you could miss it entirely. In that heat, without refrigeration, a person could start to decompose. Even an artist like Michael Seraphim would have a time with the reconstruction."

"Who is—"

"Ramona's personal mortician."

"Michael *Seraphim*?" Camille and Ellie nearly shrieked in unison.

Bridget lifted both palms. "She swears that's his real name. She visits him regularly to update her plan."

"Her funeral plan?"

"Some people plan weddings, some people plan funerals," Bridget said. "Ramona has a leather-bound, two-hundred-page will, mostly detailing her funeral plan." She sighed as she poked her fork into her salad. "Michael Seraphim had better outlive her, or she's not going. She doesn't trust anyone else to give her the proper send-off."

"The proper send-off for me is ashes in the wind," Camille said. "I'm assigning you two to see to it for me, just like in the song."

"I think that's dust in the wind," Bridget said.

"Whatever." Camille was sure it was ashes. "Ashes in the wind" was a line from something anyway.

"I'd rather turn to ashes than dust," Ellie said. "The process seems neater, more dignified."

"More dramatic." Bridget eyed the chandelier, imagining. "But I like the idea of looking your best when you go up in flames, so I want you two to do my hair and makeup."

"Are you going up or down in flames, Bridge?"

"What*ever*."

"My request is that you don't let Aunt Willi sing 'The Old Rugged Cross,'" Ellie said. "I don't care what they do with me, but please don't let that woman sing that awful song." She pointed fork tines in Camille's direction. "And you have to keep a close eye on her. If she so much as clears her throat, you stuff her in a closet."

"Why, Ellie Louise," Camille drawled, using her real name this time. "I didn't think you ever had a harsh thought for anyone, especially not family."

"It's nothing personal. It's just that Aunt Willi can't sing to save her soul, so I don't want her offending the Lord's ears in my behalf."

"Maybe we'll spike her lemonade," Bridget suggested.

"What*ever*," Ellie echoed as she turned her "but seriously" look on Camille. "You know who I'd choose to sing for me?" She ignored Camille's sidelong warning glance. "Yes, *Creed*. That's my official request, as long as we're making them."

"I'm not much for country music," Bridget reminded Ellie, who enjoyed crooning along with the steel guitar on occasion. "But when you and Creed sang together at that party, that was one of the best duets I've ever heard. You could give Dolly Parton a run for her money if you'd trade in the choir robe on some sequins. What was that song you sang?"

"I think it was a Dolly Parton and Kenny Rogers song, but I don't remember—"

"'Islands in the Stream,'" Camille supplied mechanically. She couldn't help herself when it came to trivia, especially song titles. Couldn't sing a note, couldn't forget a song. "And just how did we get onto this subject?" She turned to Bridget. "Let's take a leap back over Ramona and Aunt Willi and talk about the bride and groom. What did they think of the piece I made for them?"

"Oh, Cam, it turned out beautifully with the changes we talked about."

Camille had made the mistake of showing Bridget her design for the trellis and inviting suggestions. Most people simply approved, knowing that the finished product would have the Delonga signature. Bridget had had suggestions.

"But does *Lauren* like it?"

"She loves it. And they are going to use it as a bedstead, headboard sort of thing until they have a yard to put a trellis in."

"I hate to admit it, but you had an excellent idea. I'm going to keep making them that way, and I'm naming the new style after you." Camille smiled. "Bridget's Bridal Bower."

"It's Lauren's bridal bower." Bridget brightened. "How about Bridget's Best Brainstorm?"

"Cute, but it won't sell sculpture. Just tell me you're honored, and don't keep trying to improve on it. I can incorporate only one outside improvement per piece. That's the law."

"It's going well, right?" Bridget asked.

"The work goes well. It's a lot of solitude, so I miss teaching sometimes, but—"

"I mean the artist biz. You're making really good money on that stuff now, aren't you?"

"It pays the bills pretty nicely."

"You've built a name for your work," Ellie offered. "Even way up in my neck of the woods, we know a Delonga fireplace screen when we see one. I showed that article about you in the *Minnesota Monthly* around for a year." She tapped the middle of her palm with her fingertip. "I know her. She's my dear friend from way back. We have lunch together all the time."

"Long, leisurely lunches," Bridget said.

"During which we solve everyone's problems." Camille checked her watch. "For the moment. I've gotta go."

"Say hello to Rosemary," Ellie said. "And Jordan. Tell her Auntie Ellie heartily approves."

"Oh, Ellie," Bridget scolded. "As my daughter would say, that is *so* not likely. So completely Never-Never Land. So totally—"

"I think you've made your point." Camille bristled, and she had to avoid looking at Bridget to keep her surprising defensiveness under wraps. "We should all be so lucky. I wouldn't mind heading for that first star on the right myself, but Mama's waiting for me at the clinic." She tucked her purse under her arm and finally met her friend's eyes. "Guess I'm still a damn Wendy at heart."

Chapter 4

$\mathcal{M}$ama never spoke of it outright, but surely she glimpsed, smelled, and tasted some piece of death, had a growing sense of what the whole of it would bring. Its proximity had begun to encroach on her living space and change her body, shrink it, steal its definition, overshadow it with a hazy pall. When she looked in the mirror, she must have wondered whose face she was seeing and where these changes were taking her.

Camille wondered and wanted desperately to ask her mother what was going on, to simply ask what was on her mind the way she once did as a child, before she'd learned about the rudeness of looking, pointing, asking too many questions, making people feel bad.

Why do your eyes look funny, Mama?

Does that sore on your lip hurt?

Who better to ask than Mama? Who knew more? Maybe Father knew best back then, but Mama knew more, and she would tell Camille what she needed to know. Changes were fascinating and powerful and scary, and who else could explain them?

When am I going to have boobies like yours mama?

Jeez, Mama, is this all I get? Aren't these tits ever going to get any bigger?

How low are these boobs going to sag?

Why am I bleeding?

When will I stop getting my period, Mama? When did you?

Who will I ask when you're not here anymore?

Why can't I ask you now?

She couldn't ask because she was a coward, because she saw changes in her mother's body that smacked of finality, even as they seemed strangely like a return to a time before Camille. Was this what it meant to come full circle? Without her wig, without her hair, Mama looked babyish. Her pale face seemed softer, more serene, and Camille wondered what feelings went along with these changes.

But Rosemary offered no invitation to ask, no inclination to talk. Instead, she brought out items from her jewelry box. She unearthed old things that Camille remembered seeing in the breakfront cabinet that no longer stood in the living room, or in the dining room hutch that contained Camille's collection of pottery instead of Rosemary's china. She dug up memories and deposited them in her daughter's account.

"You know where this came from, don't you?" Rosemary quizzed, emerging from her room carrying a large glass pedestal bowl as though she were taking up an offering. She set it on the kitchen counter next to the chicken Camille was preparing to make into comfort food.

Camille had a vague memory of the lacy blue glass, but she wasn't certain when or where she'd seen it before. "Was it a wedding present?"

"From Aunt Caroline. Your great-aunt." With a badly chewed fingertip, Rosemary traced the molded glass filigree, which eddied across the slope of the bowl. "My mother's oldest sister. She was always so good to me, sent me birthday cards that she made herself. I should have saved those." She looked up, caught her daughter's eye as she slid the dish a scant inch closer to the chopped chicken. "Matt isn't going to want any of this stuff, you know."

"Have you asked him?"

"I can't bring anything like that up with him. You know how he is."

"Have you asked him to come home for Christmas this year?"

"Let's see how things go," Rosemary said quietly as she slipped her hand into the pocket of the tan slacks that lately fit her like a gathered skirt. "Look what else I found," she said, her fingers springing open, childlike, her tone suddenly as bright as the sparkling brooch she revealed. "I thought I was the cat's meow when I wore this to a party."

"The cat's meow," Camille echoed, smiling. "That's beautiful, Mama, but the *cat's meow?* That's a new one. You hate cats."

"I'm allergic to cats, but the meow doesn't bother me. And it's hardly a new expression. Don't you remember your grandma saying you looked like the cat's meow? Well, this was hers." The pavé-set stones sparkled as Rosemary angled her hand to catch the light.

"It's beautiful," Camille repeated.

"Would you ever wear it? This Art Deco period is quite collectible now, you know. You should see what they get for things like this on eBay."

Camille ran water over her hands to make them fit to touch. She had no idea whether the stylized floral design was made of gems or glass. It didn't matter. She'd never worn much jewelry herself, but she remembered getting caught using this brooch to fashion a scarf dress on one of her dolls. She also remembered the rare spanking she'd gotten for getting into Mama's jewelry box.

"You'll wear it at Christmas," Camille said as she wiped her hands on a dish towel.

"I'm serious. We should have some of these old things appraised so you can insure them. I'm telling you—"

"Mama." Camille sandwiched the brooch and her mother's hand between both of hers. "I don't need an appraisal. I promise you, I'm not going to hold an estate sale. Grandma's brooch and that whatever-it-is from Great-Aunt Caroline—"

"It's a compote."

"They're not going anywhere, Mama."

"They should go to Jordan someday."

"They'll have to pass through me first. I want to see what it feels like to be a meow."

"You know that royal blue suit with the fitted jacket?" Rosemary pressed the brooch into Camille's hands. "This will be perfect with that suit."

"I'll borrow it next time I wear the suit. If I can still get into it." Neither of them looked at it as the brooch changed hands again. "This belongs in your jewelry box, but this . . ." Camille carefully lifted the glass bowl. Its weight surprised her. "This goes in the hutch. I didn't realize we had a compote."

"Your father didn't like it. He said it looked like a piece of tacky old junk. To him, old was synonymous with poor. He wanted the latest in everything."

"Creed did, too. But we don't have to decorate around them now, do we?" Camille took the heirloom into the dining room, which itself could well become an heirloom room since it was rarely used these days. She turned on the overhead light—a chandelier that made the design in blue glass sparkle almost like pavé gems. "I'm going to rearrange the hutch so that this will really take center—"

The front door—also rarely used—opened with a squeak, followed by an exuberant "I'm home! Is anyone else here?"

Camille set the compote on the table and straightened her T-shirt, checking the front for food spills. She was a messy cook, and Jordan never used the front door or announced herself like a chirpy songbird unless she had someone with her.

"Just the cat and her meow," Camille called out.

The joke sailed right over the bright and beautiful head that peeked around the doorframe. "Mother, I have a surprise. Where's Grandma?"

Camille gestured toward the kitchen. "She's—"

"Grandma, could you come in here, please?" Jordan called toward the kitchen, but her eager gesture was directed toward the front door. "We . . . James and I . . ."

He joined her, taking her outstretched hand, looking for all the world like somebody who'd just smoked his first joint.

Camille's gut trembled around an ominous feeling. She was about to lose her chick to a wolf wearing a boy-next-door mask. Was there still time to drag him by the ear and throw him out before he got her daughter hooked on his brand of high?

Not according to the silly shine in Jordan's dark eyes.

"We have something to tell you."

Rosemary appeared silently from the kitchen.

Camille knew what was coming, and she hung on to the moment before it came for as long as Jordan would allow her to.

"We're"—she thrust her left hand out and shifted her finger, catching the light in her new ring—"getting married."

"Oh, my . . ." Camille felt winded, breathless, blinded by the light. It was a day for all kinds of sparkle. "Engaged? Jordan . . ."

Drawn to the ring, drawn to her child, she finally drew breath and sailed into a hug.

"Engaged?" She gasped again as she took the girl's ring hand in hers and peered at it. Not that she doubted the value or the weight. She'd heard the voice and seen the faces and felt the news in her gut. Therein lay the value and the weight. And the deposit on guaranteed change.

"Yes, *engaged*. We're getting married. And soon, that much we agree on." Jordan squeezed her mother's hand before she drew it away and laid it on her fiancé's arm. "The engagement ring was James's idea. The wedding is mine."

"The wedding?"

"I'd be happy with a JP," James said, "but Jordan has convinced me that we should do it up right."

God, his voice sounded deep and husky.

"Every woman dreams of a beautiful wedding," he added over Camille's thoughts of where had all the children gone.

Gone to brides and grooms, every one.

"Not *every* woman," Camille said, taking exception even as she opened her arms to her future son-in-law and whispered her congratulations.

Then back to her daughter. "Oh, honey, I'm so . . ." Another squeeze finally got the words flowing. "But this is so sudden. I always thought you'd tell me you were in love first. You know, like, 'Mom, I'm in love with James, and I think he loves me.' And then you'd start hinting about marriage, and I'd have time to get used to the idea before you'd start flashing a ring. And then you'd be engaged for a nice long while, and then—"

"Oh, Mother." Jordan gave a quick laugh. "I've already told you I was in love with James."

"When you were twelve."

"And right then I said I was going to marry him."

"Yes, but he wasn't in on the plan." Camille grabbed his arm. "I want to hear it from James."

"I'm crazy in love with your daughter, so I plan to make her my wife and you my mother-in-law." He kissed Camille's cheek.

A little too smoothly, she thought. Shouldn't he have been shaking in his boots right about now?

"And Grandma here . . ." James extricated himself from mother and daughter and headed for Rosemary.

Camille watched him take those steps, not in boots but in running shoes. For some crazy reason she breathed more easily.

"You're as much part of my plan as anybody," James told Rosemary as he leaned down to peck her cheek. "Have you met my Grandma Mayfield?"

"Briefly, at Lauren's wedding." She put her arms around James's neck and gave a happy groan. "Such good news."

"Every family needs a grandma. That's why I'm inviting you," James recited, tucking her under his arm. "Grandma Mayfield is a bust as a grandma."

"She can't be. There are no rules for grandmas. Grandma is as

Grandma does." Rosemary stepped away from James, a new sparkle in her eyes, a tint of color in her cheeks. "And this grandma has a wedding dress to make."

"Oh, Grandma, you don't have to worry about—"

"No worries," Rosemary said as she hugged her granddaughter. "It'll be beautiful. Any style you want, but you need to decide and give me a head start. I'm a little slower than I used to be."

"You know what I think about spending a lot of—"

"Money on a wedding, I know, Mama," Jordan said.

Camille wanted to bite her own bitter tongue off.

"I don't want to go overboard, but I do want a wedding," Jordan went on. "Small, simple, elegant."

"How do you feel about it?" Camille asked James.

"I know my mother went bonkers with Lauren's shindig, but it was a nice time. Innocent, kind of." He gave a boyish shrug. "Like I said, I'd be happy with a JP, but whatever Jordan wants is fine with me."

"Have you broken the news to . . . anyone else?"

"You're the first," Jordan said.

With a knowing look, James acknowledged Camille's concern for his mother. "Thought we'd practice on you."

"We knew you'd be happy for us, Mom."

"I've known you both all your lives, but you can still surprise me." *Shouldn't be able to,* Camille thought. *A good mother would have seen it coming.* But she smiled in the knowledge that James would be a good husband. "It's the good kind of surprise."

"Aren't Bridget and Ellie coming over here tomorrow for lunch?" Rosemary asked. Camille had suggested that they include her mother this time.

"We'll tell Mom tonight."

"Ask Ellie if she'll sing for our wedding."

. . .

Bridget arrived for lunch on Ellie's heels. Camille barely had time to break the news to Ellie, who gave a cheer and a hug, then glanced out the door. Bridget was coming up the flagstone walk.

"Is she okay with it?"

"We'll soon find out," Camille whispered.

Bridget's greeting was soft and cool. She asked first about Camille's mother—a polite but pointed way of avoiding mention of her daughter. *Okay*, Camille thought. *I won't ask until you tell.*

"She insisted on making her curried chicken salad for us, which is a good sign. She hasn't felt much like being around food for—"

"The answer is yes, I've heard the news," Bridget said.

Camille exchanged a quick glance with Ellie. *And she's not too happy about it.*

"They said they wanted to practice up on me first," Camille said, keeping it light. "Probably because there's only one of me. Grandma's blessing is always a given."

"Were you as surprised as I was?"

"I don't know, Bridge." Camille slipped an arm around her friend. "Probably more surprised than I should have been."

"I was stunned," Bridget said emotionlessly, stepping away, moving inside. "I still am."

"We set the table in the dining room," Camille called after Bridget, wondering where she thought she was going. She glanced at Ellie again, looking for support. She found it in Ellie's eyes.

"Are we expecting anyone else?" Bridget wanted to know, headed for the table as though she were reporting for a business meeting. "I was hoping for just us."

"Just us." Camille grabbed an envelope off the buffet. Ellie and Bridget took seats at the table she and Rosemary had set earlier with cloth napkins, matching placemats, and grocery-store daffodils in a blue glass vase. "How do you like Great-Aunt Caroline's compote?" she said of the heirloom she'd filled with fruit salad.

Praise for the piece was nominal.

Pulling a handful of snapshots from the envelope, Camille took another tack.

"Isn't this weird?" She handed Ellie a couple of the pictures and gave Bridget a few more, all of them showing Bridget and Camille wearing long hair and long peasant dresses, all in colors of the past. They were celebrating the first of their babies. "I was going through picture boxes last night, and I found these. Look at this one." She passed her new favorite of the pictures over Bridget's shoulder. "Before I'd even met Creed, before there was any thought of Jordan, here I am holding James."

"I had to keep reminding you to support his head," Bridget mumbled.

"I'd almost forgotten that I was his godmother." Camille laughed, revisiting the awkwardness she'd felt when the picture was taken. "Some friend, huh? I hope I make a better mother-in-law."

Bridget turned her head slowly, punctuating the move with an odd stare.

"I know," Camille assured her. "I wasn't ready either."

The nearly imperceptible shake of her head, more like a shudder, and the befuddled look in her eyes seemed, even under present circumstances, very un-Bridget. *Especially* under the circumstances.

"What? What's wrong?"

Bridget turned away, back to the photograph.

Camille slid into the chair at the end of the table, peering, waiting for an answer that wasn't coming fast enough.

"What did you say when you heard the news, Bridge? Did you . . . You didn't argue or anything, did you?"

"With James and Jordan?" Bridget shook her head. "They didn't stay long."

"Are you all right?"

"Not really." There was that dazed look again, as though she'd been slapped by a friend. "She's pregnant, isn't she?"

It was Camille's turn to feel the sting. Slowly, carefully she explained, "Bridget, they're *engaged.*"

"Because she's pregnant."

"Because they plan to get married. No, she's not pregnant."

"She told you that?"

The sting was turning to heat. Not a sound came from the kitchen, nor from Ellie's end of the table. This was between mothers, and Camille was hard-pressed to keep her cool.

Ellie's chair scraped the floor. "I'm going to check on Rosemary and the salad."

When Ellie was gone from the room, Camille answered softly, but there was no mistaking the warning in her tone. "You know what, Bridget? The subject of pregnancy simply didn't come up."

"Why am I not surprised?" Eyes wide with sudden awakening, Bridget squared herself. "You never ask the right questions, Camille, which is why you never have all the facts. Why else would they be talking about getting married?"

"Bridget, calm down before you say something really ugly."

"Ugly?" Bridget touched fingertips to forehead, as though she were trying to reason or remember. "In this day and age," she whispered. "And James, at his age, my God."

"What are you talking about, *age*? What is this, Bridget? Your son is marrying my daughter, and they're both *of age*. And she's *not pregnant*."

"Do you know that for sure?"

"I don't know *for sure* that she'd tell me if she were, but I think she would. It's not the first thing that came to my mind when I heard the news."

"You approve?"

"Approve? In this *day and age?*"

"You still want Jordan to go back and finish school. You've said that many times. And James . . . I can't believe James would . . ." Bridget kept shaking her head, as though the turn of events in her son's life were an insect that could be shaken away. "I thought he was smarter. I thought . . ."

"Smarter than . . ." *Not Jordan. Don't you dare say Jordan.*

The head shaking continued.

"James is a brilliant man who has so much potential, which he will never fulfill if he doesn't complete his program. I tried to tell him, just go right through. Get your Ph.D. Don't put it off. Don't take time out for some silly job. You're so much smarter than that."

Bridget was floundering, fairly babbling, on the verge of whining. It was so unlike her that it would have been laughable, had there not been an underlying tone of desperation. There was more to her anxiety than the notion of losing a bright son or gaining an ignorant daughter. No one knew Bridget quite as well as Camille did.

"Why didn't they stay very long?" Camille asked quietly, the rising anger momentarily quashed.

Bridget looked mystified.

"When they went to your house last night," Camille clarified, "why didn't they stay?"

"Because I was just going to bed. They said what they had to say, and I just . . . I was very tired." She closed her eyes, shook her head again. "Because I can't handle this right now."

"Good." Camille reached across the corner to touch Bridget's arm. "Because it's not yours to handle, Bridget. It's their choice, their life." She sat back with a sigh. "I just wish you hadn't done such a beautiful job with Lauren's wedding, because now that's what Jordan wants. A fancy wedding."

"Oh, fine." Bridget's beautiful hands went up as she glanced at the ceiling. "That's just great. I'm really in the mood for another wedding."

"Relax." Camille reached for her again, but Bridget's glance prompted her to lay her palm on the table. If not the comforting gesture she intended, at least it said *truce.* "You're the mother of the groom. All you have to do is show up."

"In this *day and age?*" Bridget shot back.

"You said that was all Anthony's parents did," Camille reminded her.

"They came from California. What else do you expect?"

"You didn't *let* them do anything else, did you?" Camille supposed softly. "Well, you've had your wedding. Now it's time—"

"For my divorce."

Camille was stunned.

"For your . . ."

"That's right." Even in a whisper, Bridget's voice rose in desperation. "Tim says he wants a divorce. Can you believe it?"

"Oh, Bridge, I'm—"

"Incredible, isn't it? The match made in heaven, the perfect couple, the ideal . . ." Her eyes avoiding Camille's, Bridget blinked back tears. "Incredible, isn't it?"

"It can happen to anyone," Camille insisted. "But maybe you two need some professional help."

"We've already thought of that. He has his attorney, and I have mine." Bridget gave a deep, long sigh. "This isn't as sudden as I'm making it sound. He agreed not to move out until after the wedding."

"Do the kids know?"

"They, um . . ." More blinking, more head shaking. "We haven't actually talked, not, you know . . ." She swallowed hard. "I didn't think he'd really do it. A phase, I thought. Midlife crisis."

"Is it . . . ?"

"Another woman? If it is, he's not saying. I'm sure it is. My attorney wants to hire a detective. Do you think I should? Did you?"

"No. I was able to go through tribal court because he's Indian. It was pretty civilized. He kept his stuff, and I kept mine. He made no claim on the house—said the house belongs to the woman. He agreed to let Jordan stay with me." Camille's wan smile was meant to be apologetic, but in the back of her mind she had a nasty, niggling thought. *No one else took you for the perfect couple, Bridget. Just you.* "I guess that's not much help."

"Didn't you feel like cutting him up into small pieces and just . . . ?"

"The anger becomes more manageable after a while."

"You make it sound so clinical. Anger management, for God's

sake. You were madder than hell, weren't you? You, Camille. You were spitting nails when we weren't looking." Bridget glanced warily at the door to the kitchen. "Please tell me you were."

"I was angry with him most of the time toward the end. Sometimes I didn't even know why. I just knew that I couldn't live with him anymore. The way he lived wasn't the way I wanted us to live."

"Was he screwing around?" Bridget whispered. "Don't look at me like it's none of my business. We've known each other forever, and now we're both in the same boat, more or less. He was, wasn't he? He must have been."

"He never admitted it."

It was less than Bridget wanted to hear and more than Camille intended to say.

"I never thought it could happen to us. I thought . . ." Bridget gave another tremulous sigh. "You know, we had our home, our family, our friends, our life. We agreed on everything, all the ground rules. We even went to church. How could he be such a hypocrite, sitting right next to me in church?" She shook her head once more. "I never thought it could happen to me."

"Neither did I."

"I know. Everybody's going to be totally shocked. You're the first person outside the family that I've told. Of course, I don't know how many people he's told. He's probably sending out—"

"No, Bridget. You missed the point. *Neither did I* think it could happen to *me*. I was just as confident as you were. I believed in our marriage." She smiled, remembering the conversation she'd had with Jordan and Mama the day after Lauren's wedding. Since then she'd thought a lot about her mother's observations on failure and success in marriage. What was the standard? Was it appearances?

She tipped her head consideringly. "In some ways, now that I think about it, I still do. Some ways, some days."

"You never got over Creed, did you? That's where that anger management gets you. I'll get over Timothy Mayfield, believe you me."

"But not the marriage. Even after the marriage is over, you'll never be over the marriage. It'll always be part of you, part of your life, because it *was* a marriage. For better or for worse. You choose."

Bridget pushed away from the table. "I'm not ready for quite this much wisdom, Cam. I want sympathy."

"You have mine."

"I'm not ready to tell Ellie yet." Again she glanced at the doorway to the kitchen.

By now Ellie and Mama had undoubtedly figured out the gist of what was going on. They were pretty quiet. Either they had their mouths filled with chicken salad or their ears to the wall. Maybe both. But they would hang out together in the kitchen until Camille gave some signal.

"Ellie and Stan," Bridget mused. "Who'd have guessed they'd be the ones to make it the longest?"

"Did we have a contest going?"

"Of course not. No, you're right, it makes perfect sense. They're both such nice, steady, everyday people."

"We aren't?"

"We're more high-maintenance. Not to mention our former and soon-to-be-former husbands. You're an artist, and I'm . . ." Bridget turned to her, looking lost, so lost. "I don't know. What am I, Cam? I'm a college graduate. That's something. I'm . . ." Shaking, shaking. "What am I going to do?"

"You're going to take it one step at a time." Camille managed to catch Bridget's hand in hers this time. It was cold and trembling. Nothing to do but hang on. "Our kids are getting married, Bridge. Let's think about that for a minute. James and Jordan."

"I think it's a mistake. They haven't thought this out." She shook her head again, this time firmly and in her own control. "I have to go, Cam. I don't . . . I'm talked out. I can't deal with another wedding. And I don't want Tim there if there is a wedding. I especially don't want—"

"You know what, Bridget, they just got engaged. We've got plenty of time to work all this out. This will be a small, intimate wedding. Simple and elegant. I know my daughter. She's not going to go overboard." Camille held on when Bridget tried to draw away. "We've got the same situation on our side. I don't even know how to get in touch with Jordan's father right now. But we won't let anything ruin this for our kids, Bridget. They're happy."

"For how long?"

"For *now*, Bridge, come on." Camille squeezed and shook as though she were wringing laundry rather than a limp hand. Suddenly she saw herself, and she almost laughed aloud. Since when had she become the cheerleader type? "A nice, small wedding. When they start making serious plans, I'm sure that's what they're going to want."

Bridget managed a wobbly smile. "Whatever," she whispered, returning the hand squeeze. "I'm just going to slip out the back, Jack. Okay?"

"Sure?"

Bridget nodded. "Ellie and Rosemary . . . you'll explain?"

"Sure."

Chapter 5

*Y*ou can come out now." Camille gave the two sheepish faces a moment to appear, one on each side of the kitchen door. "Cowards."

Ellie gave a small shrug. "I thought you two had things to work out."

"You heard?"

Both women nodded.

"The *rest* of the story," Rosemary intoned.

"Oh, Mama."

"Well, Bridget's always been just a little too high and mighty." Rosemary offered Camille a cup of coffee in one hand, a yield sign with the other. "I know, I know. This is a bad time to say that, but it's true. Of course, I'm sorry for her troubles." With the handoff complete, she folded her arms beneath droopy breasts. "But she'd better not try to spoil things for those kids, or I'll show her trouble."

"Mama!" The quick protest was necessary to thwart the speaking of the other of Camille's two minds—the one that was thinking the same way. "She won't try to spoil anything. Once the bandwagon starts rolling, she'll want to be right up there in the driver's seat."

"Which could turn out to be the *rest* of the rest of the story," Ellie said.

"We'll handle it. You two are going to help, right? No more sneaking off, then eavesdropping when things get touchy."

"We *weren't* eavesdropping."

"We just heard bits and pieces. We couldn't help it."

Camille snorted. "I didn't hear you rattling any pots and pans to drown out the tête-à-tête you didn't want to hear."

"We were just about to bring in the food when we heard the big D word, and we don't mean Dallas," Rosemary explained. She drew two puzzled looks. "I just heard that song on the radio. 'Goin Through the Big D.' "

"What station are you listening to these days, Mama? Golden country oldies?"

"I listen to all kinds of golden oldies these days. I kinda like the fact that you can't be golden until you're an oldie."

Camille started spooning chicken salad onto three plates. "I hope it's just the music that has you feeling so chipper."

"It's the wedding," Rosemary gushed. Catching Camille's glance, she adjusted tone and tune. "Oh, I'm sorry about Bridget splitting up with her husband, but I never thought he was such a prize. Seems like he's always trying to convince people that his time is more precious than anyone else's." She took the two plates Camille handed her. "You ask me, he drove his son away."

"Oh, Mama. James grew up and *moved* away."

"I think there was more to it. 'Course, I could be wrong." Her tone canceled out the possibility. Headed for the dining room, Rosemary dropped crumbs of wisdom for the next generation to follow. "One thing I can't be wrong about is James. He's a good man. I generally know one when I see one."

"Generally?"

"Some are more obvious, and others are late bloomers. But generally." Rosemary set the two plates on either side of the head of the table, the place that was now Camille's. "James is the kind you don't miss your guess on. The obvious kind."

"So he comes with a guarantee?"

"Only mine," Rosemary said. "Oh, the fruit. Ellie, help yourself to some fruit. That big ol' dish is too heavy to pass."

"That's no ordinary dish, Mama. That's a compote."

"She's learning," Rosemary whispered to Ellie as they passed each other—Ellie bringing the coffeepot, Rosemary going back for something nearly forgotten.

"This doesn't look like an ordinary spoon either," Ellie said, handing Camille the ornate silver serving piece she had just used in helping herself to fruit.

"Eight million heirlooms in the house, and every one has a story."

"Take notes," Ellie advised, her voice dropping to a whisper on Rosemary's return.

"I went out and got the mail earlier. This is your pile." Rosemary placed several ordinary envelopes beside the fork at Camille's place before taking her own seat with an armload of books and magazines. She set her collection in the chair next to hers—the one Bridget had left empty. "And this is my pile."

"I thought you'd weaned yourself off those Internet auctions, Mama."

"Not completely. I'm still a registered blue-star buyer. I was just browsing, and these caught my eye. I had a feeling. Or a wish, maybe, I don't know." She presented exhibit number one: Martha Stewart. "Wedding books." Number two: *Minnesota Bride.* "Magazines galore. I got a bunch of them for ten cents on the dollar, and that's counting the postage. All fairly recent."

When she heard neither oohs nor aahs, she assumed ignorance.

"Ideas, my dear girls. Styles. Tips. I'll need to get started on Jordan's dream dress. What do you think she wants?" Food went untouched as Rosemary flipped through pages. "I'm betting on simplicity. Something that flows over her body like sweet cream."

"Mama, I really think you're jumping the gun, bargain or not. They haven't even set a date."

"Once they pick a month or even a season, the church and the reception hall will set the date." Rosemary glanced from face to face, astonished. "There's a lot to be done, no matter what the date turns out to be. Your friend Bridget will back me up on this just as soon as she's able to get on board."

"She's already told me how much planning a wedding requires," Camille said with a groan. "Over and over and over again."

"Maybe she can use the distraction to help her get through that big D," Ellie said.

"Jordan's wedding will not be somebody else's distraction from whatever is going on in her own life," Camille insisted.

Her mother gave her one of her loaded looks. "How about from what's *not* going on?"

"I didn't mean you, Mama."

"That's funny. Neither did I."

Ellie cleared her perfectly clear throat. "I don't know what either one of you is talking about, but I do know that Rosemary's right about booking the facilities. That's the first challenge. Judging by the last Mayfield wedding, you need to think big."

"This is going to be a Delonga wedding."

"Jordan's last name is Burke," Rosemary reminded her. "Careful, Camille. You don't want to start sounding like Bridget already."

"Poor Bridget," Ellie said. "She's always been one to do one thing at a time and do it very well. But you can't pile too many things on her at once or you'll strip her threads and she'll screw right out from under you."

"Divorce isn't something most people do very well." Camille picked through her salad, separating a chunk of chicken from a slice of celery. "She did a nice job with Lauren's wedding, but I know that Jordan has very different ideas. It'll be simple. Bridget will have to cut down the list on that side, because it'll be small and elegant if I know my daughter." She smiled suddenly. "By the way, Ellie, they'd like you to sing for them. That's the first detail they've decided on."

"I'll be happy to, but if that choice is any indication of things to come, maybe you don't know your daughter as well as you think you do." Camille's quizzical look made Ellie laugh. "I'm hardly small and elegant."

· · ·

In the middle of the night the phone rang, rudely snatching Camille away from the craziest dream. In it, she'd been modeling a fluffy white dress for her mother while Ellie and Bridget did a line dance in front of the three-way mirror and crooned "Whose Bed Have Your Boots Been Under?"

Somehow too embarrassed to turn the light on, she knocked the phone off its cradle.

"Mrs. Burke? It's James," said a deep voice. "James Mayfield."

Camille still hadn't opened her eyes, still hadn't made the transition. Everything in her head was still silly, so she laughed. "Hello, James Mayfield. You're the only person who calls me—"

"Mrs. Burke, my mother needs help, and I don't know what to do for her. I know it's late, but can you come over right away?"

"Is she sick?" Couldn't be. A moment ago she was doing the Achy Breaky Shake. "Is she hurt? Should I call—"

"No, she told me not to call anyone, but I'm scared for her. She's kinda wigged out."

"Wigged out?" Bridget was out of wigs? She didn't wear wigs. But Camille was sitting up now. "Does she need—"

"I don't know. I don't know what she needs. Can you come? I know it's late."

"I'll be there as soon as I can."

"Thanks." His sigh was long and deep and full of unwarranted relief. "Please hurry."

Camille grabbed her robe off the bedpost, turned on the hall light, and headed for the kitchen and the door to the garage. Along the way she thought to pull her purse off a chair and leave a note on the kitchen counter. At the closet she had a choice between clogs and ankle-high boots. Since the last of the early-spring snow was confined to dirty ridges along the driveway, the clogs would ordinarily be her preference. But that stupid song had her zipping her bare feet into the boots. She pulled on her coat and headed out.

About ten minutes later she approached the sprawling Mayfield house. It was the only one on the street in the posh suburban neighborhood with lights on inside. Camille parked her van in the driveway beside James's car. She found the front door unlocked, so she let herself in. Down the hall to the left, she could hear water running in the bathroom sink and a woman desperately trying to control a crying jag.

In the darkened living room to the right, a masculine silhouette rose from a chair. "Mrs. Burke?" he whispered tentatively.

Camille shed her coat, unzipped the boots, and flipped them off her feet. One of them hit the wall.

"What's going on, James?"

"She called me and told me she was sorry about a bunch of stuff that didn't make any sense. She sounded drunk or something. I didn't know what was going on, so I came over."

The sobbing down the hall suddenly abated.

His voice dropped as he approached. "She said she couldn't sleep, and then she started in about being sorry again, and now she can't stop crying. I can't do anything. I try to talk to her, she just gets worse."

"Is she on any kind of medication?"

"I don't know." They stood face to face in the shadowy foyer. "You know about my father."

"I know he's asked for a divorce." Camille caught herself clutching the front of her bathrobe and wishing she'd taken time to get dressed. This was, after all, her daughter's fiancé.

But he sounded just as scared as he had the time he'd sneaked one of Creed's guitars out of its case and dropped it on the cement floor in her workshop.

"She's having some kind of a breakdown, Mrs. Burke. I don't

know how to get her to settle down. She's . . ." His gesture, a pointed plea, directed her to the sliver of light that escaped the bathroom door and sliced the dark hallway in half.

Camille leaned close to the door. "Bridget?"

The door swung open. Bridget's whole face was red and swollen from crying, and her hair, backlit by the bulbs surrounding the mirror, stood on end at wild angles. But the look in her bloodshot eyes was far wilder.

"What are you doing here?" Bridget demanded. "It's the middle of the night, for God's sake."

"I just wanted to make sure you're all right."

"Of course I'm all right." Bridget shouldered past Camille, going after James. "You called her, didn't you? What for?"

"I didn't know what else to do, Mom."

"This is family business, James." Trapped, she did a quarter turn, as though she wanted to keep an eye on both of them at once. "I was having trouble sleeping, and James was always such a night owl that I called him just to talk. He's making a big deal—"

"You're not making any sense, Mom."

"If you want to be a good husband, you're going to have to learn a thing or two about women, dear. Sometimes they cry. You'll have to learn to handle a woman's tears if you're going to get married, because women cry sometimes. And you can't just walk out."

"I'm not," he said quietly. "I won't. I just don't want you to . . ." He reached cautiously, as though she were a bird on a branch. "You had me a little scared, you know?"

"Isn't that just like a man? They can't handle emotion. It disgusts them."

"I'm not disgusted, Mom. I just don't know how to help you." He took a step back, pitifully unsure of himself and looking to Camille for support. "Maybe I shouldn't have called you. I've never seen her the way she was a few minutes ago. She—"

"Don't talk about me as though I weren't here." Bridget dug deep for a reserve of motherly clout. "I'm right here."

"Well, yeah, you seem to be now, but a few minutes ago I wasn't so sure, Mom. Are you okay now?"

"Yes, of course. I'm not a lunatic, James. You make it sound as though I'm some sort of lunatic, but I'm not. I'm just not sleeping very well anymore."

"Have you seen a doctor, Bridge?"

"For what? Drugs? I don't need any more drugs. They make me crazy, and I can't afford to be crazy." But her agitation level was on the rise. "I'm sorry I disturbed you, James." Unexpectedly, she pushed past Camille. "I'm sorry my son disturbed you, Camille. I'm sorry. I know I look like a fool, and I'm really, really sorry."

"It's all right, Bridge, we're not—"

"You go on home now. Both of you. I'll be fine." She backed into her bedroom, receding like a pale specter evaporating in the darkness. The door closed. The lock clicked.

The crying started again.

"Should I take her to a hospital?" James asked.

"No!" Bridget screamed. "I'm staying here in my house! This is my house!"

"Shit."

"You don't have to go anywhere, Bridge," Camille said through the door. With a gesture she reassured James. "And I don't feel like it either. How about if I sleep over?"

"Oh, Cam," Bridget moaned. "Why would you want to do that?"

"Why would I want to drive home now?"

No answer.

"Seriously. I came over here in my nightgown." She had been to the dentist earlier that week, and she half smiled as she remembered an item that was still in her purse. "I brought my toothbrush."

No answer.

Camille injected some sternness into her voice. "Bridget, open the door and say good night to your son. Let him see that you're okay."

"He's seen enough," Bridget shouted. And then she groaned. Finally she whispered, "James, thank you for coming over. Go back to your apartment, back to bed, back to your—"

"Open the door, Mom." He gave the knob a couple of futile twists. "I'm not leaving until you let us come in and make sure you're okay."

Punctuated by slow, audible, shaky breaths taken on the other side of the door, a long moment passed.

Finally the door opened. "Camille can stay with me," Bridget said sullenly. She lifted an unsteady hand. "I'm sorry for all this, James."

"There's nothing for you to apologize about, Mom." He took the hand she held out to him.

"Then I won't. I'm not sorry. Go get some sleep now."

"You sure?"

She nodded.

He seemed relieved to be able to back down the hallway. "I'll call you tomorrow."

"James?"

He stopped, waited.

"Please try to forget how badly I've behaved."

James left on a quick, desperate nod.

After they heard the front door close, Bridget turned to Camille. "He's going to make some woman a fine husband."

"Promise?"

"You know the saying 'Like father, like son'?"

Camille nodded hesitantly.

"He's not," Bridget quickly assured her. "As it turns out, that's not a bad thing."

"We'll talk about the fathers and the children later, Bridget. Right now let's take care of you." Camille put her arm around her friend and eased her into the lonely darkness of the master bedroom. "You're shaking. What can I get for you?"

"I do have something that I'm supposed to take to help me sleep."

"Have you taken any tonight?"

"No."

Bridget flipped on the light. Like much of the house, the bedroom had been professionally decorated, with original artwork, fine furniture, all the bedding and drapery coordinated to match the wallpaper and carpeting in the latest shades of green and whatever they were calling beige these days. She blinked several times, as though it were all suddenly unfamiliar.

"I think I left it . . ." Bridget's hand fluttered in the direction of what she called the dressing room, which was an overblown closet with enough built-in storage to house clothing for a family of five. And Bridget had enough clothes for a family of five.

Camille found the prescription bottle on top of a built-in bureau, along with an open purse and a set of keys. She checked the label— filled that day—and compared the number on the prescription to the pills in the bottle. Why hadn't Bridget taken any? Did she enjoy lying awake counting her husband's sins?

Sometimes, Camille admitted to herself. Sometimes the only pleasure to be had was just that perverse.

Bridget sat on the side of her bed, looking as though she didn't know where to put herself. Camille placed the medication in her quivering palm and insisted that she drink the whole glass of water.

Bridget gave a shaky sigh as she handed up the glass. "You know exactly how I feel, don't you?"

"I think I do."

Bridget looked up slowly, big hangdog eyes swimming in tears. "When people say they know how you feel, they don't," she muttered softly as she allowed herself to be placed, limb by limb, in a prone position. "Even if they've had a death or a divorce or whatever. They don't because they're not you. But we've been shoulder to shoulder for so long, you and I. We're so much alike."

We aren't at all alike, Camille thought. There were times when she wondered what they saw in each other, why they still got together regularly, how each tolerated the differences in the other's personality, how they had anything to talk about when their interests were so different, not to mention their values. She had more in common with Ellie. But she and Bridget had been together in the important times.

"Almost like sisters," Bridget said.

"In many ways we're closer than sisters."

"We are, aren't we? We've shared so much, Cam. And now this."

"This?"

"Divorce."

"Sisters don't get divorced, Bridge." She climbed into the huge bed and turned off the light. "Neither do friends."

"You know what I mean. It's so unreal, Cam." Bridget turned on her side, and her voice traveled through the dark, across the long road of pillows, all the way to Camille's ear, oddly like the innocent bearer of sleepover secrets. "I wake up in the morning, and for a moment I think it's going to be a regular day. And then I remember. There aren't any regular days anymore. No more nice days. They're all full of holes and bare spots. It's like I've been in an accident, hit by a train or a meteor. *Wham!* My head's spinning, and everything around me is all disjointed." Near silence. Then, shyly, "Was it like that for you?"

"Pretty much."

Not at all. Camille's course had seemed crystal clear, even though every step had been painful. If they stayed together, she would keep asking him to change, and he wasn't going to do it. If he left, she would stop asking. If he moved out, she would move on.

"Did you hate him?" Bridget wanted to know.

"Yes." When she worked at it, she could hate him.

"Then why does it hurt so much to lose him?"

"It just does. There are too many reasons for you to deal with right now, Bridge. It just does."

Bridget finally talked herself to sleep. If the pills did their job, she would sleep most of the day away.

But Camille hadn't taken any drugs, and all the talk of hatred and hurting didn't help her rest in the presence of her friend's pain. She'd lain awake all night, then slipped away early, promising herself that she would call James and let him know that his mother was alone but sound asleep.

The morning light played over the bare branches of the sugar maples and the old oak trees that surrounded her house. The daffodils on the south side had just begun to poke through soggy sod. Camille checked the newspaper box and wondered whether they'd lost their carrier. The paper was late again. She found the front door unlocked and wondered whether she was at fault.

But she found the culprit in the kitchen, sipping on coffee he'd apparently just made. The newspaper lay on the table beside the black cowboy hat that was Creed Burke's trademark. His boots had already left a scuff on the linoleum. His scent had probably already marked the erstwhile female territory. That fatal spark in his dark eyes made its claim on her sensibilities. And unfortunately it all felt good.

She hoped he couldn't tell.

His lean face was craggier than it had been in those early, innocent days, but his slow smile softened it, just as it always had.

"Hello, Camille."

Chapter 6

"What are you doing here?"

She regretted the words as soon as they came out of her mouth. It was a rude way to greet the man, even though he had no business messing in her kitchen anymore.

He didn't appear to take offense. He went right on putting cream and sugar in her old "Favorite Teacher" mug. But he'd always taken his coffee straight.

"You haven't had your coffee yet this morning, have you? You still buy the best. I still make the best." He handed her coffee with that same old sloe-eyed, sleepy morning smile. "My daughter lives here."

"Is that how you got in?"

He sipped his own coffee. "She says she's getting married. She's not old enough, is she?"

"How old should she be?"

"Older than my little girl." He boosted himself up the few inches that it took him to seat himself on the counter. His long legs dangled nearly to the floor. "I always liked Jamie. I thought he was really going to make something of himself. Pick up a couple of instruments, put a band together. He couldn't sing, but he had a good ear."

She let the "make something of himself" jibe sail past her ear.

"How did you get here? I didn't see a strange vehicle in the driveway."

"And you don't see a strange man in your kitchen. You know us both. I'm still driving the same pickup, the one I left here with."

"How old is that thing now?"

"I've lost track. But she had zero miles on her when I got her." He gave his signature wink. "Just like you."

"What a flattering comparison."

"More than you know. That pickup is the only thing I have left that I don't share, but Jordan needed it to haul some stuff." His eyes went soft, as though resting them on her felt good to him. "How've you been?"

"Fine."

"Your mom?"

"Not so fine." She tried to remember what had been going on in her life when she'd last heard from him. "You know she has cancer."

"No, I didn't know. I'm sorry." He wagged his head sadly. "Jordan said she'd moved back, but she didn't say why. How's she doing with it?"

"Jordan, or my mother? Coping, both of them." She took her mothering stance, arms folded. "You haven't given me one straight answer so far. Why are you here, Creed?"

"Jordan called to tell me she was getting married. Actually, she left a message on my new answering machine." He grinned proudly. "I can call from anywhere and check in. So I got this message from her saying she had some news. I was coming into town anyway, so I . . ."

Her undeniable curiosity must have shown, because he was quick to explain. "I've got a gig. Haven't had one here in a long time." His smile seemed almost apologetic. "Yeah, I'm still at it. And, yeah, I still work construction to pay the bills."

"So why are you here," she repeated with exaggerated patience, "in *this house?*"

"Like I said, Jordan called. Talked to her last night. She called again this morning, wanting to use the pickup. She said you were gone with the van."

"That's right," Camille recalled. "She told me she needed it today."

"Said you'd been gone all night." He shrugged diffidently. " 'Course, we weren't worried."

"I left—"

"I haven't seen the boy yet. What's he like now? Still smart? Still . . ." A trace of the worry he'd disclaimed appeared in his eyes. "I know he's not a boy, and I know I missed my chance to send the bad ones packing and give the good ones fair warning. I left it all to you. He'll treat her right, won't he?"

"I hope so," she said with a sigh. "What am I saying? If he doesn't, she's outta there." Another double take. "*What am I saying?* They'll treat each other right."

"Like partners?"

"They'll make it, Creed."

"They haven't yet?" He gave a nervous laugh. "Just kidding. I don't want to know. I'd have to break his neck, and I don't think that would look too good. A neck brace with a tux." Hunkering down, he propped his elbows on his knees and cradled his coffee between his hands. "She's got her heart set on a fancy wedding, huh?"

"Fancier than ours was, I guess."

"A ten-dollar chapel in Vegas with an Elvis impersonator would be fancier than ours was." His eyes smiled for hers, hauling her into their private memory. "But the wedding night was a different story, wasn't it?"

"It wasn't fancy."

"Neither is heaven."

"Oh?" She raised her brow. "When were you last there?"

As always, Camille lost the ensuing stare-down. The instant she glanced away, she realized her foolishness. After all these years, she couldn't stop herself from asking the stupidest of double-edged questions.

"So you're here to congratulate your daughter on her engagement," she said. "Plus you've got your own engagement."

"Not the same kind." He nodded toward the kitchen table. "I saw the note you left. What's with Bridget? They're splittin' the sheets?"

"I guess so." She lifted an eyebrow for a pointed reminder. "I hate that expression."

He chuckled. "Hey, I left all the linen intact."

"You were quite civilized." She offered a piece of a smile. "You really were."

"I surprised you sometimes, didn't I?" He matched her, smile for smile. "You surprised me from the start, coming to that honky-tonk with your tony friends, then asking me if I took requests. I had a smooth comeback for you, but I couldn't roll it past the knot in my tongue. Then you had to ask for Hank Williams."

"That was about the extent of my knowledge of country music at the time."

"Cut me to the quick. I hated to disappoint you right off the bat, but I didn't do Hank Williams then. You can't sing Hank Senior until you've done some serious suffering." His gaze held hers. "I do ol' Hank's music now. I could break your heart with it."

"I don't doubt it."

"And I still take requests."

She gave a cool smile. "I don't make them anymore."

With a deferential nod he gave her side the point, then hopped off the counter and pulled the carafe from the coffeemaker. He offered her the first refill.

"I never let myself think about her getting married," he mused as he poured his own second cup. "Going to school, going to work, all that seems okay, but it's hard to think about her getting married, becoming some guy's wife." He slid the empty carafe back into its slot, switched the machine off, finally turned to Camille. "I thought you'd get married again."

"Maybe I will."

"You got somebody in mind?"

"Yes." She lifted one shoulder, disappointed that he didn't even blink. "But I haven't found him yet. I'm not sure he exists." She reached past him for creamer. "How about you?"

"Oh, I exist. I don't know if I did when we were married, but I do now."

"I mean . . ." He knew damn well what she meant, but she explained herself anyway. Old habit. "I notice you haven't remarried."

"You didn't expect me to, did you? Once was enough for this cowboy."

"Don't give me that 'cowboy' stuff. Is that the way you exist now, the way you live?"

"That's right. I get to play the lonesome cowboy. Gets 'em every time."

"The women?"

"Right where they live." He teased her with a quick one-finger belly poke. "I couldn't make it without them."

"Well, it was them or me, *darlin'*." Because she got the "darlin'" right—his drawl with a touch of sarcasm—she was able to look him in the eye and smile. "And you chose *them*."

"We'd stopped makin' it long before that final choice was made."

"Not completely."

"Sex was all we had left, and you didn't . . ." He glanced away, undone by his own cleverness. "I couldn't hold on to you with just that."

"Maybe it was all we ever had."

"Maybe." He took a step back. "And maybe we ought to find something else to talk about. This is hard enough without us draggin' out the dirty laundry. We had some good times, didn't we?"

"We had Jordan."

"*Have*," he averred. "You still have her, Camille. You always will. As for me . . ." He glanced out the window over the sink. "She wants her daddy to give her away again. But, damn, once was enough for that, too."

"Nobody expected you to become a complete stranger, Creed."

"Honey, can we call a truce?" He turned to her, voice soft, eyes soft, clearly gone soft all over at the thought of the impending give-away. He touched her chin with one guitar-string-callused fingertip, traced the line of her jaw so softly that she couldn't make herself turn her head away.

There was a reflexive answer, a polite answer, and a good answer. She held her breath, trying to sort them out while she gave him nothing but a heated stare.

"Hmm? For Jordan's sake." He tucked her hair behind her ear, massaged her earlobe with his thumb, her heart with a wistful smile. "I like your hair. I liked it long, but I like it this way, too. The color's a little different."

"Gray looks a lot better on you than it does on me."

She wasn't trying to flatter him, but she had to say something to stay on top of her game. Or her end of *their* game. She remembered the first time she'd seen him, the first look he'd given her, the first words he'd said. She remembered the scuffed black boots, the snug-fitting jeans, the way his shoulders made that pale blue satin western shirt seem as masculine as any football jersey. She'd made her peace with the fact that every detail of that first meeting was etched in her brain for the duration of Camille Delonga.

Letting him get this close now probably wasn't doing said duration any favors, but she told herself that passive resistance was good exercise, since the knees were often the first to go.

"I've been thinkin' about the good times." He drew his hand back. "Ever since Jordie called me with the news, I've been thinking about when you and I got married. It wasn't exactly a wedding, was it?"

"Why not?"

"You didn't have all the bells and whistles you deserved. You should have had all your friends and family there, nice meal, fancy cake, big dance."

"We had a dinner. Your family put on a big feed for us at the community center a few weeks later, and your friends and relatives showered us with gifts."

"We got at least a dozen blankets," he remembered, leaning back to rest against the edge of the counter as though touching her had been hard work.

"We were given thirteen blankets and four star quilts to be exact."

"One of your many gifts." He smiled when she drew a quizzical frown. "Exactitude. Is that a word?"

"I think so, although I'm not sure it's a gift."

"It was to me. I've been off ever since we split. I pay overdraft fees like you can't believe."

She laughed.

He shrugged, giving her the same boyish smile he'd always used to elicit her forgiveness. "Okay, I guess you can. Anyway, there was a feed, and there were gifts."

There was nothing to forgive him for now, she reminded herself. He had his checkbook, and she had hers.

It was definitely something she could smile about. "And we danced on our wedding night."

"We did, didn't we?"

"And you sang to me. Not many brides have a groom who can sing to them." She settled against the counter alongside him but gave herself a few inches of space. "We had a wedding, Creed. We had a marriage, and we had a child. *Have* a daughter. 'Have' while she's . . ."

She lifted her hand. "No, you're absolutely right. She'll always be our daughter. And I don't regret the wedding we had. I never have." She turned. "What about you?"

"I didn't at the time, but later it bothered me, knowing how much you missed out on."

"You should have told me. That was one bother we could have written off." She lowered her chin to her chest, looked down at the floor, and noticed his old black boots, the toes scuffed nearly colorless. Not far away the shiny toes of the black boots she rarely wore were sticking out from under her bathrobe.

How long had it been since she'd shared morning coffee with a man, hung out in her kitchen with him in her bathrobe?

What *man*? There had been only one. Creed Burke. And no one else. She'd told herself that she had a daughter to raise and didn't need anyone else, but the truth was that she'd tried the dating ritual and hated it.

But she missed the morning coffee.

Get real, she told herself. How often had they shared morning coffee when they were married? Was she forgetting the mornings he'd been hungover? The mornings his side of the bed had been empty? Bells and whistles didn't begin to describe what she'd missed out on.

And don't you forget it, she told herself.

But aloud she said, "We should have talked more."

"I wasn't much good at it." He tipped his head back, viewed the ceiling. "Especially at first. Whenever I tried, I'd get mad when you didn't seem to get my point. At first I'd wonder whether I had one and whether it mattered. Later on I figured I could have a damn good one and you wouldn't notice."

She looked at him curiously. He'd always preferred walking out on a disagreement to talking it over. Had he actually thought about it that much?

She shook her head. "That wasn't why you weren't much good at it. You weren't always truthful."

"I didn't always tell you everything."

"And I did. I told you everything."

"So you always said. What makes you think you know better than I do?"

She opened her mouth to protest.

"No," he said firmly, cutting her off with a gesture. "Hear me out for once. I got tired, too, Camille. A guy gets tired of being told everything. Just now I took a shot at telling you why I wasn't good at talking about every damn thing that happened, and every person, and every word, and every friggin' . . ."

He let out a deep sigh, as though he'd been saving it up for a long time, and he turned, collecting himself for better control.

"I'm telling you that I can't express myself as well as you do, at least not by talking. I'm telling you that I'm not much good at it. This is me, telling you something about me, and you just"—he snapped his fingers—"just like that, dismissed. It's not some little bother, baby, it's a big concern. But you have no trouble writing it off."

He was right. She'd had her protest ready to fire, but he'd blown it off her wall. Her mind scrambled to put the pieces in order, but at the moment "I didn't" and "you never" didn't add up to a hill of beans.

"I just meant that I didn't grow up dreaming of a fancy wedding," she said quietly, feeling very small.

"And I didn't grow up talking," he said patiently. "Not like you did. So I'm not much good at it."

"You're doing fine now."

"I'm not doing fine. I'm ready to walk out that door."

Ah, the Creed she had known and . . . knew still. Prompting her to smile knowingly. "What's stopping you?"

"I'd have to keep on walking, since our daughter has my pickup."

He had to laugh, and she had to join him.

"Have you had breakfast?" she asked finally.

"I've had coffee." He shrugged, shook his head, gave her that willing look, achingly reminiscent of the young heartbreaker she'd married. "Whatever she wants," he said, "I'll do what it takes to pay for it."

"Wedding receptions?"

He groaned. "How many would I have to do, *exactly?*"

She had no idea. "Your share of fifty should cover half the cost."

"No problem," he said affably. "As long as I don't have to be sober."

Laughing, she reached for her frying pan. "I don't think they notice at weddings."

But she realized they were to become "we" for a while. The wedding people. Doomed for a time to wander from pillars of flowers to invitations to post. *We* for a while, a wee while, and then back to normal. Camille could handle it, *would* handle it, as Creed had suggested, for her daughter's sake.

When Jordan walked through the door, it seemed for just a moment that "we" added up to three again. Mom and Dad were lingering at the kitchen table, a few scraps and crumbs left on their plates, some cold coffee in their cups. Little Jordan was rushing in from school to grab a bite to eat.

Camille hung her head, smiling, undoubtedly giving the impression that she was embarrassed about having breakfast with her ex-husband, or the fact that it was nearly noon and she still wasn't dressed, or the simple fact that she was smiling. But no one picked up on it, maybe because they both knew full well that she was uncomfortable with feeling too comfortable.

So they greeted each other as though it were something they did every day. Like a normal family.

It was unusual for Jordan to come home for lunch, but she had something that didn't belong to her. "Thanks for the use of your truck. With Mom's van gone this morning, I don't know how I would have gotten that plywood to school."

"I'm sorry. I forgot that you . . ." Camille gestured vaguely in Creed's direction. "You didn't tell me that you already called . . ."

Addressing him with a quick glance, she shifted her apology. "Not that I didn't intend . . ."

He turned to Jordan, laughing. "When did she forget how to finish a sentence?"

"I don't know." Jordan's smile was tentative. "She had no problem with it yesterday."

"I've hardly been able to catch my breath since yesterday. All of a sudden everything's moving too fast for me to keep up, never mind finish a sentence."

"Dad suggested that we look at the Countryside Inn for the reception." Jordan handed Creed his keys. "His band is playing there this weekend."

"Isn't that sort of a pizza and beer motel? I don't think that would quite do for the Mayfields."

Rosemary's sudden appearance in the kitchen doorway brought Creed to his feet.

"I thought you said this was going to be a Delonga wedding," she said, reaching into Creed's easy hug. "How's my favorite son-in-law?"

"*Ex*-son-in-law, Mama."

"I don't divorce my children." She patted his cheek. "You'll be my favorite as long as there are no new prospects on the horizon. So far the horizon remains vacant."

"And there's peace in the valley," Camille muttered, cradling her cold cup.

As she recalled, Creed had been at least a dozen kinds of undesirable as a son-in-law, but Rosemary's objections to their marriage had evaporated the day Jordan was born. A dozen years and a pail of tears later, she hadn't objected to the divorce outright, but she'd sure enjoyed playing devil's advocate.

"How's this a Delonga wedding when the bride's name is still Burke?" Creed turned to his daughter. "It is, isn't it?"

"Of course it is," Jordan said promptly, having little time for detours in the conversation. "The Countryside Inn would be convenient to the church."

"What church?" Camille demanded in a tone that questioned the legitimacy of any church that would locate near a place that would hire Creed's band.

"We thought we'd use the church James grew up in since we've . . ." Jordan shrugged innocently. "Well, we've sort of bounced around church-wise."

"I haven't been able to get you to go for . . ."

Calm down. Camille took a breath as she placed both palms carefully on either side of her empty plate. She glanced at Creed, who didn't seem to know whether to sit down with Camille or hang with his apparent allies.

"Okay, I've slacked off in a few areas," she felt compelled to confess. "But I keep meaning to get back into the habit."

"You don't have to explain anything to me," he said with a chuckle.

Jordan snatched the remaining corner of cold toast off the edge of Creed's plate. "I'm putting the Countryside Inn on the list of places to consider," she said, sucking the orange marmalade off her thumb.

"There's already a list?" Camille muttered. She was surrounded by people who weren't listening.

But neither was she. She was remembering that the marmalade in the cupboard had always been purchased as Creed's favorite before it had become Jordan's.

"How many people can they seat?" Jordan asked her father.

"We play in the bar, but I know they have a nice-size banquet room." He slid back into his chair, the better to challenge Camille eye to eye. "Just because I play there doesn't make it a dive."

"I didn't say 'dive.' I just don't think we want pizza and beer for our daughter's—"

"We'll go this weekend," Jordan decided. "James would love to hear Dad's new band."

Camille suddenly remembered how she'd spent the last twelve hours. "Have you talked to James today?"

"He told me about last night. He feels pretty bad about the whole mess." Jordan brightened as she turned to Creed. "It would do James good to go out for pizza and beer and some live music this weekend."

"We don't solve any problems, but we can sure drown 'em out for a while."

"Do I get to go?" Rosemary asked with a laugh.

"Sure, if you feel like it, Grandma. And we can check the place out at the same time. I'll bet their rates would be reasonable. If it's big enough, we might want to schedule a consultation with—"

"How big are we talking?" Camille asked.

"We only have about a hundred on our guest list so far."

"There's already a list?"

"When she comes up with a complete sentence, she likes to reuse it," Jordan told Creed.

"You haven't even set a date," Camille reminded her.

"We're getting to that," Jordan told her mother, who was beginning to feel extraneous in the conversation. "We didn't know what to do about your side, Dad. They probably wouldn't be able to come all this way, would they? Wouldn't really want to, probably."

"Why not? Once they get a pass to leave the reservation, they ought to be able to get across the state line without too much hassle."

"A pass?"

"Just kidding," he said, his voice soft and tight.

Camille heard his tone over the words, actually heard him this time. With Creed there was fun kidding and there was defensive kidding. This was Creed telling his daughter that she was about to step on some thin skin.

"How long has it been since you've been out there?" he asked her.

"Since the last time I went with you, which was, what? When Grandma Frances died?"

He shook his head. "That can't be right. It can't be that long ago. That's been almost three years." He rose from his chair and stepped back from the table. "You do what you want about my side. You want 'em to come, they'll come. Some of 'em anyway."

"Which ones?" Jordan asked hesitantly.

"Which ones are welcome?"

"All of them, of course, but you have so many relatives, Dad. And we'd have to know *for sure* whether they were coming."

"You do what you want," he said. "I'm just glad *I* got invited."

"And I'm glad I get to make another wedding dress," Rosemary said, clearly as oblivious as Jordan was to the growing tension. "It'll be the best thing I've ever done, Jordie. I want you to look at some of the pictures I've collected and tell me what you like."

Jordan slipped her mother a frantic look.

Camille offered her daughter a tight smile. *We'll talk later.*

Pushing back from the table gave Camille a chance to adjust her smile for her mother. *I'm glad you're feeling better.*

Coming to her feet, she felt new warmth for her former husband, and she let it touch her eyes when they met his across the table. *It's good to see you again.*

Chapter 7

"Mom, what am I going to do? Grandma really thinks she's going to make my wedding dress."

Camille slid her safety goggles over her forehead and turned off the torch. She had to finish the autumn-leaf pattern in the fire screen by the end of the day. Her client was counting on it as a wedding gift.

Lately everywhere Camille turned, somebody was getting ready for a wedding. And, like the client who had ordered the fire screen, they were pouring in the cash as though there were endless tomorrows. The artist who made the perfect wedding gift could name her price.

In the name of common sense, the mother of the bride was determined to do the same. At the very least, she would name her limit.

"You don't want her to?" Camille asked, nearly achieving the desired artlessness in her tone.

"I'm not looking for Vera Wang or anything, but I don't want a homemade dress."

Jordan had sense to spare, and there was nothing common about it. It suited no one but her. She had her own sense of style, of direction, of timing, of what was right and wrong for Jordan. In any given situation she was able to zero in on what mattered to her and let go of the rest. Clearly the wedding dress stood at the top of Jordan's list of what mattered, which was exactly where it was for her grandmother. Rosemary's list had to be even shorter and narrower than Jordan's. But it was to be Jordan's wedding, Jordan's dress.

This would not be an easy compromise to negotiate.

"You'd have a *hand*made dress," Camille said calmly as she pulled off her gloves. "Made by the hands of your grandmother. She may not be a designer of haute couture, but she used to be quite well known as one of the best tailors in the Twin Cities."

Jordan began circling, one sidestep at a time. "She makes *quilts*, Mother, and it's been a while since she's even done that."

"There was a time when people would bring your grandma a picture or even a sketch and she would copy it perfectly, make them something better than what they could buy in a store."

"But not a wedding dress."

"Why not a wedding dress? A dress is a dress."

"This is *my* wedding dress we're talking about, Mother."

"We're also talking about your grandmother, who's made all kinds of dresses." Camille took her daughter by the arm and led her to the cushioned settee she'd made to resemble climbing roses tumbling over a fence. "You've seen the pictures of her wedding dress."

"And I've seen pictures of me wearing those frilly little dresses you said she made for me, and they looked cute, but, Mom . . ." Jordan lifted her plaintive gaze and obediently sat. "A wedding dress? She's not up to anything like that now."

"Like what? What do you have in mind?"

"I'm not sure, but I don't want it to look . . ." Jordan shrugged off the temptation to presume something unflattering. "She's not well enough."

"She seems to think she is."

"What if she's not?"

"Then you might have an unfinished dress and a dead grandmother, Jordan. Which part of that picture screws up your plans more?"

Jordan glared. "That's not fair."

Granted, but under the circumstances, the judicious pulling out of certain stops was a mother's prerogative.

"Okay, put it this way." Camille shifted toward her daughter, knee to knee. "Which part of the picture is irreplaceable?"

"She screwed up your wedding, didn't she?" Jordan challenged, choosing to ignore the question. "If she hadn't hated Dad so much, you wouldn't have had to go to a justice of the peace."

"She didn't hate him, honey. She didn't know anything about him except that he was a musician."

"And an Indian."

"Well, that's all water under the bridge. They made their peace when you were born. Your dad and I did it our way, and you and James will do it yours. It's easy for me to support you, because I've known James since he was born. I like to think I'd back you no matter what, because I know *you*. But maybe that's not fair." She shrugged and glanced away, grateful to go untested.

The rift between Camille and her mother had been painful. One of those "I'll never treat my daughter the way my mother treated me" lessons on the one side, "May you be cursed with a daughter just like you" on the other. Time and the birth of a child had brought new perspectives to both of them.

"So I'm braced," Camille declared with a stiff smile. "What's your way going to be?"

"We won't go overboard. I know you think it's a waste of money, but, Mom, James and I are going to be married. *Married*. It's such a big step."

She nodded, gratified that her daughter saw it that way. Camille believed in marriage, believed in marrying for love and loving the marriage enough to preserve it as long as it would last. She hoped her daughter's would last forever.

"It's not the money, Jordan. It's the way—"

"Our way is to do it once and do it right," Jordan said, firmly enough to cause a sting. "Make it special. It's important to me to mark the beginning of our married life by celebrating with the people we care about. I want it to be a day that we'll all enjoy and remember."

"Have you been shopping already?"

"Without you and Grandma? Of course not. But I can't ask Grandma to go shopping with me for my wedding dress when she's bound and determined to make it herself."

"Are you bound and determined that she can't?" The answer was in Jordan's eyes. "Are you going to tell her this?"

"I was hoping you could talk her out of it," Jordan pleaded softly, slipping back a few years, taking her turn at glancing away.

"All you have to say is that you don't want her to make your dress."

"It's not that I don't *want* her to." Jordan's eyes challenged her now. "Any more than it's not the money."

"I don't know how long she's been gathering books and pictures and fabric swatches."

Jordan groaned.

"She's waiting for you to find the time to look at them with her." Camille laid her hand on Jordan's bare knee. "Honey, this is her gift. Her talent, her special skill."

Jordan stared at the work her mother had set aside. Camille could almost hear Jordan processing the guilt she'd unabashedly piled on, filtering it through her secret hopes and dreams, coloring them with lackluster shades of *homemade*.

"How long has it been since she did anything like this?" Jordan asked finally, beginning to resign herself to the first compromise.

Disappointment already, Camille thought. Jordan was bracing herself to settle for less if her mother had the first say. Because Jordan's wish had always been her father's command, it could never be her mother's. Camille had held the line on spending for so long that it was ingrained in her, embedded in every decision. When Jordan had asked for Nike or Guess, Camille would find something that looked almost the same at half the price. But "almost" didn't count for anything but disappointment.

And now Camille's push was on for less wedding.

Not that Jordan couldn't buy her own wedding dress. She'd been buying her own clothes since she'd started working. But money was not the object in this instance. Maybe it had been with the Nikes and the Guess, but not with the wedding. She had told her to put her savings toward the future purchase of a home. She truly wanted her daughter to have a nice wedding, but she wasn't sure Jordan believed that completely. To Bridget and Lauren, "nice" meant "expensive," and Jordan was about to become a Mayfield.

Jordan would still be Jordan, Camille reminded herself. Head-strong, a bit willful sometimes, but good at heart. She didn't understand the extent of Rosemary's skill, but she understood that refusing her grandmother's offer, no matter what the reason, would hurt.

But if Jordan accepted, what then? How long *had* it been?

"You'll have to ask her," Camille said. How did that old hymn go? Faith of our fathers? How about faith of our mothers, *in* our mothers? Living faith, against all odds. "Tell her what you have in mind. If she can't do it, she'll let you know."

Please, Mama. If you can't do it, say so.

"What if she thinks she's up to it and it turns out she's not?"

"We'll buy a dress."

"You can't just walk in and buy a wedding dress, Mom."

"You look great in everything you try on, Jordan," Camille said with practiced patience. "You're not hard to fit. And you've never been this hard to please before." Not quite true, but it sounded good.

"I've never been a bride before. What if she makes something that turns out looking . . ." Jordan's grimace said it all. "Well, *homemade*. I'll have to wear it, won't I?"

"Boy, that's a tough one, Jordan. It would have to be your call."

The grimace gave way to a sick smile. "Thanks."

"And I would have to sit back in silence and watch you make it."

"Is that what they call the mother's moment of truth?"

"It wouldn't be the first, would it?" Camille laughed. "Remember the Cabbage Patch debacle?"

"You mean when we got the last doll in the store, and that other kid was bawling because her sister had snapped up the second-to-last one?"

"That poor little girl. That was their shopping trip with their weekend dad. He offered you an extra seven dollars, which was all the money he had."

"Oh, Mom, they were working on your obvious weaknesses. Long faces and great bargains."

"I left it up to you because I was sure you'd let the little girl have the doll."

"After we'd been to at least a hundred stores that were sold out of Cabbage Patch dolls? You didn't see me bawling over it, did you? No, I sucked it up and kept on hunting. Once I got mine, I wasn't letting her go for seven dollars or seven hundred."

"You wouldn't have taken seven *hundred?*"

"From that poor man and his pitiful little girl?" Jordan laughed. "They say that God doesn't give us more teachable moments than we can handle."

"Or more kids," Camille said, delivering a parting pat on the knee as she stood. "You work this out with your grandma."

"I need your help, Mom. I can't say no to her."

"If you can say no to that sad little girl . . ."

Jordan groaned.

"And her poor dad's last seven dollars . . ."

Jordan growled.

"Little girl, I know you've got unselfish bones in that woman's body of yours. You've just got to drink more milk to strengthen them up."

"Be serious, Mother. I really need—"

"I'm completely serious," Camille claimed.

But she was laughing. She didn't know why. She really didn't know which way Jordan would jump on this dress thing, but it was up to Jordan. Camille had seriously given herself complete leave not to worry about it, to let Jordan handle it herself.

"A little milk, a little trust," Camille mused as she headed back to her metalworking. "You'll be amazed at how far you can go."

· · ·

Her mother was turning into one of those insufferable wise women in her old age. Jordan would have to settle the wedding dress issue on her own. She wanted to get straight to the point, but when Grandma looked up from her magazine and smiled, she decided to take a small detour.

"What are you doing this weekend, Grandma?"

"I'll have to check my calendar." Grandma scooted closer to the arm of the living room sofa and patted the space she'd left all warm and sunken in. "Are you still planning on going to hear Creed's band this weekend?"

Tight-lipped, Jordan nodded.

"You ought to get your mother to go along."

"What about you? I was thinking maybe you'd like to join us for a while."

"I have to go to the clinic tomorrow. That always wipes me out, but if I bounce back in time, I'd love to go. Either way, try to drag your mother out of the house. She loves listening to him sing."

"What if he's got someone else there, listening to him sing?"

"What if he does? They've been divorced almost as long as they were married. At this point they can probably handle it, both of them." Grandma patted the sofa seat with added insistence. "Come sit with me for a few minutes and tell me about the most beautiful dress you've ever seen in your life."

"The most beautiful dress?" She'd know it when she saw it, but the politic response to her grandmother was to shrug innocently and take a seat. "It's funny, isn't it? I'm always wearing jeans and slacks."

"How about your prom dress?"

"Oh, God!" Jordan hooted. "That was a disaster. I liked the *idea* of that dress, with all those sequins and that cutout back. I thought I was going to make quite a nice little splash in it. Maybe they'd even try to kick me out of the dance for exposing too much skin."

"Wouldn't that have been exciting?"

"More exciting than the prom turned out to be. Boy, what a let-down after all that preparation."

"But the dress . . ."

"That thing was so uncomfortable." Jordan laughed. The mere memory made her boobs itch. "It kept hiking up, and I kept feeling those sequins under my armpits. By that time I had broken up with Paul, but we decided to go to the prom anyway, and I hated having him put his clammy hand on my bare back. And, as it turns out, it's not so great going without a bra. I felt naked."

"I'm surprised your mother went along with that."

Jordan lifted one shoulder. "The dress was on sale."

"Ah, that explains it. I taught her not to be wasteful. I didn't teach her to be cheap."

"It was the dress I wanted," she explained quickly. "And Mom was willing to overlook the minor drawbacks because we got such a good deal. But by the time prom night rolled around, nobody liked my dress except the guy I didn't want to be with."

"So the sequined backless halter dress is not your style."

Jordan hooted again, then hung her head, wagging it, wondering what had happened to that dress and whether she really had a style, whether she even wanted one. It sounded like a label, something to be known for that was really of no consequence.

"The most beautiful dress I've ever seen," she mused, thinking that was all she wanted. Not a label, not a style, not a look. She wanted to wear a beautiful dress on her wedding day.

"Cinderella at the ball?" Grandma prompted.

"That's Lauren."

"Princess Diana? Queen Noor? Madonna?"

"More like Jean Harlow, or Rita Hayworth, or Lauren Bacall," Jordan decided. She hadn't thought about it that way before, so the comparison was as much a revelation to her as it was to her grandmother.

Maybe more so. Grandma didn't look at all surprised. "But not backless," she said.

"Definitely not backless."

"I knew it." Grandma reached across the arm of the sofa and came up with an old scrapbook. "Let's look at some pictures."

"What have you got here?" Jordan thought she'd seen all the picture albums her mother and grandmother had ever kept.

"I've made some beautiful clothes in my time, Jordie. I used to have a waiting list of customers who wanted something very special, something custom-made." She opened the scrapbook and started paging through it. "Granted, these clothes are a little dated, but these are some of the things I made. Just to show you that we're not talking about your ordinary Simplicity pattern book here."

Jordan leaned closer.

The scrapbook contained swatches of fabric, sketches, old photographs of ordinary women with brand-new-dress smiles on their faces. No forties drab or fifties kitsch here. The suits and gowns were classics. Had Jordan seen these pictures before? She had the feeling she'd seen without looking, been present without interest. But here were styles reminiscent of the looks she associated with ageless beauty, black-and-white movies, sensuality and grace. Princess Grace. Jacqueline Kennedy. Audrey Hepburn.

"You made these, Grandma?" She could've kicked herself for sounding surprised, but her grandmother laughed. "Of course you did," Jordan said, laughing along. "I knew that. They're wonderful."

"I'm not a designer, but I can copy to beat the band." She offered Jordan a recent bridal magazine. "You show me what you see that you like."

Ignoring the magazine, Jordan petted a swatch of silk that was glued to a scrapbook page. Her grandmother had made these beautiful clothes a lifetime ago. But still, she'd made them. There would be no saying no. Whatever she made, Jordan would wear.

"Just something simple, Grandma."

"You don't want sequins. What do you think of seed pearls?" Grandma would not be sidetracked from her pursuit of Jordan's dream dress, be it simple or ornate. She flipped pages until she found a style with clean lines. "What do you think of something like this?"

"It's too complicated, Grandma." Over her grandmother's "Pshaw" she added, "Well, look at all that little stuff. Can you buy the material with beads already applied? That would take forever to do by hand."

"I don't have forever, but I do have time." She covered Jordan's hand over the scrapbook and squeezed, reassuring both of them. "I know I do."

"Of course you do. I just don't want you to overdo."

"Don't worry about *over*, Jordie. But please let me *do*. Let me show you what I do, what I once did and know I can still do. Give me something important to do. You won't be disappointed."

"Why did you quit?"

"I didn't quit sewing, but I stopped doing it professionally. I had my home, my family. And times changed." Rosemary looked at the dress in the magazine again, smiling wistfully. "I didn't want to go into the wedding dress business, which is stressful and demanding, more so all the time. There was only one other wedding dress I wanted to make besides yours and mine. But it's pretty hard to make a dress for someone when you're not speaking to each other."

"She didn't want a wedding dress."

"I could have made something else—whatever she wanted to wear. I was stubborn. She was proud. It was a missed opportunity, one that you can't do over again." Grandma looked up, bright-eyed with anticipation. "Give me a challenge, Jordie. Give me lots of handwork to do, plenty of details to apply. If you make it too easy, I'll have to take it apart every night so I have something to do the next day."

"I love the simple lines of your wedding dress, Grandma. But this delicate beadwork is beautiful, too. Do you do this kind of embroidery by hand?"

"Do I ever!" She displayed her hands with new pride.

Ten chewed nails and myriad age spots on shriveled skin didn't deter from their beauty for Jordan. They were Grandma's hands. She'd watched them stitch quilts. An infinity of tiny stitches taken in bright, practical cotton. Years ago Jordan had asked for a blue quilt because all those stitches had always reminded her of stars. A bit of fancy applied to something serviceable, worth the effort because Jordan would use it daily for years to come.

She would wear her wedding dress once. All that money spent for a dress you wear for one day, her mother would say.

How about all that work? What if it turned out to be her grand-mother's swan song, the ephemeral notes stitched in diaphanous white? Jordan imagined tiny stitches rising in a trail to the stars. Her throat burned. All that work for a dress she would wear only once. One day only.

"And here's a blessing I hadn't thought of," Grandma warbled happily, flexing her fingers. "I've got my share of health problems, but arthritis isn't one of them. Jordie, you'll have a dress like no other."

"An heirloom," Jordan said.

"Don't store it in the basement if you live in a flood plain." She pulled a shopping bag off the floor next to her feet and reached inside. "Your mother picked up these fabric swatches for me, but we're not limited to these. This silk satin is beautiful. And the silk organza—"

The white strips fluttered across her knees, one at a time. Pure white. Star-bright white. Safe-surrender white.

"*Mom* shopped for these?"

"They're just swatches. Of course, there are so many shades of white, you want to get the bolt and drape a large piece . . ." She traced the drape on Jordan, shoulder to shoulder, then lifted her chin for a look in the eye, age to youth, grandmother to granddaughter. "I can do this, Jordie."

"So much to decide. I haven't even looked in the stores yet."

"That's a good idea. Try some on for style."

Jordan nodded. "What about the attendants? I'm thinking I'll have three. Maybe four. We'll want a complementary style, won't we?"

"That's all up to you, honey. Try to pick girls who have grandmothers who sew." She laughed as she turned more pages until something caught her eye. "What do you think of this neckline?"

Jordan tipped her head, a noncommittal gesture. *One commitment at a time,* she thought. She would marry James. She would wear a homemade wedding dress. No, not homemade—*handmade.*

Handmade it would be.

.　.　.

"Get dressed, Bridget. You're going out with me tonight." Camille pushed on the front door, widening the wedge until Bridget stepped back and let her in. "We have a date with destiny," Camille declared with more cheer than she knew she had in her.

"I'm still married. Maybe after the divorce is final, I'll try changing my orientation." Bridget turned away, scuffing across the polished wood floor in slippers and satin robe.

Camille closed the door. "Actually our children's destiny." She tossed her coat across one of a pair of foyer chairs. If Bridget wanted it hung up, she could be a little more hospitable. She followed Bridget to her bedroom. "They're looking at a possible reception facility, and I'm not going alone."

"You're going with them."

"They're going with each other. Creed's band is playing at the Countryside Inn."

"Creed?" Blue funk gave way to curiosity. "What's *he* doing here?"

"I just told you." Camille ducked into the huge, meticulously organized walk-in closet and emerged with a denim shirtwaist. "Wear this. Perfect for pizza and beer."

"Pizza and beer? Creed's band?" Bridget grimaced. "The *Countryside Inn?* They can't use that place for their wedding reception."

"My thoughts exactly, but I need some backup. Especially with—"

"Creed being there?" Bridget accepted the dress and held it up for inspection. "Is this mine?"

"It's in your closet."

"I'm really not in the mood for country music sung by my best friend's ex-husband," Bridget claimed as she disappeared into the closet. "Not that he isn't good," she called out. "Ellie's right about that. I never understood why he didn't go a lot further than he did with it."

"Fear of success," Camille said, screwing up her face at Bridget and the dressy skirt and blouse she carried from the closet. "No, don't wear that. Too stuffy. Just find some jeans. Do you have jeans?"

"You're not wearing jeans," Bridget pointed out. "And Creed never struck me as the fearful type. Why didn't he give it a shot? There are places right here in Minneapolis where you can make those demo recordings."

"I don't know, Bridge. He's too good for Main Street, but maybe he's not good enough for Music Row."

"But maybe he is. You don't know until you—"

"He's no longer my problem," Camille snapped. Then she sighed. Bridget was going to wear that fussy surplice blouse. "At least he wasn't until Jordan told him she was getting married."

"Country music at my son's wedding?" Bridget sank into her satin-tufted boudoir chair with a groan. "I can't think about this right now, Cam. It's just one more thing that's too unthinkable to deal with."

"I don't know about the music, but Creed Burke will be part of your son's wedding. That's a given, I'm afraid. But I'm not facing him alone again, not tonight."

"The Countryside Inn." Bridget thought for a moment, then sat up straight, untying the sash on her robe. "You're right. We have to be on hand to nip that notion right in the bud."

"Open mind, Bridge, open mind. This is Jordan and James, not Lauren and Anthony. Different wedding, whole new ball game. We have to keep an open mind."

"Or the appearance of one." Bridget slipped into her designer blouse. "You're not in favor of this place, are you?"

"My preference went by the boards long ago. With my limited experience in the wedding department, I have no idea what we're in for, but I'm sure it'll be interesting."

"We'll look at their choices, and then we'll suggest some irresistible alternatives."

"Practice saying this, Bridge: 'This is not my wedding. It's James and Jordan's.'" Camille glanced at the tall bureau. Bridget and Tim's wedding picture had been removed, but Lauren and Tony's remained. "And I'm not taking out a second mortgage to pay for it."

Chapter 8

⌒

They were seated, like five mismatched peas in a pod, at a corner booth upholstered in green vinyl. Bridget stood out, put together in unrivaled style for the first time in weeks, content to outclass her surroundings. Rosemary, at the other end of the booth as well as the style spectrum, was content to be outside the house for reasons other than medical ones. At the center of it all, James and Jordan were content in their pod within a pod.

But Camille, seated next to her mother, was far from content. The Countryside Inn Café didn't take reservations, and her group had waited forty-five minutes for a table. She hoped the line for tables meant that the food was decent. The menu offered standard fare.

When the waitress finally greeted them,

Camille slapped the menu shut and looked up as though she'd decided to spring a pop quiz. "What's your specialty?"

"Have you tried our pizza? It's the best in the Twin Cities."

"I just moved back from Chicago, where the pizza is hard to beat," James said.

"Give us a chance," the young woman wheedled. "I'll give you my personal money-back guarantee. Now, you can't beat a deal like that."

"Where else but Minnesota for *such a deal?*" Jordan put in, slipping her fiancé an inside-joke glance. They both laughed. "We understand you do wedding receptions," she said to the waitress.

"All the time, but not too many brides ask for pizza, which is a mistake in my book. It's cheaper than chicken Kiev and looks just as good on the front of the dress as butter sauce." She gave an appreciative look at the hand Jordan had laid possessively on James's arm. "Pretty ring. I'd say this guy's a keeper. When's the big day?"

"We haven't booked it yet," James said. "I'm up for the pizza challenge. Who's with me?"

Bridget opted out, but everyone else agreed on the house special.

"I think they're setting up for a reception tonight," the waitress said as she collected the menus. "You might want to go through the bar and take a peek at the banquet room. Your order will be up in twenty."

"And so the hunt begins," Camille muttered to Bridget as she slid across the booth.

"I wonder when the band starts."

"We probably won't stay too long. Right, Mama?"

"Who's 'we'?" Rosemary grinned and did a little hip swing. "I'm here for the music."

"And I'm here for the drama," Bridget said, following the conga line they'd formed as they made their way through the bar. "At some-one else's expense."

"It won't be mine," Camille said blithely. "I'm here for pizza and beer."

"The first round's on me."

Camille did a quick about-face, surprised that she hadn't noticed Creed from the back. He swiveled, gave her a look that said she wasn't getting by him that easily as he slid from the barstool. He greeted his daughter with a hug, gave everyone else a general nod. "Nice to see you, Bridget. Congratulations."

"On what?"

"Your son's good fortune." As though the possibility of a miscue had just dawned on him, he added, "Hey, I'm sorry about the split, but it doesn't surprise me. Mayfield's no brighter than any of the rest of us guys."

"Which Mayfield?" James offered a handshake.

"You'd better be the exception, young James. If there's one excep-tion in the entire male race, you'd better be it."

"Men aren't a race, Dad. They're a gender."

"Jordie, if this guy doesn't treat you right, he'll find himself in a race, trying to escape your ol' man. Hell has no fury like a father whose son-in-law turns out to be dumber than he is."

Creed laid a hand on James's shoulder, man to man.

James chuckled. "Pretty hard to respond to that one without put-ting my foot in it. Let me just go on record with a promise to love my wife and respect my elders."

"You raised a damn fine diplomat, Bridget," Creed allowed. "If you need a date for the wedding, I can fix you up with my fiddler. Sam, come over here and meet my family." He waved across the bar at a small, white-haired man. "Sam has a little age on him, but it takes years to become a good fiddler and a gentleman both. I wouldn't fix you up with anything but a true gentleman, Bridget."

"I don't know about the fiddler part."

"You had enough of that, huh?" He laughed. "What'll you folks have to drink?"

"We were on our way to take a look at the banquet room," Camille said. "Our first look at a possible reception site."

"No kidding?" Creed reached back to the bar to stub out a cigarette and claim his beer. "I can vouch for the hotel rooms, but I haven't been invited to any banquets yet."

He hadn't been invited to join the inspection party either, but he tagged along anyway.

Beyond the double doors, preparations for a celebration were almost complete. Round tables were set, and gold and silver balloon bouquets floated throughout the room. A tiered cake took center stage. A bit on the spartan side, Camille noted, but she was impressed with the two walls of floor-to-ceiling windows. She approached the woman who appeared to be supervising the setup and asked how many people the room could accommodate and the size of the party they were expecting tonight. She still had no idea what they were looking for, but she wanted to look as though she did.

"This is surprisingly nice," she mused, imagining more candles. Lots and lots of candles.

"In a utilitarian sort of way," Bridget allowed grudgingly.

"But it has windows, Bridge. That's what Lauren's reception was missing. Windows double the candlelight."

Bridget scowled. "Lauren's reception wasn't missing anything. Not a thing."

"You didn't have windows."

"Lauren's reception was beautiful," said Jordan, stepping between her mother and James's. "And ours will be beautiful. But different. We're starting at square one." She took another look around. "I agree, Mom. The windows are a big plus. And people can go outside on the patio."

"It's pretty small. Of course, I don't know how many people you're planning on." Bridget inspected the burgundy upholstery on one of the dining chairs. "Have you chosen your colors, Jordan? I guess you could always rent nicer linens and maybe chair covers."

"I think you've skipped a few squares, Mom," James said, slipping his fiancée a subtle wink. "This looks great to me. It feels friendly and comfortable."

Jordan *would* go for a winker, Camille thought. Her father's favorite brand of flirtation and her own worst weakness. *Former weakness.*

"We're easy to work with," the supervisor volunteered. She took a hotel business card from her skirt pocket and handed it to Camille. "Here's the name of the lady you'll need to talk to." She glanced at Creed. "Aren't you with the band?"

"Yes, ma'am. I'm also the father of the bride."

"That works out well. Is the groom's father a judge by any chance?"

"Why not the groom's mother?" Bridget demanded. She was checking out the wedding cake.

"Either way, you'd have some major bases covered." The woman had clearly turned her interest to Creed. "I heard you guys practicing. They're out there putting the name up on the sign now. Word's gonna get out fast. Great name for a country band, hey."

"What is it now?" Camille asked.

"'Only the Lonely.' We thought about 'Pretty Men,' but then we thought again."

"Good thinking," she said dryly.

"You got time to hang around and catch a few songs?"

"That's what we came for," Rosemary reported before anyone had a chance to say otherwise.

"Rosie, you're the most loyal fan I've got, not to mention the most beautiful. And to think you're my mother-in-law." He turned to the fiddler, who had also tagged along. "Sam, we'd better strike 'Mother-in-Law' from tonight's playlist."

"He's kidding," Sam assured Rosemary. "That's not our style. I wanted to call us 'The Country Gentlemen,' more in keeping with our true nature. Creed says the appeal of country music is that people don't have to get up for it. They can be low down. The music will reach in and get hold of people right where they live. Even if they've hit bottom, it'll find them." He gestured to demonstrate. "'Only the Lonely' was Creed's idea, so I guess we know where he's living."

"It sounds like a shameless bid for female sympathy to me," Bridget said. "What is it they say about lonely women?"

"They make good lovers," Creed said. He cocked a finger at Sam. "Take that song off the list, too."

Sam slapped Creed on the back. "Damn, by the time you're done hiding your true feelings, we won't have much left."

"We're not staying long," Camille said. "Save the true feelings for the bottom feeders."

Creed laughed. "You wound me, Wild Thing."

"Wild Thing?" Jordan aped, bouncing an incredulous glance between Creed and Camille.

"Haven't you ever seen your mother boogie?" Creed asked.

"Mother? *Boogie?*"

"Sounds like somebody else is hiding her true passion. Once she starts gettin' down on the dance floor, you'll be here till last call."

Maybe once upon a time, Camille thought, but she gave her daughter a suggestive smile. It wasn't that she didn't want to go out every so often. She didn't have time. She had no reason to make the time.

Her married friends had long since stopped trying to fix her up with that friend on the rebound who's just the nicest guy. Men on the rebound generally tried too hard, and nice guys generally bored her. Everyone finally believed that Camille enjoyed her independence.

But independence didn't lend itself to going out on the town. There was no place for a fifth wheel on the boogie buggy.

Creed turned down Jordan's offer of pizza. He'd already eaten the supper he was about to sing for. His music drifted into the café while his family dined. Camille had almost forgotten how much she enjoyed hearing the sound of his voice. She had planned to make her excuses and leave after supper, but that wasn't going to happen now that she'd heard him and remembered how much fun it was to watch him.

After they finished eating, they moved to the bar, where they got the last empty table. Camille laughed off James's invitation to dance, but underneath the table she couldn't keep her feet completely still. Not only was Creed's music impossible to resist, but so also was the pleasure he took in making it. Creative juices were delicious. Camille had come to savor that particular taste in herself, and she knew how addictive it was, how the pungent taste would burst forth in the instant when vision became reality. But it would fade in its own attainment, and you had to start chasing it all over again.

Oh, she understood that now. She knew how he felt when he

closed his eyes and crooned "A Thousand Miles from Nowhere." It was undoubtedly a song made popular by another singer, but Camille hadn't heard it before. She'd stopped listening to his brand of music the minute Creed had moved out of their home.

He didn't write his own music. He "covered" other people's songs, but when he sang a song his way, it became his. He lived it, loved it, caressed it with his whole sexy, soothing self, and gave it life. But because he didn't record it, his song was fleeting. Beyond the moment, it lived only in the memories of those who'd heard it.

Maybe that was the beauty of it.

He sang for the crowd, which grew. People who had come in for a drink ended up staying for the music. He would have them as long as he wanted them, and the booking as well. A few weeks, probably, and then he would want a change of scene, a different crowd. But for now he gave unstintingly, and everyone in the room loved him for it.

Everyone.

He sang for Camille, a song called "The Heart That You Own." For the moment she believed every word, every soulful sentiment. The rest of the band played on as he laid his guitar down, stepped off the riser, and drew Camille out of her seat, onto the dance floor. He had the grace not to sing, the style not to pose her in some sticky clinch. He knew her rhythm, and she knew his. No need to press. Their bodies touched and acknowledged each other and moved together like the two becoming one that they had once been.

"Damn, they look almost as good together as we feel." James hooked his arm around Jordan's shoulders and gave a quick squeeze. "You see, Mom? It's going to be okay after some time passes and you get your feet back under you. You'll be able to . . . I don't know, maybe be friends or something."

"I don't see that happening." Bridget scowled, her attention, like that of everyone else at the table, glued to Jordan's parents. "I don't see *this* happening. She's lost all sense of dignity."

"Would you mind if we decided to have the reception here, Bridget?" Jordan asked. "We'll look around, but if this turns out to be what we want, will that be okay with you?"

"I suppose." Bridget shrugged, shook her head, sipped her wine, and grimaced. She'd been served the house Chablis. "It's not for me to say. I want to help, of course, but it's not my decision."

"We want you to be comfortable with what we decide." Jordan turned her attention to the dance floor again. She smiled wistfully. "Dad has offered us his band."

"And they're good," James said. "This is great stuff."

"I don't see how your mother would be comfortable with that," Bridget said.

"We'll deal with your comfort levels separately, Mom."

"I'll be comfortable having no decisions to make. I don't suppose I could recycle the dress I wore for Lauren's wedding? I guess not. That would show in the pictures. So one decision—a new dress. That's it." Bridget tasted her wine again, making no faces this time. "I can't handle any more right now." She drank again, then cast a forlorn glance at her son. "I hope I'm not letting you down. One parental letdown is—"

"Don't start with that now, Mom. We're having a good time." James took the wine, then took his mother's empty hand. "Dance?"

"You have a lovely fiancée to dance with."

"Yes, I do. And I will. But sometimes a man feels an irresistible urge to dance with his mother."

"I guess that's no weirder than a woman's urge to dance with her ex-husband." Bridget allowed James to draw her to her feet. She was watching Camille and Creed as though they were doing something distasteful. "How can she resist giving him a piece of her knee right where it—"

"Mom, this is your firstborn *male* child you're talking to." James clucked his tongue, took his mother in his arms instructively. "We're dancing. I get to lead now." He looked down at Jordan and gave her a parting wink. Bridget finally took his cue. "Very good. No more scary talk. You're doing just fine tonight, which is a great relief to me."

Bridget glanced back at the table and gave an apologetic smile, which she turned up to her son as he danced her into the crowd.

Jordan watched and wondered whether they ought to consider eloping. Planning a wedding around two incredibly unorthodox and unpredictable families might not be the best way to begin the perfect marriage.

But if two negatives made a positive, maybe two *un*s cancelled each other out the same way. After all, her parents were dancing with each other. Her grandmother was somehow able to ignore the war between two poisons being waged inside her body and enjoy the dance music. And the perennial runner-up was the future bride of the man most likely to marry the girl with the crown.

A celebration was in order.

Chapter 9

The wedding date was set for the first Saturday in October.

After visiting two more reception possibilities, Camille realized that Jordan and James were stuck on the Countryside Inn. A subconscious bid to please Creed, no doubt, but she wasn't going to get into that with them. At least the price was right and everyone was comfortable with the size of the room.

The guest list was another matter. They had haggled over the guest list *and* come up with a preliminary count, but Camille figured she had more weight on her end of the seesaw than Bridget did. The list of names might change during the coming weeks, but the limit would hold. She enjoyed the irony of playing the conservative to Bridget's liberal, but her amusement was lost on

Jordan. Bridal stress was already beginning to take its toll on her sense of humor, not to mention her loyalties. Wasn't she still, after all, a Delonga?

"Burke, Mother," Jordan reminded her over Saturday-morning coffee. "My name is still Burke, and I don't know what to do about it."

Camille scanned the list of surnames—Mayfield, Marsh, Delonga, Burke. There was also an Iron Kettle and a couple of Spotted Horses. Bridget had been trying to add a whole host of Fraziers—Lauren's new high-toned in-laws. Camille had finally given Bridget a number and told her to live with it. Privately, she'd given James his own number, but he'd said she could keep that as a cushion. His closest friends were taken care of in the wedding party.

James was such an agreeable young man.

"Do you want to keep your name?" Camille asked. "My romance with the idea of becoming 'Mrs. Creed Burke' was probably imprinted on us from birth in those days, but the name game became an issue with me. Part of it was identity, part business, part—"

"I don't have time for an identity crisis, Mother," Jordan interjected. She snapped up the neatly written list she had made on yellow paper and laid it next to Camille's notes, hastily penned on the back of an envelope. "I'm talking about a list of names, not some big symbol of my personhood. I don't know what to do about the Burkes."

Camille shrugged. Question marks still dotted her list. "Invite them."

"All of them? I don't even know half of them. I don't want to hurt Dad's feelings, but he's got so many relatives."

"Do you have a problem with that?"

"Of course not. But where do you draw the line?"

"When it comes to hospitality, Indian people don't send out invitations and they don't draw a line. After we got married, they just spread the word that they were putting on a feed to celebrate, and people came."

Camille smiled wistfully, remembering the night she and Creed had attended their first social function as Mr. and Mrs. Burke. He'd asked her whether she would mind going with him to "this thing my sisters insist on doing for us."

"Why would I mind?" she'd asked. He'd shrugged diffidently.

Later she realized that once courtship was over, he didn't know what to expect from her. He'd understood what she wanted from a suitor and a lover, but as her husband he was about to take her beyond the intimacy of two. He'd asked her to be his wife, and she'd surprised him by asking him to be her husband. Two affirmatives made a positive, which was pure bliss. But how would she take to the everyday truth of being the wife of whoever this man was beyond that handsome face and seductive voice? How would she fit into his family, his life, his very different world?

And how would he fit into the living ripples surrounding the one woman he'd promised to love?

She'd called her mother, who had declared her daughter's bliss to be born of ignorance and refused to participate in the ritual sealing her ruin.

"Let's just get a license and get married," Camille had said.

He couldn't comply fast enough. If his bride didn't mind a civil ceremony, who was Creed to argue? They'd hopped into his pickup and headed for the courthouse.

She recalled the quick, sharp, unexpected pang of sadness she'd felt when the courthouse clerk had said, "The judge is ready for you now." Camille had had her share of romantic fantasies about wandering troubadours and candlelit bowers, but a frou-frou wedding had never been part of her dream. Still, it would've been nice to have someone else there to witness their vows and wish them well. Some family member, some friend.

The long oak bench they'd waited on might have been a pew. The old courthouse corridor's creaky floorboards might have made an aisle, and the judge's chambers might have served as a sanctuary. But, oddly—perhaps because "might have been" were said to be the saddest of all sad words—Camille might have turned and run had the man beside her not taken her hand to his mouth and kissed it when they reached the door. It was a gallant gesture—a first for him. He'd wooed her with charm and sex, but now came a soft, sweet brush of icing on the cake. Gallantry.

She'd looked up as he raised his head. The confession in his eyes had startled her, then endeared him to her all the more. He was just as scared as she was. And just as eager.

There was no turning back, and no wish to do so.

Why, then, would he think she would mind when he took her to that little run-down community center for his sisters' "feed"? She remembered feeling heartened and lifted by the good wishes she saw in the eyes of the people who had come to celebrate with them. His family. His boyhood friends. His community had wished them well from the very beginning, and with that simple celebration they had made a good beginning.

"We're going to have to be flexible," Camille told her daughter quietly. "I think your dad can help us find out who'll come."

"I hope so. But I don't think they'll show, and I don't want to waste—"

"Let me worry about waste," Camille said. "That's my department."

"I'm worried about wasting invitations."

"They're not *that* expensive."

"*Spaces,*" Jordan barked. "If they don't show, that's a space wasted."

Camille stared at her daughter. Pre-wedding jitters, she told herself. She was the bride, the queen for a day. A little self-centered attitude was to be expected. She glanced away, mentally reciting the Mother's Motto: *This, too, shall pass.*

Again she found herself resorting to a reserve she hadn't used in years. "We'll talk to your dad about it."

"His band's really good. *He's* really good. You guys, when you were dancing, you looked really . . ." Jordan's voice dropped like a barometer. "Are you still in love with him?"

It was one of those heavy-air questions you could always feel coming.

"I still care about him."

"Don't play word games with me, Mother."

Camille laughed. She wasn't getting away with the easy lob. Apparently her days of soft-pedaling the topics of love and marriage were over with Jordan. It must have had something to do with being engaged.

"Caring about him is easy, but being in love with him is something else entirely."

"What else?" Jordan urged. "Tell me what else, Mom. Woman to woman. It must have been love to begin with. Where did it go?"

Into you, Camille thought, then bit her tongue, thinking, *How the hell do I know?*

If she had to lie to somebody, it might as well be herself.

"Oh, sweetie, I can't go there now. You don't have time for an identity crisis. I don't have time for a Creed Burke crisis." Abruptly she reached for her new bible, flipping it open to the first chapter. "Now, according to Martha Stewart, we start planning for our flower order and our baubles and bows by determining our color palette and getting a theme going."

"Color palette, Mom?" Jordan tossed aside her list. "Are you kidding? *Theme?*"

"I guess I know as much about color and theme as anyone, including Martha. Might as well get with the program. Do you have anything in mind?"

"A purple haze."

Disgust? Derision from the girl who had started all this? Camille was doing her best to take this production seriously, and her daughter was being a smarty-pants.

"Purple is nice," she said artlessly, squelching a laugh. "I don't know about the haze part, unless you want a sixties feel. Maybe we should think seasonal."

"Halloween?"

"He'll wear black." Camille touched a finger to her chin, making a pretense of pondering the possibilities. "You'll wear ghostly white and carry orange mums. Bridesmaids on broomsticks would be cute. Bridget suggested chair covers, which made me laugh, but now I can see turning them into tombstones."

"People actually do stuff like that, you know. You've got your Renaissance weddings, your rodeo weddings, your sky- or scuba-diving weddings, your—"

"Church weddings," Camille put in. "Which seems pretty novel to me, as often as I've been to church lately. Notice I said 'I.'"

"I do like purple," Jordan said. "I don't think we have to—"

"Girls!" Rosemary shouted on her way into the kitchen. "Look what I found! This"—ceremoniously, she placed a silver cake server, then a matching knife, on the table—"and this. They were in with my quilt fabrics, along with the scraps from my mother's . . . well, that'll be a surprise if I get to it, but I knew I'd put them all in a place where I would find them at the right time.

"And look what else I found." Now on a roll, she spread the newspaper on the table between them and pointed to an advertisement. "A full-service wedding boutique has just taken over that big corner space in the Clear Lake Shopping Center. That's practically right next door. They do almost everything, according to this. Flowers, tux rental, dresses, invitations—all that stuff. Of course, your dress is taken care of. Well?" Breathless now, Rosemary touched both women's shoulders. "What do you think? Should we check it out?"

"I think we should shop around," Camille said, sparing the paper no more than a glance. She was busy trying to remember whether she'd seen the cake-serving utensils before and wondering when her mother had started squirreling away her old treasures.

Rosemary stabbed the center of the ad with a blunt finger. "It says here they give discounts on multiple services. The more of their services you use, the better the discount."

Camille took a second look at the newspaper, scanning with new interest. "We should definitely check that out."

· · ·

The shop was called Your Dream Wedding. Owner Valerie Florin promised to simplify everyone's life by providing under one roof all the services a bride could wish for. A florist by trade, she was particularly proud of her picture albums showing bouquets and flower arrangements from past weddings. She admitted that it was generally the bridal gown samples that drew customers in, but when she was told that Jordan's dress was already under construction, Valerie claimed that it was really her floral creations that sold her services.

Camille agreed that the flowers, which would determine the color palette, were a good place to start. She'd resigned herself to thinking about a one-day affair in such high-end decorator terms as "color palette." She was an artist, after all. Putting her own talents to work would make Jordan's day more personal. Not to mention less pricey.

From photographs and catalogs Jordan chose bouquet styles and varieties of flowers—sterling roses, purple iris, white stock and stephanotis, blue delphinium and periwinkle, hydrangea and freesia. Valerie made notes and headed for her flower coolers in the back of the shop to gather samples of real blooms. Camille was left in the showroom with her suddenly starry-eyed daughter. They were really doing it. They were ordering the first of many accoutrements deemed by the experts to be requirements for a beautiful wedding.

They had been seated at a small table, surrounded by more sample elements, soft lights and colors—lots of white, splashes of pink and lavender, touches of green and gold. Camille watched as Jordan took a turn around the small space, examining tall candelabras, lattice panels draped with white tulle and strings of tiny lights, a garden trellis covered with fake ivy, an arch. In the blink of a mother's eye her child had leaped from dreams of sugarplum fairies to one of wedding sweets and bridal bouquets.

"I like the little white lights," Jordan said. "They remind me of your Christmas branches on the fireplace."

"We could do willow branches," Camille said absently. But with the words a vision started taking shape in her mind. They had the bones—the room, the windows, the tables and chairs. "There's such tradition in willow. Women's baskets, men's sweat lodges. We could use that wonderful curly willow, which would be related to tradition but more decorative."

Inspired by her own resourcefulness, Camille rose from her chair to the impending occasion. "We could do the lattice panels with lights, too. And we could do swags with lights."

"We?" Jordan turned to her, strangely alarmed. "You mean we'd have it done?"

"We'll see. Maybe some of it, but I can do some of it myself. You decide what you want, and we'll look at their prices."

"As far as the room goes, I'm thinking just some—"

"Not balloons," Camille said firmly, then remembered her role. "We're not doing balloons, are we?"

"I don't have any problem with balloons."

"I'm sure Bridget does."

"Aren't you the one who keeps saying it's not Bridget's wedding?"

"I happen to agree on that point. Balloons are for birthday parties."

Jordan turned on her with folded arms. "And you're agreeing with . . ."

"You. It's your wedding. Whatever you want." Camille smiled. "You know, within reason."

"I want beautiful flowers."

"That's my personal specialty," said Valerie, returning on cue with a handful of fresh flowers. "And just look what you've chosen. These varieties complement each other beautifully, and with your garden theme you'll want to feature your flowers throughout your decor."

"Do we have a garden theme?" Jordan asked Camille.

"I thought someone said garden theme," Valerie said. She named each flower, handing them to Jordan one by one.

Enchanted, Jordan smelled and touched and oohed and aahed.

"Would you like to make an appointment to plan your order?" Valerie asked her.

"I thought that was what this appointment was for," Camille said.

Valerie drew herself up, assuming the expert's stance. "Usually I sit down with the bride and we go over all the details."

Not this time, Camille decided then and there. They'd already spent an hour and a half at this, and it wasn't as though she didn't know flowers. She wanted to know what they needed and what the cost would be.

"We'd like to do that now, if you have time. You'll be working with both of us. I'm paying the bill."

Valerie glanced at Jordan, who was sniffing her flowers with all the sweetness of a Disney character.

"Shall we begin with the bridal bouquet and work our way down from there?" Valerie said with a smile. She had them, even if it wasn't quite where and when she might want them.

They went through all the members of the wedding party, choosing the shapes and sizes of bouquets, the number of stems. Valerie was amenable to Camille's adding herbs from her kitchen garden. "Sage is very spiritual," Camille explained. "And it's symbolic of wisdom. That would be nice for the boutonnieres. Rosemary in the corsages for remembrance."

"All right, now we have the wedding party, parents, and grandparents," Valerie said. "Let's move to godparents, favorite aunts and uncles, clergy—"

"Wait," said Camille, coming down from the satisfaction of adding her herbs. "We're putting flowers on *all* these people?"

"Organist, soloist, host and hostess at the church, host and hostess at the reception, guest-book attendant, gift attendant, personal assistant . . ."

"Whose personal assistant?"

"The bride's." Valerie leaned back and claimed the upper hand. "Are you sure you're ready to do this? Perhaps I should give you a list of what you'll need."

"I have a better idea," Camille said, leaning across the table and into the space Valerie had unwittingly vacated. She laid her hand on the notes Valerie had made. "You go down the list, and I'll tell you whether we need flowers."

"You see, that's why I like to meet later with the bride. We need to determine not only who should get a corsage but also what size. And if you have stepmothers, you'll want to use a different variety of flower. There's a hierarchy of corsages, starting with the largest for the mothers, a bit smaller for grandmothers, and then down to—"

"People are supposed to be able to tell us apart by the size of the corsage?"

"That's not the point, Mrs. Burke. The bride wants large, lush corsages for both mothers."

"Jordan," Camille began, turning to her daughter with a mischievous smile, "I have told you, haven't I, that size doesn't matter?"

"Mom . . ." The word was injected with a serious warning tone.

"What? It's just us girls. What counts is quality." Camille turned back to the florist. "We don't have stepmothers. Not at the moment anyway. We can't get into aunts because there could be a lot of them. Or not. We don't know. And I think the guest book can tend itself."

"It won't get signed unless it's tended." Valerie tried to be subtle in her attempt to ease the list out from under Camille's hand. "Mrs.

Burke, if money is a big issue, then maybe you should tell us what you'd like to spend, and we can help you decide how to put that amount to the best—"

Camille wasn't budging.

"I'd like to hear all your suggestions, Valerie. But we'll decide. Jordan likes what you've come up with here, so we're making progress. Let's go down this list and put flowers to names. I've been studying up, and I know there are lots of other places we'll want flowers besides wilting on shoulders."

"Martha Stewart," Jordan quietly explained to the shop owner.

Valerie smiled when she heard the name. Martha loved flowers.

"We do have a special running on our cake- and punch-table packages. That includes flowers and greenery."

Camille's ears fairly tickled. "A special?"

"And if you rent the candelabras from us, we do flowers on those, and you can get twice the mileage out of them if you use them in the church and have them moved to the reception."

"Twice the mileage?" That sounded good. "Tell me about the special."

They spent another thirty minutes making their list, checking it at least twice.

"Now, your dress is taken care of," Valerie observed again once the flower list was finally complete to everyone's current satisfaction. "How about your attendants?"

"We've looked at some styles, but we haven't found what we want," Jordan reported. "It should be something they can get some use out of. Something wearable."

Camille smiled. Given a few more years, she trusted that Jordan would turn out to be a lovely little chip off the sensible old block.

"But my gown will be vintage forties style," Jordan continued. "I'm thinking two-piece suits for my attendants. Long, slim skirts, maybe a little shoulder padding in the jackets. Do you have anything like that?"

"We can have it made. We can provide any style you want." Valerie turned to Camille. "And we offer a multiservice discount. The more services you use, the bigger the discount. What other services might interest you? We do rent tuxedos in a variety of styles."

"And tux rental is pretty standard, isn't it?"

"At Your Dream Wedding, the groom's tux is complimentary if you order the rest of them through us."

"Good deal," Camille agreed. "And you do invitations. What else is there?"

"Decorations and centerpieces generally fall in with flowers, but you're already talking about four services. You'll get a very nice discount."

"Really? Well, that does sound good. It's not that I'm unwilling to spend the money, but I always like to get a substantial bang for my buck."

With her list safely bracketed by her elbows, Valerie smiled over steepled fingers. "We can certainly provide you with a first-rate bang, Mrs. Burke."

By the time she stopped laughing, Camille had forgotten to correct the woman on her name.

Chapter 10

Jordan borrowed a book of wedding sta-
tionery samples from her new wedding adviser,
Valerie Florin. She couldn't wait to go over them
with James and tell him all about their flowers.
Driving home alone after the heady visit to Your
Dream Wedding, Camille let the radio "seek"
button sail right past *All Things Considered* and
settle on oldies rock, where she knew all the
words.

As long as no one was listening, she was
hoping for "Goin' to the Chapel," grooving to
her own unanticipated enthusiasm for frou-
frou. One shimmering idea after another popped
into her head. If she wanted to, she could turn
the banquet room at the Countryside Inn into a
veritable paradise. She had the ingenuity, and
she could get the goods.

Finding Creed's pickup in her driveway seemed to cap off a head-ful of wackiness just perfectly, although she wasn't too crazy about finding him messing around in her kitchen again.

"Rosemary let me in," he explained, as though the look she gave him meant something besides *Just because you know where everything is doesn't mean you're allowed to drag it all out.*

"That's fine," she said.

No greetings. He'd never been the "Honey, I'm home" kind of a husband, but by the end of their marriage they'd long since fallen out of the habit of exchanging hellos. She'd wanted explanations, and he'd stopped giving them.

But he seemed to realize that explanations were back in order now that he was not.

"I'm getting us something to eat." With a gesture he indicated the open cupboard, where they'd always kept the canned goods. "She says she's not hungry, but she also admitted she hasn't eaten today. That can't be good."

"It isn't. She was sewing when I left, so I took her some . . ."

He pointed to the plate of raisin toast with peanut butter, untouched and undoubtedly turned to cardboard.

"That's what she said she wanted," Camille said with a sigh. She tossed her keys on the kitchen table, noting the tray he'd set there, arrayed with eating utensils, napkins, salt and pepper.

He'd thought of a tray?

"I didn't ask her what she wanted, but I know she's not going to let a guest eat alone. It's not polite. And I'm hungry." He opened the dish cupboard. "How about you? I made plenty."

"What . . . ? I mean, why . . . ?"

"Oh." Dishes aside, he shoved his hand into the pocket of his jeans and pulled out folded cash, which he handed over like an install-ment on some debt. "I got paid for last weekend, and we're booked into next month." He caught her quizzical look. "For the wedding."

"What are you going to live on?"

"Your charity." His eyes sparkled with his teasing and his contri-bution to her cause. "I hired on with a roofer. Maybe I'll work for him through the summer."

"You hate roofing."

"I said *maybe*." He reached into the cupboard and pulled out three soup mugs, one at a time. "Maybe something better will come along."

"You're providing the music, Creed. That's a big contribution."

"I want to do more." He turned, studying the third mug as though there were something in the bottom of it. "I had a college fund for her, you know. I started it up three or four times. But then I'd have to dip into it for something, and pretty soon there wasn't enough to buy books, so I'd clean it out. Figured there was still time to start over. I don't know where it all went. You know, the time."

He looked up at her, chuckling, his eyes filled with a telling help-lessness, as though the joke was on him. "Those are about the lamest words a person can say, aren't they? 'I don't know where the time went.' "

"You were pretty good about helping support her."

"I'm *pretty* good at a lot of things. I should've done better for my daughter. I didn't always send as much as we agreed on."

"Sometimes you sent more."

He shrugged, wagged his shaggy head. He needed a haircut. She wondered whether she would still know how to give him one.

"How much does a wedding cost?" he asked. "You know, a nice one."

Stop acting so damned innocent and looking so damned . . .

"Not as much as college, which is what I wish we were paying for."

"She can still go back. Some people need a little more time than others. Take me, for instance."

"I did."

He laughed. "That's right. For better or for worse, you said."

"As I recall, our civil vows didn't include that line."

"What have you had since? Better or worse?"

She gave him a look that should have burned a hole between his eyes.

He raised his brow. "Doesn't hurt to ask, does it? You used to ask me all the time." Palms up, he surrendered. "Okay, sorry. I just answered my own question. It does."

"I'm not asking anymore, am I?"

He cocked a finger, gave a cluck and a wink. "I knew I was missing something."

"Anyway, I never asked about better or worse. If there's someone else, who cares whether she's better or worse?"

He laughed. "More proof that we come from different planets."

"All right, I'll ask, even though it's none of my business and it doesn't matter anymore." She had that corsage list to consider. "Are you—what's the current phrase—with someone at the moment?"

"At the moment I'm with you."

"There, you see? Typical Creed Burke answer."

"Straight as an arrow." He jerked his chin in her direction. "That was a typical Camille Burke question. Carefully phrased so I could answer it without telling you anything. So I did." He shrugged. "My answer never mattered. Your question was always more important to you."

"Meaning what?"

"Meaning I finally realized that the question would always be there no matter what I did."

"So what did you do?"

"I did a lot of things. Some things I'm proud of, some I'm not." But he smiled. "When you said you weren't asking anymore, I thought, *Good for you.*"

"That's not what you said."

"I know. Old habit." He gave a quick nod. "But the truth is, I thought, *Good for you, Camille.* You seem happy. I don't know if letting all that shit go is the main reason, but if you're happy now, good for you."

"Are you 'happy now'?" she chirped, trotting out a bit of mimicry and sass. "Good for you."

"That's not what I said either, is it?"

"No, not exactly."

"Even if you've had better since me." He tried to touch her shoulder, but she saw it coming in time to step away, leaving his hand outstretched and empty. "Good for you."

"I haven't gone looking for better." She snatched the cold toast off the plate and tossed it into the sink. "I haven't had time."

"Twelve years?"

"I've been very busy. Besides, men are so much work." She ran cold water over the toast, using a fork to feed it to the snarling disposal.

The flip of a switch, the slap of a faucet handle, an uneasy silence.

"Did I tell you how good you were the other night?" She turned, smiling because he looked genuinely perplexed. "Your music."

"Thank God. I was afraid I blinked and missed something else."

"It's really a good group, and you're better than you ever were. Do you think you might record something?"

"Only the demos we use to get jobs." He turned his attention back to the soup he'd left on the stove.

"But you're so good. You could—"

"I like what I'm doing." He turned, saw what was coming, and warned her with an upraised soupspoon. "Don't, Camille. I like the part where you said I was good. But you always want more."

And *he* always choked on any confidence she showed in him. She thought better of saying she didn't want anything, that he still didn't get it, that he still couldn't take even the simplest compliment from her.

He saw the storm coming, too, and he shifted gears smoothly, giving a sly smile. "Now, if we were talking about sex, no problem. Right? If you want better, you come to me."

"You're as good as anyone on the radio," she muttered.

The *ding* from the toaster startled her.

He laughed. "Thanks, honey, but I know you're just saying that. Not to flatter me, but because you don't know what you're talking about. I know you haven't been around that much."

"Cut it out, now, I'm serious. I'm not pushing either. I have no reason to push you. I'm just trying to encourage you because . . ." She wasn't sure he was listening. He was reading the label on a peanut butter jar. "Well, you never liked roofing."

"No chunky?" he asked.

"Only my hips," she quipped, but she opened another cupboard and handed him a new jar.

"Much better," he said, spinning the lid. "No wonder Rosie didn't eat that other stuff. Got any Marshmallow Creme?"

"Why haven't you gained any weight?"

"I would if my cupboards were stocked the way yours are," he said when she handed him another jar. "I never liked roofing because it's hard work, and I'm basically lazy. Funny the height doesn't bother me."

"You've never had problems with height."

"Oh, yeah, I have. That stage at the state fairgrounds was too high for me." He scooped a dollop of Marshmallow Creme out of the jar and sucked it off his finger. "Mmm, sweet. I like what I'm doing. Bigger gigs pay better, but I never was very good with money. You know that. You always handled it better than I did."

"I just hate to see things like money and talent go to waste."

"Really?" He offered her a fingerful of marshmallow.

Camille thought about giving him something he'd never expect from her. A shock. A thrill. Slickery, lickery lips closing over his finger, throat sucking, tongue slip-sliding, drawing that sweet sticky white stuff into her mouth. Pressing her lips together, she stared at his finger. Lots of other women would.

Lots of other women undoubtedly had.

She snatched the stuff quickly, a bird stealing a treat from his hand. Her teeth scraped his skin, and the taste of him came with the confection. Or maybe the taste of him *was* the confection.

Maybe she did need to get out more.

"You want it with peanut butter?"

"What?" she asked innocently. "Talent? Or money?"

"I gave you all I had, sweetheart. All I have left is my hands, but at least they're clean." Another sly smile. "By the way, I took a tour of the workshop a little while ago. Great stuff back there. You've got a lot of talent, Camille. Why are you wasting it making stuff for rich people to stick in their yards?"

"That's what artists do for a living," she said, easily shrugging off his cleverness without giving him the touché she knew he deserved. "They make things for rich people to do whatever they want with. Stick in their yards or hang on their walls or decorate their tombs."

"So if Bill Gates stops in at the bar tonight and listens to a set, I can call myself an artist?"

"You *are* an artist, but so few people ever get to . . . enjoy what you do."

"Yeah, but at least those few are alive. Mostly. The Countryside Inn is damn sure no graveyard." He grimaced. "People really use your stuff to decorate graves?"

"Not my stuff."

He nodded, as though the sparing of her stuff consoled him enough that he could get back to fixing soup.

"Not *graves*," she insisted, trailing him to the stove. "Tombs. Michelangelo was commissioned to make statues for rich people's tombs."

"And that's not a waste of money and talent?"

"I'm paying you a compliment on your music, and you're being difficult."

"Like I said, I enjoy what I do." He turned, soup pot in hand, grinning. "You ran out of answers, didn't you?"

A long time ago, she thought, but she decided to let him have the last word. *I can't live like this* had long since been her final answer.

He was about to pour soup into the mugs and splash it on her counter. She opened a drawer and handed him a ladle. Without looking up, he took the ladle, set it down on the counter, and proceeded to pour cream of something soup into the three mugs.

"Jordan chose her flowers today," Camille reported as she reached for the sponge. "We put in a preliminary order. There's no getting around it; weddings are expensive. Now that we're into it, I want to make it special for her."

She looked for splashes to wipe up behind his back while he was returning the pot to the stove. There were none.

"I want to help." He glanced at the sponge in her hand. "But I don't have to come around if you don't want to see me."

"No, it's fine."

"I don't drink much anymore."

"You were the other night," she pointed out, meeting his gaze.

"I had a couple of beers. Did I get out of line?"

She shook her head. The sponge slipped from her hand, into the sink.

"You don't have to worry about me at the wedding," he promised quietly.

"I'm not worried."

"Liar." He tipped his head to one side, considering her eyes. "Do you mind if I bring a date?"

"Of course not."

He laughed. "Damn, you can lie."

"That makes two of us, I guess."

"I guess." He turned away, looking for something more to do with the food. "You want toast?"

"Just the soup," she repeated. "Is it still hot?"

"Rosie showed me what she was working on for Jordan and how it's gonna look." He handed her one of the mugs. "I didn't know she did that kind of sewing. That's gonna be some dress. Have you found one for yourself yet?"

"I'm not ready to shop for my dress yet. I need to lose"—she glanced at the cream soup and smiled sheepishly—"well, a little weight. Does it show?"

He lifted one shoulder. "I'd say there's about twenty pounds more of you than there was when I first met you."

"Oh, boy, that's quite a candid answer. When we were married, you would have dodged that one for sure."

"When we were married, I had more to lose by telling the naked truth. As for whether you need to lose . . ." He gave her a quick once-over. "You look real good to me."

"Understand that this is a sensitive subject. You wouldn't just say that, would you?"

"What would it get me? It takes a lot of effort to lie, and I don't go to that much trouble for nothing."

" 'You look real good to me,' " she aped. "Effortlessly said."

"Not for you."

She questioned him with a look.

"You've done that twice now, and it's not easy for you. You want me to think it is, but you don't really like to mock people. So you can't quite pull it off."

"Bullshit."

He laughed. "You can't quite pull *that* off either."

"I heard a rumor that somebody was making us something to eat," Rosemary said by way of announcing herself. "Did I just over-hear the last word on the rumor?"

"No, ma'am. I've got it all fixed right here." He pulled a chair away from the table and held it for her. "But I'll have to heat it up again. Your daughter's one powerful distraction."

"I'm sure I heard cussing."

"It was too lame to count, Rosie. Sit down and start with some toast while I nuke the soup."

"Oh, yeah, you'll eat *his* toast," Camille complained when her mother took a bite. She punched Creed's shoulder. "You big brownie."

He laughed. "You got that right, hon."

Chapter 11

I'm going to make you earn your lunch today," Camille warned her friends. She ushered them into the dining room, where the table was set up for what Rosemary had lately termed "the craft of the week." A pile of little twig nests from the craft store was the centerpiece. "We're going to make favors."

"Make favors?" As though checking for bird droppings, Bridget chose one little nest for close, squinty-faced inspection. "Or make-do favors?"

"Not 'make-do' favors. These are going to be fabulous favors. Sit," Camille ordered on her way to the kitchen. She returned with a pot of tea and began pouring it into the cups she'd already arranged. "When you do it yourself, you give of yourself. It's a personal touch."

"She's become a Martha Stewart disciple," Ellie told Bridget across the table.

Bridget was checking out the rolls of satin ribbon and the plastic bag stuffed with iridescent shred. "Aren't you afraid this is all going to look sort of homemade?"

"That's exactly what I'm hoping for." Camille took her seat at the head of the table. "I call it 'personalized.'"

"What kind of tea is this?" Ellie asked between sips. "We should be drinking green tea. They've discovered that green tea gives us some percentage less chance of something. I don't remember now whether it has to do with menopause or cancer. Or bone loss. Something really bad."

"Turning into a witch," Camille suggested as she handed out the scissors to go with the rolls of purple and lavender ribbon. "Green tea keeps you from turning into a witch. Prevents the warts, the stoop-over, and the raging crabbies."

"How about the green skin?"

"As long as you add milk, you're all right. All we're doing is decorating these to hold the traditional candied almonds. Jordan's almonds, as it were. Make sure you use the piece of ribbon I gave you as a guide for length on those."

"Yes, teacher," said Ellie.

"Well, I determined the amount of ribbon for this project by the number of pieces we're making, and I'm not going back to the craft shop again until next week." Camille sighed. "If I don't get some real work done this week, it really will be 'yes teacher.'"

"The truth is, she doesn't want to go back to the craft store until another coupon comes out in the Sunday paper," said Bridget.

"What's wrong with that? Saving money is not a bad thing, my friend. You wait and see how all this comes out before you turn your nose up at my personal touches."

Bridget glanced askance as she snipped off a piece of ribbon. "I see that somebody finally did some personal touching up on that back door that's been broken forever."

"What are you talking about? My trick door?"

"I noticed that, too," said Ellie, who had already devised a method of measuring and cutting a whole roll of ribbon in two snips. "All I had to do was turn the knob. No pulling up on the knob, twist, jiggle, whistle the 'Minnesota Rouser' while you're standing on one foot and pushing in. I just turned the knob—and *wahla*."

"That's 'voilà,' Ellie," Bridget said. "It's French. So, Cam, did you finally call that handyman I recommended? He's better than a husband."

"You can pay him in regular U.S. currency?" Camille asked with a smile.

"*After* he does the job and you're completely satisfied."

Ellie knew better. "Is Creed still in town?"

"For the summer," Camille said.

"What else is he repairing besides your doors?"

"He didn't repair any doors." But Camille knew better, too. If the door had been fixed, Mr. Fixit had done the deed. Whether he did it to be helpful to her or to himself, she didn't know. She shrugged. "Or maybe he did. It's just like him to be gone forever and suddenly wander back into the house and start messing with things."

"We're going to sing a duet during the wedding," Ellie announced quietly.

Camille turned on Ellie as though she'd pinched her from behind. "Who says?"

"It's going to be a surprise for Jordan. You two are sworn to secrecy. I just wanted to make sure you wouldn't mind."

"Whose idea was this?"

"Oh, I don't know. Mutual, I think. You brought it up not long ago, that you thought we sounded good together. Wouldn't it be fun if we could surprise Jordan and James?"

"I think I was the one who brought it up," Bridget claimed. "It's a great idea. You'll be Creedence Clearwater Revival meets Eleanor in the church where a wedding . . . is being?" She glowed with her cleverness. "That's where Creed got his name, isn't it?"

"He's been Creed since birth, which obviously predated Creedence Clearwater Revival," Camille said. "He says it came from his mother's mission period. He has a sister named Faith."

"His mother was a missionary? I thought she was an Indian."

"I think it's possible to be both, Bridge," Ellie said.

"In this case it was his father who was the missionary. I guess when he decided his work in the Dakotas was done, he left her with the kids and headed for Alaska."

"You mean you can't even depend on a man of the church?"

"Sometimes they're the worst."

"Now, cut that out, you two," Ellie scolded. "We're working on a wedding here. A *church* wedding. In case you two haven't heard, the Lord works in mysterious ways." It was her turn to instruct Camille. "Obviously Creed's mother didn't depend on Mr. Burke. After he left, she went right on living her life, raising her children, probably still going to church and—"

"She actually died way before her time."

"You mean she was too young and too dear to the people who loved her, but who's to say when it's time? Who but . . . ?"

Ellie glanced from Camille to Bridget and back again, trying to decide whether to say the word and be forced to defend it. Not that they weren't believers. They simply couldn't hold a candle to Ellie, even though on occasion when she got started on the subject, they'd threatened to do just that.

Ellie lifted one shoulder as she pulled on the loops of a purple bow. "Well, I just think time is an illusion, and death is like the river flowing."

"What sense does that make?" Bridget asked.

"Sense is an illusion, too," Camille said, reaching across the table. "Ellie's way out there, Bridge. Have another nest."

"So Creed is more spiritual than musical," Ellie mused.

"*Way* out there," Camille said. "And, Bridget, you're behind on your nests. Look at my pile already. You've made exactly two. We've still got shower favors to do."

Bridget looked up from her work, scandalized. "You're not giving the shower, Cam. The mother of the bride does not give a shower. That is simply not done."

"What would Martha say?" Ellie teased.

"I'm just helping out the bridesmaids with a few of the details."

"Hello, girls." Rosemary had suddenly appeared in the doorway. "Speaking of bridesmaids, guess what I just scored on eBay. A complete bridesmaids' breakfast set."

"Set of what?" Camille asked, dreading the answer. Her mother had already "scored" at least a score of antique wedding handkerchiefs, an assortment of crystal votive candleholders, and three Victorian birdcages.

"It's a gorgeous rose pattern, almost like chintz. I printed out the picture." Rosemary swept aside strips of ribbon and placed the paper on the table next to Camille's teacup. "It's a service for eight, but look." She pointed out each piece as though she'd unearthed an assortment of pre-historic tools. "These darling coffee- and teapots, cream and sugar—all porcelain. No chips, no cracks, no crazing," she recited from the listing. "And look, it even has eggcups and dome covers for the toast plates."

"Mama, have you taken leave of your senses?"

"Sense is an illusion," Ellie reminded Camille, eyes twinkling.

"I couldn't resist," Rosemary chirped. "I got such a great deal on it. The starting bid was really low, and hardly anyone bid against me."

"I wonder why," Camille said dryly. "Who's ever heard of a brides-maids' breakfast set? What did you pay for it?"

"None of your beeswax." Rosemary's smug expressions—facial and verbal—were equally impish. "We *are* having a bridesmaids' breakfast, aren't we?"

"I guess we are now." Camille turned to Bridget. "Did you have a bridesmaids' breakfast?"

"We went out for a nice lunch."

"Brunch would be fine, as long as we can use the eggcups, but we must host it here in our home." High on bid-winning adrenaline, Rosemary slipped into the empty chair at the end of the table. "The bridesmaids' breakfast is a wonderful southern tradition. Like the groom's cake. My people are from Virginia, you know." She drew a quick frown. "We *are* having a groom's cake, aren't we?"

"We haven't gotten around to cakes yet, and I don't recall any of *your people* ever purchasing a complete bridesmaids' breakfast set for any wedding," Camille quipped. "And does this have anything to do with that new magazine that appeared in the rack in the living room? *Southern Weddings?*"

"I subscribed," Rosemary confessed. "*And* I had a groom's cake and a bridesmaids' breakfast for my wedding. We used my grandmother's china."

"Which would have been just fine, Mama."

"I told you, I couldn't resist." Rosemary rested her chin on the heels of her palms and smiled wistfully, a bewigged cherub. "It's so sweet and elegant. The little eggcups and toast covers."

"How's the dress coming, Rosemary?"

"Slowly but surely," she told Bridget. "I wish I could show it to you, but I don't want anyone to see it until Jordie walks down the aisle. I think it's the best work I've ever done."

"What a special gift," Ellie said.

"I found something else on the Internet that I'd like to contribute." Rosemary withdrew a folded piece of paper from the pocket of her long cotton jacket and unfolded it with some hesitancy. "This might seem a little foolish to the 'everything's up to date in Kansas City' crowd, but with the forties-style dress, I think we must have this 1949 limousine."

"What a great idea." Ellie craned her neck to get a peek at the picture. "Who cares what they say in Kansas City? That's awesome."

"I can't believe this, Mama." Camille shot her friend a cool-it glance. "What happened to your favorite line from Shakespeare?" She waved an instructional finger and quoted, " 'Thrift, Horatio.' "

"Well, if I die right before the wedding, I expect you to *remember me*," Rosemary said with histrionic, haunting emphasis on the last two words, followed by an impish smile. "By not letting the leftovers from the funeral table go to waste. But since I'm not dead yet, I'm having a little fun with my money."

"Spend it on . . ."

Camille glanced at the ink-jet print of the dishes, delicately hand-painted with sunny yellow, pink, and blue flowers. She looked at the picture of the old car with its ornate hood ornament and gleaming grille. She could sense her mother's knowing smile, knowing the appeal, the sentiment, the way their strong female minds made their apologies about going soft and finding meaning in such matters.

"What do the kids think of the limo?"

Rosemary shook her head. "It's been two or three days since I've seen Jordie."

"When she's not at work, she's spending every waking minute with her fiancé," Camille explained.

"Isn't school out yet?" Bridget asked.

"This is the last week. Then I'm hoping she'll get more involved in these plans. We'll start looking into cakes."

"Oh, you must use Barnett's Bakery," Bridget advised. "They're the best. That's where we got Lauren's cake."

"It was beautiful. What did you pay for it?" Camille felt her face flush. "Sorry. If I may ask."

"Right around a thousand."

"*Dollars?*" Camille nearly choked. "I think I'd better take a cake-decorating class."

"Now, this has to stop, Cam," Bridget said, tossing aside a tiny flower with a wire stem. "If you try to do it all yourself, how are you supposed to enjoy the wedding? This is going to be an important day for you, too. You don't want to miss it."

"Okay, scratch the cake decorating. But wait till you see my plan for the banquet room."

"Are you renting chair covers?"

"No, but I promise you won't miss them, Bridge." Camille decided to turn the tables. "Have you picked a place for the rehearsal dinner yet?"

"No. I haven't been able to get Timothy to commit to . . ." Bridget stared down at her hands, slowly pulling a piece of satin ribbon between her thumb and forefinger. "He's selling my house." Her lower lip trembled. "That son of a bitch is selling my house."

Camille scowled. Not that it missed the mark in any way, but "son of a bitch" rolled surprisingly trippingly off Bridget's tongue.

"He can't sell the house." Ellie searched for confirmation in the faces around the table. "Can he?"

"How can he sell the house?" Camille demanded. "It has to be in your name, too."

"He agreed to take out a second mortgage for the wedding, and now he claims that was all my idea. He says there's no way I can keep the house in the divorce settlement."

"What does your attorney say?"

Bridget shook her head quickly. "I think I'm going to have to find a better attorney."

"He suggests selling the house," Camille deduced.

"*She,*" Bridget corrected her. "I thought a female attorney would be more apt to look after my interests, but I'm beginning to wonder if she knows what she's doing. All you need is a good attorney." She paused, hoping for confirmation. When all she got was silence, she insisted, "Well, isn't that right?"

"Bridget . . ." Camille was very much afraid she already knew the answer to the question she was about to ask. "I don't mean to sound nosy, but how much equity do you have in the house?"

"I don't know," Bridget admitted sadly.

"You *must* know, honey," Ellie said. "You just took out a second mortgage."

"Actually, we haven't paid off Lauren's college education yet, so maybe it's a third mortgage. Is there such a thing as a third mortgage?"

"Oh, Bridget."

Four pairs of eyes stared at the two piles of little nests in the middle of the long oak table. The smaller pile had been feathered up with ribbon, flowers, cushy iridescent shred. They were ready for nesters. The larger pile still needed attention, but suddenly the mood for attending to frivolous party favors had passed.

"It's such a big house, hon," Ellie said finally. "You don't want to be rattling around in that big house all by yourself now. Think of the upkeep. You can take your share of . . ." She caught Camille's worrisome glance. "Or just rent something. Let the landlord worry about keeping the sidewalks shoveled."

"Or become a bag lady." Bridget's hollow humor echoed out of a vacant stare.

"You'll be the only one on the street with designer clothes in her bags." Camille laid her hand over her friend's forearm. "You'll be Bridget, the stylin' bag lady."

"You think this is funny, Camille?" Bridget suddenly came to life, jerking her arm away. "Oh, I get it. Now it's my turn, right?"

"Your turn for what? You made the bag-lady comment, which I took as my cue to lighten up. Although, as a rule, I don't laugh at bag ladies."

"Are you saying I do?"

"Oh, for Pete's sake. I'm saying . . ." Camille shook her head. She wasn't going to let Bridget wallow in it too much, but she did have some sympathy for her. It was a vision she'd had herself from time to time. "I'm saying it's a scary thought."

"There but for the grace of God—"

"Knock it off, Ellie," Camille said. "We're not holding a prayer service here. Nobody's going to be a bag lady." She offered Ellie an apology in a glance.

Ellie was still smarting, but the pain was heavier on Bridget's side of the table, and there was only so much sympathy to go around before things turned sloppy. Be damned if Camille would let it all turn to sap right there in her dining room.

"Bridge, the only thing we're taking turns at is being mother of the bride. I'll welcome any advice you can give me."

"Don't try to do too much of it yourself," Bridget said quietly, welcoming the chance to advise. "Hire people or . . . ask your friends. If I had known . . ." She drew a deep, steadying breath and shook her head firmly. "I wouldn't have done anything differently, and I don't regret one penny of what it cost. It was a beautiful wedding."

"Yes, it was."

.   .   .

Creed found the door unlocked, as promised. The house was dark and quiet except for the ticking of the clock on the mantel, which sounded like someone thumping a hickory stick on the floor in the schoolhouse. It felt like the old days. Not the old school days, when acting like a boy was justified, but the crazy days when a man enjoyed feeling like a boy sneaking into class late. He'd been a smart boy, terrified of riling the teacher. But as a man he'd miscalculated. His wife had been somebody else's teacher, somebody else's mother, but he wanted her to play all the roles for him as well. He had expected too much and taken her way too lightly.

Sneaking into the house in the middle of the night had felt a little risky, which was the part he'd always enjoyed. He was a night owl. Being stealthy was part of his nature, part of his game. It was too much to hope that he'd hook up with a woman who shared his nature, so he'd married simply for love. He knew Camille had done the same. It had been good while it lasted, but miserable as hell when it had all started going south.

"Creed?"

The whisper came from the living room. He followed it to the sofa. A flailing hand found his leg. He grabbed it and knelt, catching his elbow on the arm of the sofa when his knee threatened to pain him. Getting old was a bitch, all right. You never expected it to happen to you, and you didn't anticipate the changes that it brought with it. Aging was full of surprises, just like the hand he was holding. Certain things you expected when you reached for a familiar hand. Not the cold or the weightlessness or the feel of dry tissue paper passing for skin.

"I came as quick as I could, Rosie. What's going on?"

"I'm going to need a little help getting to your pickup." She struggled to sit up. He lent his arm to her effort. "How far away is it?"

"You told me not to pull up in the driveway, but it's not far. Rosie, we have to tell Camille about this."

"No we don't." She sat up briefly on her own support, then sighed as she swayed against him. "You'll have me back here before she wakes up."

"Damn, Rosie, you're like a rag doll. What's the matter?"

"The matter is . . ." She slipped her arm around his shoulder. "I got turned into a rag doll. Can you carry me?"

He wrapped her in the blanket she had brought from her bed and lifted her in his arms. His knees cracked.

He chuckled. "Never thought I'd be sneaking around with my ex-wife's mother."

"Oh!" Her limp arm suddenly found enough strength to flop her hand to her head. "Oh. Forgot my hair."

"You mean you didn't fix up for me?"

She laughed a little as she rested her head on his shoulder. Against the side of his neck he could feel the fine down that covered her head. He might have been carrying a long, skinny baby.

They'd reached the door. Fortunately, because he'd repaired it a week ago, he was able to open it easily, noiselessly.

"Rosie? You gonna make it?"

She made a sound that passed for affirmative.

He carried her down the driveway, stopping once to adjust the slipping blanket. A streetlamp guided him past the dappled shadows of the huge maple tree in the front yard. He treaded softly, no dragging his boot heels against the pavement, no displacement of gravel. Only the crickets and the squeaky door on the passenger's side of the pickup disturbed the wee-hour quiet.

"I should've called for an ambulance," he said under his breath when he slid behind the wheel.

"Too noisy. You—"

"I can be pretty sneaky, all right. I guess you've heard." He wanted an answer from her. "Rosie?"

"I'm here," she assured him, head back, eyes closed. "Still here."

"Don't worry, Rosie, there are some advantages to having a sneaky son-in-law. I know how to get you from here to there and back before anybody knows you stepped out."

"Stopped thinking of you as a bad boy . . . long time ago."

169

"I know you did, Rosie, but I tell you what." He covered her baldness with his big, callused hand. "You listening?"

She nodded.

"If my daughter told me she was gettin' married to some honky-tonk man, I'd lock her in the tower and wish her luck growing out her hair."

Chapter 12

*C*reed knew he had to tell Camille, but he didn't know what to say to her. He was still pretty shaken up about finding her mother in such a weakened state. The woman who had always been a rock had suddenly become a feather. The only thing he'd refused to do for her on the way to the emergency room was to roll down the window and give her some air. He was afraid she'd drift off the seat and he'd lose her to the night sky.

He hadn't slept. Maybe he'd dozed off in the chair for a minute or two waiting for Rosie to release him from his promise to take her home, but he hadn't really slept. Top to bottom, he felt wrung out. The coffee wasn't kicking in, and he was thinking about pulling up a chair and putting his head down on the table when Camille finally waltzed into the kitchen and gave him her cool, crisp "Good morning."

He nodded. "Coffee?"

"It's always nice to have it waiting for you, even if it is just like old times. Meaning I've slept all night, and you obviously haven't."

He gave her a steamy cup of coffee and a similar smile. "What do you say we complete the picture the way we used to, back when old times were good times?"

Unless he missed his read on her, she was tempted.

But she took the coffee and her interest in him away, opting for the newspaper. He'd never been interested in the paper himself, but he'd always brought it in and left it on the kitchen table.

"Mama let you in again?"

"She did."

"Where is she? Out in the yard?" She checked the weather corner above the masthead on the *Star Trib*. "It's such a beautiful morning, isn't it?"

She looked cute in her fluffy robe. He wasn't going to tell her that, because cute and cuddly probably wouldn't sound like a compliment to her ears. But it would be. He would have liked nothing better than to keep his mouth shut, close his eyes, and cuddle up with her right about then.

"She's in the hospital," he said.

Camille looked dubious, glancing behind him, as though he might be hiding her mother behind his back.

"She's fine now," he added quickly. "They said she was gonna be fine. They just need to build her up a little bit. Her blood count is low. They said there's some medication they can—"

"How did you get in on all this?" she exploded.

"She called me and asked me to come get her and take her over to the emergency room."

"When?"

"During the night. I don't know what time, but it was late. You know, my side of the rotation. I guess she was hoping to get fixed up and be back in her bed before you woke up."

"*Why?*"

"Why do you think?" And why was she yelling at *him*, for chrissake?

The answer to that question shone in her eyes. They were talking about her mother.

He kept his cool.

"She doesn't want to spoil anything for you and Jordie."

"Spoil . . ." She wasn't keeping hers, of course. She was setting aside her coffee, backing off, staring at him wide-eyed, as though he'd just ripped something out of her hands. "She called you. She makes me drop her off at the clinic and pick her up later, but she calls *you . . .*"

"Hey, it's not like I brought her over a pint of blood that I just sucked out of somebody's neck."

"No, but . . ." She flung her arm toward the other side of the house. "I was just in the next room."

"You were sleeping. I wasn't." He took a step closer and explained very calmly. "Listen to what I'm saying, Camille. She doesn't want you to worry. She doesn't want her illness to take away from all the excitement. It's her way of hangin' in, and it's a damn good way, if you ask me."

"How . . . how bad . . . ?"

"Like I said, she's doin' good. They said she did the smart thing to get over there right away when she started feeling woozy or whatever. We can probably bring her home later today. She really doesn't want Jordie to know. She's afraid she'll get taken off the dress detail."

"She's going to die, isn't she? My mother." She glanced out the window toward the sunny backyard and whispered again, "My mother."

"Sooner or later she will." Because the truth of it made him sad, he ached to hold her, trade solace with her. If she would turn, look, move, invite him in any small way, he would take her in his arms the way he'd done with her mother. He could give her a lift, easy.

But there was no invitation, so he gave a chuckle. "If I know Rosie, she'll make it later. She's got an important job to do, and by damn she'll get it done."

Her glance out the window had become a hard stare. "I hate this."

"I know." He had to touch her. An easy hand on her shoulder, the touch of an understanding friend. "We're not going to tell her that. How's the dress coming?"

"It's going to be breathtakingly beautiful." She turned to him, brightened, didn't seem to notice his hand. "She's putting so much effort into it. And all that detail . . . I don't know how many seed pearls and tiny crystal beads, all sewn on by hand."

"Then she'll be around awhile. She's not about to leave it unfinished." He stepped away, ostensibly needing a refill for his cup. "Starting this week I'm gonna be working in the neighborhood. If you need me for anything, I'll be close by." Laughing, he gestured with the pot to offer her the first refill. "You're thinking, *Hey, that's quite a switch.*"

"I'm thinking I can be quite a bitch." She held out her cup. He filled it, then took what was left for himself. "Is that why she called you?"

"Come on, stop feeling sorry for yourself." Clearly she hadn't heard a word he'd said. "Your mama loves you, and she's decided I'm okay, even if I'm not Mr. Perfect. I told you why she called me. Take it or leave it."

"You're right." She sipped, nodded, sipped again. "As soon as she's strong enough, would you like to go with us to sample cakes?"

"Cakes?" He smiled. Cakes had frosting, and frosting was like marshmallow cream. "Can we sample with our fingers?"

. . .

The order for the bridesmaids' dresses came first. The girls arrived at the appointed time to be measured for the outfits that were to be custom made. Rosemary had sketched the design, but she was not up to attending the meeting with Valerie Florin at the bridal shop. Camille found herself missing her mother's perspective, particularly when Valerie filed a magazine clipping with the order rather than Rosemary's sketch. Valerie had asked for a picture, and Jordan had come up with one she said was close to what she wanted, but she gave a few verbal instructions for more of this and not so much of that. Camille tried to point out that the sketch was exactly what they wanted and that Grandma was a professional seamstress.

"Mom, they need a picture," Jordan said.

"Maybe Grandma would like a job," Valerie quipped as she noted Lauren's waist and hip measurements in her file folder. "We have such a time finding good seamstresses. Nobody sews anymore."

"Grandma has her hands full with Jordan's dress, but I do think you should go by her sketch." Camille reclaimed the drawing from the table, where it lay virtually ignored. "This has all the right—"

"But it's just so sketchy. Don't worry." Valerie laughed, bypassing the drawing in Camille's outstretched hand in favor of giving Jordan's arm a quick squeeze. "I know exactly what the bride has in mind. The basic construction will be done by a company out of state. When the suits come in, we'll call the girls back in for another fitting," she explained as she took the tape measure to the next girl's hips. "They'll be custom fit and well worth a little extra cost because they'll be exactly what you want."

"Don't worry, Mom."

Camille scowled at her daughter, a signal that she didn't appreciate the public loyalty switch. "Have you ever noticed how you're more likely to worry when people tell you not to?" she asked pointedly.

"Oh, Mom."

Oh, Mom? Camille was getting the old "Oh, Mom"?

Oh, Mama.

Was this what was known as a mother's justice? Camille remembered wearing the daughter's shoes, the cool ones that were so far out, while Mama's were just plain *out*. It had taken her more than a few *Oh, Mama*'s to realize that, like the prophesies of Cassandra, Mama's caveats generally had some merit. It was irritating when Mama knew, aggravating when Mama was right. But there was also a measure of reassurance to be had—if secretly—in those moments.

Oh, Mama. Who will I turn to after you're gone?

In the back of her giddy mind Camille heard her mother's likely response:

Don't rush me.

. . .

Fortunately, Rosemary's health had improved two weeks later, in time for the first fitting of the bridesmaids' suits. The blue lavender crepe fabric was perfect. All four suits were several sizes too large, but Valerie assured them that they always ordered on the generous side.

"You gain some, lose some, it won't matter," she told Lauren when she emerged from a dressing room looking like a child playing dress-up.

Lauren flashed her lacy bra as she lapped the front of the jacket and boasted, "I'll never be *this* big."

"Of course not, dear." Valerie went after the excess fabric, gathering a handful in the back, another at the waist. "We're going to take this in. It'll be fine."

"That's a lot to take in across the shoulders," Rosemary said. "You'll have to do a complete reconstruction."

"Maybe we have the jackets mixed up." Valerie examined a tag pinned inside the back of the neck, eliciting an ouch of protest from Lauren. "Here's the problem," she proclaimed loudly, as though someone on the other side of the shop might have an interest in the proceedings. "This is the fourteen. This must be Beth's jacket. Beth is at least a fourteen."

Standing on the platform in front of the three-way mirror, a forlorn Beth Praeger turned from multiple views of her ample figure. "But this jacket almost fits me," she said softly.

"No, dear, that doesn't allow for any . . ." Valerie motioned to Beth. "Let's switch, and then we'll pin."

"What about the skirt?" Lauren grabbed two handfuls of fabric.

"Don't worry about that. That's easy to fix." Valerie shooed both girls back into the changing cubicles. "Makes you feel good to find yourself swimming in it, doesn't it? Sort of like those diet commercials where they hold up the huge pants."

Camille leaned across the arm of her observer's chair and confided to her mother, "If Beth develops an eating disorder after this fitting, I don't know whether I'll sue that woman or strangle her."

"I hope she has some good seamstresses working for her."

Camille nodded and called out, "Valerie, how good are your seamstresses?"

"The best." Valerie looked up from taking a hem measurement for maid of honor Amy Boulet. "They don't speak English very well, but they can stitch up a storm."

"A storm isn't what we need."

"Those jackets are too long and too boxy," Rosemary said, gesturing with an aged but expert hand. "My design had simple but feminine lines. You'll be taking these apart to make them—"

"Mrs. Delonga, this is why we have fittings." Valerie rose to her full height, adjusted her glasses, and looked down her nose. "After I check everything out here and get the garments properly assigned, I'll have Jenny take care of the rest. She's with another customer right now." She checked her watch. "She'll be with us in a minute. We had to squeeze in an unscheduled bride."

"So Jenny's the fairy godmother with the magic wand?" Rosemary asked.

"She works magic, all right. Just wait and see." Using Amy as a model, Valerie pointed out each area of concern. "We'll mark the point of the pelvic bone on each girl, determine dart placement, sleeve length. They'll be beautiful. Don't you love the color? I would call it sterling rose, wouldn't you?"

"The color is very nice," Camille agreed.

Valerie smiled victoriously and flipped open the Burke file.

"Now let's talk about the hotel decorations again, because I want to make sure you reserve everything you need from our garden collection. You say you've purchased brandy snifters, so you don't need our rose bowls for centerpieces?"

Camille slid Jordan a quick glance and nodded. She'd forgotten to mention her latest find, but since it was an upgrade, Jordan would surely approve.

"That's fine." Valerie made some notes with a pencil. "But we want to use the mirror tiles and several votive candles per table."

"We want lots of candles. Gobs of candles." Camille jumped at the chance to make up for her consultation oversight. "Don't we, Jordan?"

"I guess. As long as they blend in with *our theme.* This is the first I've heard of brandy snifters instead of rose bowls. When did you decide that?"

"When I found two dozen beautiful crystal stems on clearance for less than what they're charging to rent rose bowls. And they'll be yours to keep."

"What am I going to do with two dozen—"

"You'll have a brandy-tasting party," Camille said with a bright smile. "I don't know. It was a great deal, and they're much prettier than the rose bowls. Trust me on this. Valerie, we definitely want the lattice panels decorated with white lights and tulle. Four double panels. Make it five."

"And the curly willow in the floor pots?"

Camille stuck out her hand, palm up. "Let me see the price list."

"I don't have a printed list. My clients usually tell me what they want, and I do it for them."

Not this client. Camille had her own running total.

"I'll take care of the curly willow. I do my own willow arrangements every Christmas." She smiled at her daughter, who had more or less suggested the lights on the branches. "That way it's all ours."

"Great," Jordan said dryly.

"Mrs. Burke," Valerie began, stepping up to Jordan's side.

Camille answered with a cool gaze.

"Delonga, I'm sorry. The thing is, you're the mother of the bride. *You* should trust *me* on this. No matter how creative you are, you don't want to saddle yourself with a lot of details that might prevent you from enjoying this special day."

"I'll have it all ready ahead of time."

"My mother is a graduate of the if-you-want-it-done-right-do-it-yourself school." Jordan folded her arms, taking a standing-on-sarcasm stance. "You're a founding member of the Twin Cities Clearance Sale Club, aren't you, Mom?"

"Really?" Valerie looked at Camille with new appreciation. "Do you have a large membership, or does it fluctuate with the economy?"

"It's really more a matter of principle than economy. We actually take an oath." Camille slid Jordan another look. No guilt this time. Just pure fun. "I'm thinking of advertising our Web site in *Minnesota Bride*. We could help save a lot of mothers from vendors without price lists."

"I have a list. It's just that people don't usually ask for a printed copy. My services are tailored to the bride's wishes." Valerie offered Jordan a sympathetic glance. "Generally."

"She's putting you on, Valerie," Jordan said.

"You started it, sweetie." Camille touched the bride's advocate's arm. "I'm sorry, Valerie. We were kidding, of course. Your services are a godsend."

"If you were to hire a wedding planner . . ."

"I had a wedding planner." Adjusting the blouse she'd just tucked into the waistband of her slacks, Lauren joined them. "My wedding planner took care of everything, and it turned out perfectly."

"We're doing it differently," Camille said. The other three girls had also emerged from the dressing rooms. "However it turns out will be our version of perfect. Right, girls?"

There was an affirmative chorus from Lauren, Amy, Beth, and Kelly.

"Right, Jordan?"

"Right, Mom. Absolutely."

. . .

Jordan stood before the floor-length mirror in her grandmother's room watching Rosemary adjust the front of her hem. Her dress was a perfect fit. Her grandmother knew every measurement of her body, along with its history. The lines of her wedding dress would enhance the long torso she had inherited from her great-grandmother. Her strong shoulders must have come from her father's side, but she had her mother's long neck and Rosemary's legs.

There was a time when Jordan would have protested being made up of other people's parts. She looked like herself, not the stern old woman wearing the silly black hat in the black-and-white four-generations photograph her mother kept on her dresser. Not the dear, frail woman who knelt at her feet on toothpicks rather than legs. Not the Indian women who used to tell her she was too skinny and needed to eat more frybread and sweet, fruity *wojapi* when she went to the powwow to hear her father sing. Certainly not her mother, whose husband had gone away. Or astray. Jordan had tried not to wonder too much about the details. But she wasn't like her mother. She was like herself.

And she was also like them. A little bit. Maybe. Her mother was smarter than she was. Her grandmother was more skilled. Her aunts were stronger in so many ways.

But she was younger than any of them. She looked beautiful in the long white dress that draped sumptuously over her every curve. And James Mayfield was in love with her. James Mayfield loved Jordan Burke. She smiled at the image in the mirror. Maybe she had some smarts and some skills and some strength somewhere in there.

She was, after all, made up of good parts.

"You're pleased," Grandma said, looking up from the floor and catching the reflection of that smile.

"It's incredible. There simply aren't any words to describe it."

"It's not nearly finished." Rosemary poked fine pins into finer fabric. "I'm moving slowly on the handwork."

"Grandma, don't wear yourself out over this. It's already the most beautiful dress I've ever seen."

"Wait until you see the finished product. I'm taking my time, working slowly and carefully." She used the arm of an upholstered chair to gain a boost to her feet. Then she stepped back to assess the work she'd just done. "Once I have the edges in place, I'll start applying the seed pearls," she said as she disappeared into her closet.

Grandma emerged with a froth of gossamer white silk laid across her forearms. "I think I've finally got the veil right, but we still need the perfect anchor. What do you think? Crystal or pearls? Maybe both?"

Jordan was almost afraid to touch the delicate-looking fabric, which was trimmed with tiny crystals and pearls.

"Grandma, this is so beautiful. I can't stand the thought that I'll only wear it once."

"Neither can I, which is why . . ." With a flourish, Rosemary gathered the length of fabric and draped it around Jordan's shoulders. "It converts to a shawl."

"Oh, Grandma, you're a genius."

"And I have something else to show you." She ushered Jordan to the corner desk, where her computer stood ready to connect an old woman with an active mind to the outside world. "I want to do this for you myself, but only if you and James both like the idea."

A few clicks, whirs, and beeps unveiled . . . a car?

Grandma gestured as though she were presenting the crown jewels. "What do you think?"

"It's an old—"

"It's a 1949 Packard limousine. The handsome fellow holding the door comes with it, dressed in his vintage uniform."

Jordan laughed. "I get it. You want to meet the chauffeur."

"He's also the owner, and he does have a pleasant voice. I just thought it would be a nice touch with the forties theme."

"I thought we had a garden theme."

"With forties-style dresses, maybe it's a victory-garden theme. You're marrying your childhood sweetheart, which seems like a victory to me."

"We weren't sweethearts, Grandma. He was my hero, and I was his pest."

Rosemary laughed. "I'll make a note to tell your mother to add garden pests to the decor. She wants every little detail to have some meaning. Now let's e-mail the link to James and see what he thinks of the limo." She rolled her mouse on its floral pad and called up her address list. "And then you'll have to go away, because one of my auctions ends in a few minutes, and it's something I don't want you to see."

"Grandma," Jordan warned.

"Don't 'Grandma' me, young lady. How else am I supposed to do my shopping?"

Jordan's wedding dress was back on its satin hanger, and

Grandma was enjoying her latest hobby. There was no point in arguing with her, no reason to discourage her. Jordan was convinced that her grandmother would keep on truckin' as long as she believed in what she had to deliver.

But it wasn't necessary to humor her mother. Jordan found her in the kitchen preparing supper.

And she was just as pleased with herself as Grandma was.

"I've almost finished the arrangements for the doors to the banquet room," Camille said, closing the oven door on some kind of casserole. "Want to see?"

"Mom, don't you think this is getting out of hand?"

"One thing about a wedding: With stuff like candles and flowers and little accessories, you almost can't overdo."

One thing about her mother: She'd never been oppressively perky, and she'd certainly never been an obsessive accessorizer. Not until she'd caught this weird wedding bug.

"Have you been possessed by some sort of demon cherub?" Jordan asked.

Camille's laugh irked Jordan all the more. Her mother simply didn't get it.

"I'm serious," Jordan said. "You don't even ask me half the time. You just do it. Are you trying to show me yet again how to make something out of nothing? I'm well aware that you're a magician and that all the world is your stage, but do you have to—"

"Wait a minute, Jordan. Your father is the performer, not me. I'm just trying to do what I can to make this wedding very, very special."

"*This* wedding? Whose wedding is it?"

"Yours," Camille said innocently. "Yours and James's."

Hers and James's?

The innocence was a crock. Her mother wasn't getting it because she didn't want to get it. Getting it would mean giving up on doing it her way, which always turned out fine, looked good, worked well. But it always had Camille Delonga written all over it.

"Why do I feel as if James and I are fast becoming an afterthought? Walking, talking decorative elements?"

Camille looked up from the utensil drawer, the hurt shown clearly on her face. Not a big wound, but a little sting, which was all that Jordan intended.

"If there's anything in the works that you don't like, just tell me."

"*I am.*" Jordan glanced away, then back again, steadying herself. "Whatever happened to simple, tasteful, and inexpensive?"

"Still my mantra," Camille said with a quick shrug. "I embrace all those principles, but wait until you see what I can do within those parameters."

"I know what you can do, Mom. And I know you're doing it all for me. But I want . . ."

What did she want? What did she *not* want? The dress was beautiful. She'd never seen sweeter favors, and she'd been pleasantly surprised at how nice the brandy snifters were. She knew James would get a kick out of that antique limo. They were all great ideas. She liked them.

But they hadn't been hers.

"You want it all to go smoothly," Camille said. "No screw-ups. No wilted flowers, no flat tires. You want—"

"I just want to get married!"

Jordan had to hold on to herself to hide the awful shakiness that had suddenly struck her inside. She didn't know why or where it had come from or what to do about it.

And she didn't know who would, other than the person who always did.

Her mother.

Chapter 13

"Mom! Guess what?"

The childlike sound of Jordan's voice threw Camille for a bittersweet loop as she looked up from her drafting board. She held her breath, half expecting a much younger Jordan to come bounding into the workshop. She felt ridiculous when she caught herself. Misty eyes. Prickly throat.

Damn hormones.

"We've found a house. Maybe. We think we have."

Oddly, the news hit Camille like a bucket of ice water.

"A house? A rental?" No wonder Jordan was excited. It was hard to find a single-family house for rent in the Twin Cities suburbs.

"To buy!" Jordan enthused as she claimed

her favorite workshop perch—the tall blue stool that Camille herself had used to gain a good view of her father's woodworking. "We've been looking for an apartment, but rent is outrageous, even on a place as small as the one James is living in. The agent we've been working with showed us a house that has renters in it now, but the owner wants to sell it."

She clasped her hands, barely able to contain herself. "Oh, Mom, it's perfect. Almost exactly halfway between his office and my school, and not too far from you."

"I thought you were planning to stay in James's apartment until you had a little more—"

"In savings, I know, but this is such a great opportunity. We have almost enough money for the down payment now. In fact, if we skipped the honeymoon, I think we could do it."

"Skipped the honeymoon?" Skipping wasn't good. Not now. They were too far into the fairytale-wedding plans to lop off the tail and leave any ends loose. Camille swiveled her stool toward Jordan. "What does James say about that? Most men want to skip right *to* the honeymoon."

"He likes the house," Jordan said, her effusiveness fizzling.

"And?"

"And we'd need a little help." Her eyes gave away her request with an advanced apology. "Obviously, we can't ask his parents, so . . ."

"Are you asking me?"

"At the moment, only hypothetically. I'm just asking whether you would consider helping us with a down payment on a house if we were to ask."

"I would *consider* doing anything you asked me to do, Jordan. You know that. But right now . . ." *Please don't ask.*

"You'd do it?"

"Right now we're up to our eyebrows in wedding plans, and I don't know why you'd want to cancel your honeymoon."

"Not cancel, but maybe postpone. It's a great house, and great starter houses are scarce right now." Jordan grabbed Camille's hand, which was an unusual gesture for Jordan. "I'm just wondering whether it's an option."

"I guess I would need to hear more details." Camille hadn't realized that buying a house right out of the gate was under consideration. "You know, I did suggest—"

"I don't know the details yet," Jordan said quickly. "So you're saying you would consider helping us out once I have more details?"

"The word 'consider' is fairly broad, honey. As I said, without really committing much, I can honestly say that I would *consider* anything you ask. But right now we have our hands full with your wedding."

Jordan's grin was infectious. "I'll take that as a definite maybe."

"I wouldn't try taking it to the bank," Camille warned as the roar of a familiar engine encroached on the conversation.

"Dad's here." Jordan popped off the stool as though she'd been sitting on a spring. "Maybe I could take him to the bank."

"He doesn't even know where the bank is." The affronted look in her daughter's eyes took much of the satisfaction out of Camille's clever sarcasm. The rest was lost in guilt. She touched Jordan's cheek in a motherly gesture. "He'd find it for you, though. Don't . . . don't take him to the cleaners."

"What's that supposed to mean?"

"He's helping with the wedding. Your dad's always been an easy come, easy go kind of a guy. Never tight with his money when he has it, never too worried about it when he doesn't."

"Worrying was your job," Jordan acknowledged.

"That's not the best plan for division of labor if you're looking for marital bliss. But I guess you know by now that if you want something, and your dad has the money, it's yours. Make a wish in his presence and he'll find a way to grant it. He loves to be able to pull a wad of cash out of his pocket and plunk it in your hand."

"*Your* hand."

"Sure," Camille agreed as she took a peek out the window. "My hand, your hand, whatever."

Pulling a final drag on a cigarette, Creed was out there in the driveway, hunkering down to examine the cracks in the asphalt. She missed having a man around to fix things, and she knew she'd come home one day and find the driveway patched and resurfaced. But with Creed the caveat had always been *if he stuck around long enough.*

"You're his princess," Camille said, turning from the window. "If you need a crown or a coach, you tell your dad. Just don't ask him for the everyday stuff. Unless it's something he can fix with his own hands."

"I was only kidding. I'm not going to ask him. I asked him for a car once."

"A car?"

"After I got my license, I wanted my own car. Remember?"

"How can I forget? I heard it at least twice a day for two years. But I didn't know you asked him."

"I always thought that when you said no it was just because you didn't want me to have something. He never said no the way you did. He always made me feel like he wanted to say yes in the worst way, that he hated letting me down when he had to say no. I ended up feeling just terrible about asking him for the car. He had such a sad look, like somebody had pulled the rug out, landed him on his butt, and when he looked up, he saw that it was me."

Camille knew that look. Hearing its architect open the back door, she laughed. "But it never bothered you when I said no."

"Of course not," Jordan said. "You did it with such flair."

"Just for future reference, I'll let you in on a little motherhood secret. If you expect to hold the line with your kid, you have to adopt an attitude. Use it. Believe in it." Creed appeared in the doorway just as she was admonishing, "Stick to it. Otherwise you'll be caving in all over the place."

"The Camille Delonga attitude is hardly a secret." Jordan slipped her arm around Creed's slim waist. "Right, Dad?"

"I would have to say 'No comment.'"

"I would have to say that the Jordan Burke attitude is pretty obvious, too." *Along with the old Daddy's-girl routine,* Camille thought. But it was okay. Although it was hard to look at the two standing together in her workshop like that, one just visiting, the other soon leaving. Her feet located the clogs under the desk. She looked up smiling as she slipped them on. "Our attitudes sort of work in tandem."

"No way."

"Sorry. You can pick your friends, and you can pick your fiancé, but you can't pick your mother. One of these days you'll hear yourself sounding like me."

"No way!" Laughing, Jordan led the way to the kitchen. "Whose car are we taking?"

"Mine." Camille found her purse on the counter and checked for keys. "Why don't you ask James to stop in later, and we can talk about your housing needs over supper."

"Not tonight."

Camille knew a loaded answer when she heard one, but she managed to contain the automatic *Why not?* behind a smile. "Whenever you're ready. Right now are you ready for cake?"

"I know what I want." Grateful for the change of subject, Jordan pulled a magazine clipping from the side pocket of her purse and showed it to her parents.

"That's an ad for Barnett's Bakery," Camille said. "They're supposed to be pretty spendy."

Jordan pouted in disgust. "But *really* good. Of course, a cake is a cake. Let's just go to the grocery store and buy something in a—"

"Let's compromise," Camille suggested. "I've done some research, and I've made an appointment with the Bakery at Byerly's. It's not Bridget's first choice either, but I understand they're a little more reasonable. We'll sample. If it's not what you want—"

"I don't care what it tastes like. I don't even like cake that much." Jordan smacked the clipping with the back of her fingertips. "But I want it to look like this. This is classy, and it goes with my dress."

"Bring the picture. You pick the style, your dad picks the flavor, and I have the final word on price. Is it a deal?"

"You're going to let me eat cake now?" Creed snapped to attention. "Where's James? I need some male backup."

"I'm carrying his proxy," Jordan said.

"Meaning he's staying out of it?" Camille supposed. "Wise man."

"As long as he shows up at the church with a ring in his pocket," Creed said as he punched the garage-door button.

. . .

Thanks to a helpful pastry chef named Belle Jensen and her tasty wares, they were able to please Jordan with the look she wanted at an affordable price. Belle explained that the white chocolate rolled fondant in Jordan's picture could be done in plain white fondant, which she could "pearlize" with some sort of shiny confection. By serving a chocolate groom's cake decorated with a trout on the hook, they could get away with a smaller, more elegant wedding cake. Creed played the role of buffer as well as taster, helping to steer the decisions toward the happy compromise Camille was hoping for.

With the removal of each calendar page, compromise seemed harder to come by. In all the excitement Camille wondered whether Jordan was beginning to believe she'd had an infusion of royal blood. Being the center of attention was bound to take its toll, Camille decided. And it couldn't last, not even for a princess. The ephemeral bride would soon be a normal woman, settling down to everyday life. For now she ought to be able to have her pearlized cake and eat it, too.

. . .

Three weeks before the wedding the bridesmaids hosted Jordan's bridal shower at Bridget's house, which Bridget intended to occupy until the day Tim and his lawyer pried the key from her hands. Camille tried to stay out of the shower planning, but she had ideas, and she ran into bargains, and such serendipitous finds could not be ignored. She personalized scented soap for party favors and made centerpieces and floral place-card holders. Rosemary shopped her favorite Internet auction sites for hand-trimmed hankies and costume jewelry from the 1940s for game prizes. The games became competitive, the jokes risqué, and the laughter riotous.

Inevitably Rosemary ended up on the sidelines with Ramona Mayfield. They were the grandmothers, after all. They exchanged what they knew of the other two grandmothers. Creed's mother had passed away sometime ago, Rosemary explained. Ramona had heard that Bridget's mother, who had moved to Florida, hoped to be there for the wedding.

"She's older than we are," Ramona said.

Rosemary wondered how Ramona had come to that conclusion, but she wasn't curious enough to ask. Ramona dyed her hair black and wore it long. One big mistake on top of another. Not that Rosemary could win any beauty contest at the moment, but if they decided to hold an American Grandma pageant next year, she'd be ready. For now she had her wigs in several colors, but no black. She tried to imagine herself with black hair. She'd probably look worse than Ramona. The image of two black-haired crones perched side by side on Bridget's antique deacon's bench made Rosemary laugh out loud.

Heckle and Jeckle.

"Look at that little veil thing they put on Jordie," she said in response to Ramona's what's-so-funny? look.

"They shouldn't have these things so close together," Ramona said. "Wedding, divorce, wedding. My Lord, how are we supposed to keep up with it all? Isn't there some sort of unwritten rule about spacing? All we need is a funeral between now and—" Ramona caught herself and quickly offered a ghoulishly red-lipped smile. "You seem to be holding up well, Rosemary."

"You do, too."

"Well enough. I don't usually come to these things, but with my son's recent descent into absurdity, I wanted to be here for the Mayfield side of the family. It's only right."

"You were at Lauren's wedding."

"I make an appearance at the important events. Funerals, weddings, the occasional holiday gathering. Just to keep up with who's doing what, you know." She patted Rosemary's hand. "At our age you have only one thing left to do, and you want to make it count for something."

Our age again?

"What's that?"

"Divvy up the worldly goods." Ramona fairly cackled. "I'm keeping my eye on them. They know it, too. Just like I used to tell them when they started making their Christmas lists. Santa sees your every move. You'll only get what's coming to you." She turned toward Rosemary with new interest. "Have you a plan in place?"

"I don't have a lot. I'm giving Jordan some things now that she'll be setting up her own home."

"I mean a funeral plan."

"For myself?" Rosemary laughed. "That's one family event I don't plan on attending."

"But you don't want them making decisions about your final arrangements when they're grieving. Who knows what they'll come up with?"

"Well, I've—"

"And you want the affair to do you justice, to make a statement. I could recommend a wonderful planner. He is an absolute artist."

"I think I'll get myself a little more coffee." Rosemary stood abruptly, ready to scream, set to bolt. But not without proper comportment. "Would you like some?"

"Oh, no, dear, that stuff'll kill you." Ramona arched a penciled eyebrow. "I wonder what's in that decanter on the buffet?"

"It looks like sherry."

Ramona nodded once. "Sherry would be very nice, thank you."

.   .   .

"Will you all excuse the bride for a minute?" Lauren called from the kitchen. "The groom is on the phone."

Jordan sprang from the wingback chair that had been designated the seat of honor. "Maybe he's heard from the real-estate agent."

Camille presented another round of game prizes. Bridget served another round of snacks, checked her watch, caught Camille's attention with a pointed glance at the pile of wrapped gifts. Camille shrugged. Bridget redirected the pointed glance toward the kitchen. Camille had a feeling she didn't want to go there. She tried a signal from the doorway, but Jordan ignored it. The conversation was looking pretty intense, which reminded Camille of Jordan's first boy-girl birthday party. The girls had spent much of the party talking on the phone, trying to persuade one guy that even though her mother was home she wasn't *at* the party and another that he could bring his video game with him.

"Jordan. Honey, this party is in your honor."

"I have to get back, James. We'll talk about this later." Jordan scowled. "But there *is* something to talk about. I know this isn't the only house, but it's the perfect house, and if—" She glanced up at Camille, then quickly turned her back. "No, I'm not. But you're not treating me like an equal partner either." Pause. "Don't say that. Don't even—" Jordan sighed. "I have to get back to this stupid party now. Yes. Thanks a lot. Bye."

She slammed down the receiver, turned, glanced at her mother, then back at the phone. Wrapping her arms around herself, she quietly admitted, "He's mad at me."

"The house?"

"Sort of." Her lower lip trembled as a tear fell. "It's more than that. He thinks I . . ."

"Come on and open your presents, Jordan." Lauren's bright smile vanished. "What's wrong? Was that still my brother on the phone?" Lauren rushed to Jordan's side, augmenting the drama with a bride-to-bride embrace. "Don't pay any attention to him. He's just a big bunch of hot air sometimes."

"He's just my future . . . h-h-husbannnd."

"Jitters," Lauren translated for Camille. "Oh, Jordan, it's perfectly normal. This close to the big day, I was the same way."

"He says I'm not . . ."

"He's got jitters, too."

"But what if he . . ."

"He won't. They say they will, but it's their last gasp of bachelor-hood. Like a fish flopping around on the dock." Lauren leaned back, bugged her eyes, thrust out her lips, and turned her hands into makeshift fins. Her fish imitation extracted a blubbering giggle from the bride.

"All it takes is a wife to make a man of the poor dear."

"Says the old married lady," Camille said, laughing.

"A fishwife!" Jordan wailed.

"We're taking her out after the shower," Lauren told Camille. "All she needs is a night out with her maids. Don't worry. We'll have a designated driver, and Jordan doesn't even have to call *not it*."

"Do you want me to drive?" Camille offered.

"Sorry." Lauren grinned. "No moms allowed."

Ramona was the last to leave. Bridget, who had brought her, was amused to discover her tippling. She made a deal with Lauren to take her grandmother home in return for relief from cleanup detail.

"Rosemary, you rascal," Bridget teased after the girls had left. "You got my mother-in-law drunk."

"I found a way to add spirit to the conversation. It was either get her to change the subject or hit the bottle myself, and I'm trying to keep the spirits at bay these days." Rosemary wagged a finger. "That's the last time you're putting me on grandma detail."

At home, Rosemary went to bed, leaving Camille to post-party blues. She had a pair of fire screens in progress, but working on them seemed too much like *work* work. She needed a gradual letdown, a bit of play work. Applying silk flowers to grapevine wreaths was more appealing, but she wondered about the length for the swag that would go with the wreaths. She needed to take another look at the room, which would require a visit to the Countryside Inn.

It was Saturday night. The place would be busy. Probably something going on in the banquet room. If there was a band playing, the bar would be crowded.

If there was a band playing?

She wouldn't hang around. She just needed to take a peek.

The doors to the banquet room were closed for a conference dinner. No decorations, no ideas to be gleaned. Camille took a few measurements, made a few notes about the collection of doors that surrounded the foyer, but she was drawn to the music coming from the bar. She'd noticed a new poster on display inside the front door. NOW PLAYING—ONLY THE LONELY. She wondered who had taken the photograph. Creed had never been much good at promotion, and he'd never wanted a manager. *I've got a wife,* he would say. *Why in hell would I hire a manager?* But she hadn't heard anything about being replaced. Not by a manager anyway.

She found an inconspicuous place to sit and ordered a glass of Chablis, which she changed, on second thought, to a more festive margarita. She could now check "bridal shower" off her mental to-do list. That left the bridesmaids' breakfast, the rehearsal, and the groom's dinner leading up to what was fondly termed "The Big Day." She *deserved* a margarita. Anyone who celebrated such significant milestones alone in a crowd of her former significant other's fans actually deserved a whole parade of margaritas.

To the mother of the bride, she toasted silently with her first salty sip. Then she sat back to watch the father of the bride ride his music as he would a horse. He still connected with the women in the audience, singled them out individually, sang to them, sucked them in. They lapped it up, just as Camille had done. If she were sitting up front, she would probably do it again. There was no denying his appeal.

This was good practice for the reception, when she would be front and center. He would choose heart-melting music, and she, by that time, would be a bowl of emotional mush anyway. Yes, practice was a good thing.

She ordered another margarita.

Chapter 14

Creed hadn't seen Camille enter the bar. He didn't notice her tucked into the corner table at the back of the room until some fat guy tried to get her to dance to a country version of "Suspicion." Creed had added the song to the playlist years ago because it hit so close to home, which was the hit people wanted from his brand of music.

Just say no, he willed as he watched her. It felt weird, catching some guy hit on his ex-wife. The young cutie at the front table thought Creed was smiling for her, and she smiled back. Hell, she winked at him. He wasn't smiling *for* the girl. He was smiling at her because she was sitting in front him. He was smiling for the shutdown Camille had given Mr. Big. She didn't need that tub to be tromping on her toes.

It was the last set. Then it was last call. If Camille had come out to check up on him, Creed was inclined to let her get away with it without getting caught, whatever her reason. But he'd given her the chance to slip out, and she didn't take it, so he sauntered back to her corner. He wanted to thank her again for including him on the cake tasting. He wanted to tell her he'd made the appointment to get sized up for his tux like she'd told him to and to ask her what was next on the wedding agenda.

He wanted to sit with her for a while.

She saw him coming. She made no move to take off, which he figured to be a good sign. Then she smiled at him, and he realized that she was totally blitzed. He smiled back. This was a first.

"What are we drinking?" he asked as he slid in beside her.

"We are drinking margaritas." She raised a glass. The smile in her low-lidded eyes was sweet, unabashedly flirtatious. "On the rocks, with salt."

"Good choice." He noticed that she had a fresh one waiting.

"Have one. I'm buying." She lifted her hand and snapped her fingers. "Garçon!"

"Honey, I don't think there's anyone at the Countryside Inn who answers to that name. Besides, the bar's closed."

"They haven't brought me my last-call drink yet. That'll be the one I buy for you. I think I've had enough."

"What about that one?" He pointed.

"I don't want that one." She eyed the drink suspiciously. "Some guy ordered that for me after I said 'No, thank you.' Politely but quite firmly, making myself quite, quite clear, *if* you know what I mean. But I have *defi*nally had quite enough."

He laughed. "Margarita has a way of sneaking up on a person, does she?"

"Is it ob—ob-vious?"

"Only to someone who knows you as well as I do."

"You do, don't you? You know me very well." She toyed with the soggy corner of the napkin under her glass. "I think it's fair to say we know each other pretty well."

"What I don't know is whether we're celebrating or feeling sad."

"Celebrating, of course. I don't know why people go to bars when they're depressed. You just get more depressed."

He leaned back, enjoying the look of her. She rarely looked this vulnerable. "What do you do when you get depressed?"

"I don't get depressed. I don't have time to be depressed. If I feel something coming on and I think it might be depression . . ." She lifted one shoulder. "Well, I don't know for sure, because I don't get depressed, but if I think I might get depressed, then I get busy doing something. I make something, or I read something, or I plan some-thing out."

"You ever talk to someone?"

Squinting against the closing-time lights, she looked up at him and smiled. "I used to."

"So what are we celebrating?"

"The bridal shower at Bridget's. Our daughter made a nice haul. And everyone had a good time, I think. We had games and prizes and good food." She enunciated with exaggerated care. "I made the favors and some of the decorations, and I made lemon bars and three kinds of tarts. You remember my tarts?"

"I can't have a tart without thinking of you."

"I can't tell you how much it pleases me to hear you say that." She gave him what was supposed to pass for a haughty look. "What's your favorite kind of tart?"

"Chameleon."

"No such thing."

"Chamomile."

"That's a kind of tea."

"Margarita, then. Margarita is very tart."

"Very tart." She waggled her finger, signaling him to lean closer. "I think I need your help," she whispered.

"Sure. You need a ride home?"

"First things firtht," she said. "Firsst. I'm afraid to stand up. Once I manage that, I'm not sure I can execute a graceful exit."

He lifted a single eyebrow. "This sounds like some serious inebriation."

"I'm quite sure I could walk out under my own, you know . . ."

"Steam," he supplied.

"Yes, I have plenty of that. But it's that graceful part that worries me."

"You don't want to wobble at all."

"Weebles wobble, but they don't fall down," she recited, recalling a commercial for a toy Jordan had loved when she was a toddler.

"Come on. I won't let you fall down." He stood, offering her a hand.

She leaned against him, slipping her arm around his waist. "Don't let me wobble either."

"How wobbly are you feeling?" One look at her pale face clued him in. He steered her across the hotel lobby. "Hang on, hon. I've got a room close by."

"I'm not going to be sick," she assured him as he slid his key card into the lock on his door. Because he was in a hurry, it took three tries to open it. He flipped on the light, and she pushed him aside and made a beeline for the bathroom. "Go away, Creed."

"Sounds familiar," he grumbled as she closed the bathroom door on him. But she wasn't kicking him out for long this time. "You've got five minutes."

"Go away!"

"I'll get you some"—he pocketed his plastic key and grabbed a plastic bucket, typical trappings of a temporary home—"ice."

Returning after the promised five minutes plus a few more, he found her stretched across his bed. He thought she'd passed out, but not Camille. Passing out was beneath her. Her face was buried in his pillow, and her shoulders were trembling.

Camille was crying?

Creed set the ice bucket on the table next to the pull-out sofa and sat beside her on the bed.

"I always wondered what kind of a drunk you'd make. I wouldn't have guessed you'd be the cryin' kind."

"Why not?" She lifted her face from the pillow. "I have feelings, you know. I cry sometimes."

"How long has it been?"

"I don' know. A while." She rolled to her back, swiping at her tears with a childlike fist. "I don' exac-ly enjoy it, you know. But now that I got started, I don't know what . . . how to make it . . . st-stop."

"I could hold you."

She went still for a moment. "Do you want to?"

"I really do, yeah." He stretched out alongside her, slipped his arm beneath her shoulders, and drew her to his chest. He smiled, thinking that of all the scents that had ever assailed him when he'd climbed into bed with a woman, the smell of his industrial-strength Listerine on top of her regurgitated margarita had to be the most endearing, if not the most pleasant.

He rubbed her back. "Yeah. Cry all you want. You never used to let me do this. Hold you while you cry."

"I was too mad . . . usually crying . . . over you."

"Good song material," he said with a chuckle. "But you never even let me see you cry."

"What difference . . . ? Wouldn't change . . . anything."

"Is that why you're crying? What do you want to change?"

"Nothing. There's no reason." Her gasping and sobbing had given her hiccups. "Just . . . that stuff doesn't taste very good . . . coming up."

He couldn't help laughing.

"Stop it," she whined. Another hiccup. "You'd cry, too."

"Damn straight, I would. I have once or twice. But you're right. It didn't change anything."

She looked up at him. Big, sorrowful puppy eyes. "Can I stay here?"

"Sure."

"I don't know what it is. I just feel so weird sometimes."

"Weird, how?"

"*Hou,* Creed." She put her palm in front of his face, being silly again. "*Hou,* weird white woman."

He groaned. "As weird as it gets, funny girl."

"It gets pretty weird. Like, I was washing my face this morning, and all of a sudden I was just watching the water run through my fingers. Fill my hands back up, tight fingers." She drew back, holding her hand up high, the way she'd described. "Can't stay that way very long.

It still runs out. Just takes longer. So I'm standing there, leaning over the sink, my throat getting all tight, and it's just water. There's plenty more water."

"Plenty more." He brushed his fingertips across her damp cheek. "Here's some, mixed with a little salt of the earth."

"Stupid. I'm acting stupid."

"Everybody gets the blues, even Camille Delonga." He ought to be singing to her, he thought. Wouldn't that be corny as hell? But that was the way he felt—corny as hell, with a song in his heart. "You need to let go once in a while, go with the flow."

"But it was a good day. I had a really good day. The shower was fun." She snuggled against his shirt. "Jordan and James had a little lovers' tiff on the phone, though."

"About what?"

"She didn't exactly say. She hung up bawling. Then she went out with the girls. No moms allowed." She giggled. "Mums." Hiccupped. "The queen mum, the princess bride. Mum's the word."

"He's gonna be good to her, isn't he?"

"Prince James? I hope so. I hope they're good to . . . *for* each other."

"So Jordie went out with the girls. What about your mom?"

"She went to bed." After a pause she projected softly, "I don't think she's telling me everything."

"About going to bed?" He looked down at her, grinning. "Are you gonna tell her where *you* slept tonight?"

"She'd pin a medal on me, probably. She's changed. Still changing." She pressed her lips together, blinking back more tears, and then took a deep steadying breath. "Going somewhere. It feels like she's getting ready to go somewhere, but she won't tell me."

"Does she have to?"

"I suppose I should go with the flow," she allowed, voice raspy. "But you know me—I can't just float along. I want an engine. I want a steering wheel and a rudder."

"I know you," he said, rubbing her back again. "And you know me. I'm satisfied with a raft."

"That's why she called you to take her to the emergency room. No ambulance. No . . . no . . ."

"You can only push this one so far, hon, this time-and-the-river-flowing bit. Right now it's about Jordan."

She looked up with a tremulous smile. "The river or the daughter?"

"Damn, I should've seen that coming." He smoothed a damp bit of hair back from her face. "Jordan, the daughter and granddaughter. Jordan, the bride. Your mom ain't goin' no place else before we have that wedding."

"You're sure?"

He nodded.

"Do you know whether she had any more tests done without telling me or anything like . . . like more . . ."

"No, I don't. I really don't. It looks to me like she wants to handle it herself for now. I think she'll let you know when she can't do that anymore." He could tell she wasn't convinced, so he moved on. "Jordie says the dress is beautiful."

"Oh, it is. Wait till you see."

"I'll let you in on a little secret." He put his lips close to her ear. "I'm kinda nervous about the whole thing."

"You?" She leaned back, gave him that incredulous, don't-be-ridiculous look. "You get up in front of people all the time. You'll be fine."

"I'm telling you something personal here. I'm worried about getting all choked up in front of everybody."

She waggled her eyebrows. "Go with the flow."

"Right." There was something else he'd thought about, felt foolish about, figured only she would understand. "I don't want to be alone that day. I don't want to feel . . . divorced."

"Neither do I," she whispered.

"Let's make a pact, okay? On Jordan's wedding day we go with the flow together."

"It's a deal." An easy moment passed before she switched gears. "I wish Bridget and Tim could make the same pact."

"Their wounds are pretty fresh."

"Creed, I don't know what she's going to do. She's losing everything, and she hasn't supported herself . . . well, ever. I tried to tell her she could stay with Mama and me, but I think she was insulted. She said I was just being kind."

"Were you?"

"No. We've been friends . . ." She leaned back on another double take. "What's wrong with being kind?"

"Nothing. I think it's great. Maybe when I get old, you'll even let me come home."

"What, so I can mash your food and change your diapers?"

"Maybe we can mash each other's food, huh?" He laughed. "Let's not think about the other part."

"Let's not." Another moment passed before she asked with sleepy curiosity, "What kind of an old man do you plan to be?"

"A dead one. I was never one for goin' back to the blanket. I sure ain't puttin' on any diapers."

"What happened to go . . . mmm . . . with the flow?"

"I don't know. It sounded good when we were talking about other things." He looked down at her. "Why are we talking so morbid anyway?"

"Seems like the logical follow-up to getting drunk and puking one's guts out."

He smoothed her hair back again, marveling at how young she looked with her eyes closed and her lips all moist and puffy. "One is feeling better?" he asked gently.

"One is feeling very tired."

"Figures."

. . .

It had been a long time since Camille had turned over in bed and bumped into an erect penis. Its owner's eyes were closed, but that didn't mean he was asleep. Beneath strange bedcovers she moved her hand slowly up her midriff until she encountered underwire.

"You're covered," he said. "Bra and panties."

"What about you?"

"You wanna check me out?" Eyes still closed, he smiled. "Again?"

"I wasn't checking you out. You were invading my space."

His eyes flew open. "How do you figure? I'm paying the rent on this bed, lady."

She lifted her head, then eased it back to the pillow as lightning stabbed her in the temples. "Oh, dear. My head's throbbing."

"Join the club."

"Are we getting up now?"

His laughter shook the bed, which made the pain worse.

"What I meant was . . ." She had to join in. "Oh, God, it hurts to laugh. I was going to offer to look the other way if you will."

"There's nothing under here you haven't seen before."

"I don't remember taking my clothes off."

"I do."

She tried to think, which also hurt. "I did?"

"*I* did."

"You did," she echoed, drawing out the words and the thought. "I don't remember that either. What else don't I remember?"

"I've gotten pretty good at reading your mind, but not good enough to pick up on anything that isn't there."

"I don't remember having sex last night."

"Well, that's good, because I don't either."

"We didn't?"

"I didn't. I don't know about you." He rolled toward her and propped himself on his elbow, grinning. "If you'd had sex with me, I guaran-damn-tee you'd remember."

"Don't be too sure." That grin of his was way too bright, along with the sunlight crashing through the partially open drapes. She closed her eyes. "I don't know what's happened to my memory lately. Margaritas notwithstanding."

"Your memory was always way too sharp for your own good. Maybe the good Lord's taking pity on you by filing the edge off a little."

"It's mainly the short-term memory that's gone bad."

"Maybe we can find a cure. Let's see if this brings anything back."

She felt a kiss coming on. The warmth of his bare chest, the soft whisper of his breath, and the brush of his lips gave fair warning. It would take too much effort to turn her head. It would be too jarring, hurt too much. It was so easy to part her lips and lift her chin and receive his open-mouthed kiss as though she wanted it, respond as though she meant it.

He raised his head. "Remember that?"

She nodded.

"Long-term, or short-term?"

"Long."

"Too long?"

"Much too long," she admitted, but feeling that second kiss coming, and thinking of the way she must taste and smell and look, she turned her head away and whispered, "No."

He took his weight and his warmth from her as abruptly as she had turned from him. She felt bereft, and she thanked God, for what a mistake this threatened to be.

"Creed?"

"I'm not lookin'." He struck a match and lit a cigarette. "Get dressed."

Chapter 15

There was no denying that Creed and Ellie were good together.

They were practicing their surprise wedding duet in the living room while Camille and Bridget sorted out the invitation replies on the dining room table. Rosemary had moved one of the captain's chairs closer to the bay window for more light on her seed-pearl application. The next craft project—garden-scented soap and candles in beribboned baskets—was waiting in the wings at the end of the long table. Somewhere in her literature Martha Stewart had advised Camille that a small gift left in a wedding guest's hotel room was a "good thing."

Hearing Creed and Ellie's voices blending together beautifully gave Camille a thrilling, chilling shiver. She thrilled to the near perfection of "The Rose," imagining the sterling roses in the wedding bouquets just beginning to open. But the thought of any part of Creed blending with anything another woman had to offer still chilled her, even though the other woman was Camille's most trusted friend and Creed was no longer Camille's to be thrilled or chilled by.

But did he have to be *hers?* Why couldn't she let herself take his kiss for what it was, which was simply a great kiss?

She gave herself a mental smack. *Enjoy the rose, you idiot. It sounds as sweet as it smells—no blast on it except in your head.*

Somebody in the living room had screwed up the words, and they were both laughing over it. Camille was laughing with him pretty often these days, too. They'd always been able to make each other laugh, especially when they weren't making each other crazy. He laughed with lots of people—especially female people. He was every woman's favorite kind of a guy.

Damn him.

Damn herself. Camille turned her other mental cheek and mentally smacked again.

Just enjoy the damn music.

"I have an idea for plate chargers," Bridget was saying, totally oblivious to all the smacking that was going on right across the table. She pulled out the ubiquitous wedding-magazine clipping, this one a picture of a dinner plate nested in dry flowers and moss in a big terracotta saucer. "Going along with the garden theme. I think I could get them from a friend who owns a greenhouse. You've got the plates nested in these chargers, and your little nests on the plates. It's perfect."

"It's cute, Bridge, but I don't think the banquet staff would go for it. Besides, we're doing elegant garden. This would be more like country garden."

Bridget pouted briefly, then sailed on with another suggestion. "If we're going for elegance, I still say we do chair covers. Something rich, maybe a brocade, so we bring in the floral motif. Or frothy. We could do silver froth. We'll get them from—"

"No chair covers," Camille said firmly, hoping *she* wasn't frothing. "The chairs look fine. But what you could do for me is gather up a few pictures of James growing up."

The spark in Bridget's eyes dimmed, her sails deflating as she shook her head. "But we already did the slide show at Lauren's wedding."

"I remember. Don't worry, we're not going to do a repeat." Half an hour of baby pictures flashing on the wall had nearly put everyone to sleep. "This is James's wedding, so I need pictures of—"

"You're not going to put up a big collage, are you? I've seen that done. It's a little tacky, if you ask me."

"Not in our elegant garden. No, I'm going to scan the pictures and make an album that people can look at if they feel like it."

"You want me to go through picture albums," Bridget said, slipping from deflated to glum. "Can you scan Timothy out?"

"It'll be mostly the kids growing up."

"You don't want it to look as though they grew up in a vacuum," Rosemary said. "Include some family. Show where they came from. I was telling Ramona that we'd never met Creed's mother, and it occurred to me that I don't even think I've seen a picture of her."

"That's a good idea, Mama. Pictures of grandparents. Even great-grandparents. You can be sure Creed doesn't have any, but I'll ask his sisters. I have to call them anyway and see who's coming."

"You can be sure Creed doesn't have any what?" asked the man himself. The music had stopped, and the musicians had come to the table.

"Pictures of your parents or grandparents."

"I don't know if anybody does. Maybe my Aunt Patsy, but I haven't seen her in a while." He'd found the mint melt-aways in the candy dish in the kitchen. He offered Ellie the choice of a pink or green sweet from his hand as he popped a yellow one into his mouth. "What do you want with them?"

"A little history," Camille said. "A sense of roots. You know, for the garden theme."

"They're all pretty much planted in the ground, that's for sure. On my side anyway." He caught the surprise in Ellie's eyes as she glanced up from helping herself to the candy. He grinned. "Indian humor."

"A wedding brings two families together," Camille said, studiously ignoring the fact that he had Ellie literally eating out of his hand. "Let's celebrate that this time around."

"This is one wedding that's making some strange and interesting bedfellows. You wanna celebrate that?" He waited for Camille to oblige him with a pointed glance so he could give it right back to her with a mischievous smile. "I don't think you have to worry. I doubt if anybody from my family's gonna show up."

"Have you talked to them?" No answer. She sighed. "You said you would, Creed."

"There's a lot of things about you I really miss, honey, but that tone of voice ain't one of 'em."

"Not keeping your word is something I don't—"

"Children!" Rosemary smacked the arm of her chair with a flat hand. "Creed, I want you to tell your family that anyone who can come to the wedding will be my guest at the hotel. They'd be my guests in this house, but it's no longer my house. Anyway, the hotel is where all the action will be. I'll be staying there myself if I'm feel-ing"—she settled back into the chair, as though she'd expended more energy than she'd meant to—"up to any action."

"You mean, if it works out with the chauffeur?" Creed asked, grinning.

"His name is Jacques, and he's French-Canadian." Wearily, wist-fully, Rosemary returned Creed's smile. "Lovely voice, almost like yours. After we chatted awhile, he cut me a deal on the deluxe wed-ding package and offered to give me the sunset tour of Lake Min-netonka whenever I have an evening free."

"Jacques the Canuck sounds pretty slick, Rosie. Probably part Indian." Creed wagged a finger at her. "You make sure he stays in the front seat on that sunset tour."

Rosemary wagged her finger back at him. "You make sure you get in touch with your family so I can make reservations."

"Better yet, how about if I give you a phone number?"

"Creed, you—" Camille began.

"No, he's right," Rosemary said with a nod. "This is my call to make."

Creed helped himself to a pen from the table and the last page of Camille's guest list, where there was room at the bottom. "My sister Faith is like the family honcho and the keeper of the telephone. Here's her number." He wrote it down. "I haven't talked to her for a while. I guess I owe her a call, too. Between the two of us . . ."

"We'll get it done," Rosemary promised Camille.

"I'm really impressed with the way you're getting involved, Creed," Bridget said. "Considering the circumstances."

Creed glanced at Camille. "Was that a compliment?"

"Maybe there's a reconciliation in the offing," Bridget suggested.

"Where's the offing?" Creed asked, deadpan. He'd always gotten a charge out of knocking the legs out from under Bridget's high horse. "You mean like an offed marriage getting on again?"

"Close," Bridget said.

"Or just getting it on again with your ex," he teased, slipping Camille a sly glance. "Oh, *in* the offing. I get it. You're talkin' about in church, when they pass the plate."

"Just agree with him, Bridge," Camille said, trying hard not to laugh.

"You mean I can toss in a reconciliation instead of an IOU?" Creed popped the last piece of candy into his mouth and brushed his hands together. "Hey, Ellie, you think that would square me with the Great Accountant upstairs?"

"From what I've heard about your record keeping, that's the only accountant you have any chance of squaring with."

"It must be nice to be able to laugh about it all," Bridget said.

"*It?* That one was on me." Creed patted Bridget's shoulder. "The trick is to get the unsuspecting ex-husband into a house filled with your choice of hens," he said, finally coaxing a smile from Bridget. "But Miss Ellie's gonna get hers when I start our song off in *my* key."

"Will it be a duet or a duel? Stay tuned," Ellie said. "Shall we get something cold to drink and try it again, Mr. Chanticleer?"

Unsuspecting, my foot, Camille thought. A houseful of hens was all it took to get him up onstage for some rooftop-style crowing.

"That rustic charm has a way of sneaking up on you, doesn't it?" Bridget noted.

"Sure does, if you let your guard down. Never judge rustic charm by the condition of the jeans it comes in."

"That sounds like good pillow philosophy," Rosemary said. "If we can fit that motto on a pillow, we can add it to our catalog."

"What catalog?" Bridget asked.

Rosemary laughed. "The catalog business that's going to make us rich someday."

"As long as it doesn't have anything to do with making wedding favors," said Camille.

. . .

Creed had been invited to stay for supper with Jordan and James, and he'd offered to do the cooking. Camille wasn't certain what kind of help the kids were going to ask her for, if any, but she'd decided that the best way to make sure that everyone was on the same page was to open the book when they were all in the same room. But James showed up well before the hors d'oeuvre hour.

"Jordan's still at the bridal shop," he explained as he took a seat on the sofa. "They're having some problems with the bridesmaids' dresses."

"I thought they had them ready for a final fitting," Camille said. With little more than a week to go, this couldn't be a good thing.

"I guess they're not all done, and the ones that they thought were done don't fit. She said to meet her here, but I'm early."

"Well, you're in for a treat. Creed offered to make us his special Sonuvabitch Stew. I know that sounds ominous, but it's really quite safe. And very tasty, especially if you enjoy a bitch with a little bite."

She laughed at the wary look her future son-in-law gave her as she sat on the ottoman, putting them almost knee to knee. She reassured him with a motherly pat on his knee. She knew he didn't know quite what to make of Jordan's family sometimes, but she wanted him to know that she was harmless.

"Are you getting nervous?" she asked.

"Nervous as in cold feet? No. I'm in love with Jordan, and I'm ready to be married." He planted his elbows on his knees, leaned forward and laced his fingers together. "Tomorrow would be good."

"It's a lot of fuss, this wedding stuff, but I think it's going to be worth it."

He nodded, pulling his fingers apart and pushing them together again, a young man's way of working up to something. Finally he said, "I guess you know about our little disagreement over the house."

"I don't know about a disagreement. I thought we were going to talk about your house plans tonight."

He sighed, looking up rather sadly. "She asked for your help without talking with me about it first."

"You didn't . . ."

He shook his head.

They should all be in the same room now, she thought. They should be opening the book together. If she knew her daughter, a tiny bit of manipulation had been in the works, which meant that Camille and James were on the pages Jordan had assigned them. But it was transition time, a rollover of roles, a swift moment of passage when there was truth in triteness; love would find a way.

"She didn't . . ." A flurry of excuses lightened the weight of Camille's instincts, and she tossed one out for James. "She really only asked whether I would consider helping you get into the house if you two were to ask me."

"It doesn't matter how she phrased it. The point is, she asked you. I didn't have anything to do with it." Hands on his thighs, he sat upright, taking charge. "The thing is, we're ready to be married, but we're not ready to buy a house. We were looking to rent, and we stumbled onto this deal. I ran the numbers on it. It isn't feasible right now, even if we skip the honeymoon." With a sigh, he leaned back, slouching, suddenly looking more like the boy she remembered as her good friend's son than a man about to be married. "Frankly, I could use a honeymoon."

"Not until after I give her away." Creed came in abruptly, crossing the living room toward the sofa.

James sprang to his feet. "No, I know. I mean—"

Creed offered a handshake. "How's it going, James? Could you use a beer first?"

"Before . . . ?" James glanced at Camille. "No, sir, I'm fine. I was just saying that the wedding couldn't come soon enough for me."

"Myself, I can't get it straight in my head that my little girl has found Mr. Right. Did Camille tell you I'm cooking up my special recipe of Sonuvabitch Stew?"

"Yes, sir, it smells great. Sounds like it might be a little hot?"

"We named it after Jordan's last fiancé," Creed said as he took a chair. "He thought he was pretty hot, you know, pretty tough. But we tenderized him, didn't we, hon?" He winked at Camille. "I'm glad to see you kept that ol' meat-tenderizing mallet around."

"He's kidding, you know," Camille assured James.

"I was pretty sure, but he wasn't smiling at all."

"Indian humor, son," Creed said. "Give it half a chance, it grows on you. Camille still owes me."

"Owes you what?" she demanded.

"Maybe a quarter of a chance?"

"Your humor is one of the few things I don't mind you putting over on me." She laughed. "And I kept the tenderizing mallet around for grizzled ol' meatheads."

"You wound me, woman."

"How long have you guys been divorced?" James wanted to know.

"Not as long as we were married," Creed said.

"You still seem to like each other. That's kind of encouraging." James glanced back and forth between them, taking his seat again, still unsure. "This whole thing with my parents is such a mess. I don't know who's got the bad timing, them or us, but I want Jordan to have the wedding she deserves."

"There's never a bad time for a wedding or"—Camille looked down at her bare hands, her eyes avoiding Creed's—"a good time for a divorce."

"Jordan doesn't know that I'm paying for the rehearsal dinner myself," James said quietly.

"But your mother planned it."

He chortled, rolled his eyes. "No kidding."

"I thought your father—"

"She thinks he is, but . . ." James shook his head. "I don't want anything from him. And my mom doesn't need to know any of this. She's kind of day-to-day at this point. I don't want to think about what happens after they sell the house." He glanced between Creed and Camille again as he squared his shoulders. "The point is, I'm taking care of it, which is the way it should be. We're going to have our wedding and our honeymoon, and when we can afford to, we'll buy our house. And I wish Jordan hadn't gone to you looking for help for that. It's . . . kind of embarrassing."

"Oh, James. There's no reason for you to feel—" Camille caught a sharp look from Creed and shot back, "Well, there isn't."

"James, you're talking to someone who's never felt embarrassed." Before she could protest, Creed explained. "You've *been* embarrassed, maybe. For reasons. But if you had ever *felt* embarrassed, you'd know that reason doesn't figure in."

"I just meant that . . ." She looked at James, then back to Creed. They were clearly on the same wavelength. "Is this a man thing?"

"Exclusively?" Creed asked. "That, we wouldn't know."

"You should tell Jordan about the rehearsal dinner," she said to James. Then to Creed, "Shouldn't he?"

"My wife might have asked for my advice once in a while if we'd had a son," Creed supposed in James's direction. "Honey, the man's caught between a rock and a hard place here. He's got a divorce on one side, a wedding on the other."

"Can I ask a question?" James squirmed, suppressing a smile. "Is the wedding the rock or the hard place?"

Creed laughed heartily. "You'll do okay, son. You'll do just fine." He nodded at Camille. "He should do what's right for him, honey. For them."

"She should have talked with you before she asked me about helping you guys out," Camille said to James. "Maybe she was afraid I'd say no. And then she'd be embarrassed." She shook her head quickly. "Or feel embarrassed, or whatever. But that's not important. You two need to be open with each other first. It's the two of you foremost, and then you can decide who else you let in. But don't keep secrets from each other." She looked James in the eye. "Talk with each other."

"They really open up after a couple of margaritas," Creed commented at her back.

"Creed Burke," she warned. "I'm serious about this part."

"Why did you two split up?" James asked, turning to Creed. "You just called her 'honey.' "

Creed chuckled. "And she called me Creed Burke."

"And he calls all females 'honey.'"

"All I know is what I see," James said. "You're not like my parents."

"Marriage is complicated" was Camille's reply.

"But not when you're about to marry our daughter," Creed said. "Then it's simple. You be good to her or you deal with us." He flashed Camille a you-and-me smile. "And we are hell on wheels when we get goin' on that stew."

Chapter 16

The bridesmaids' breakfast was a celebration of Jordan's closest friendships. She'd known Lauren the longest, but she'd asked Amy Boulet to be her maid of honor. The choice had surprised Camille, even though Jordan couldn't be expected to select Lauren after Lauren had chosen her college roommate over Jordan. Camille had assumed that Amy was Jordan's tit for tat. Jordan had been the educational aide in Amy's third-grade class for two years, and she loved her job. Amy was the first to acknowledge that they worked like a team of teachers rather than teacher and aide, and her mention that Jordan had signed up for a program in which she could earn class credits on the job was the first Camille had heard of a renewed college effort.

"I just got into it after school started," Jordan explained over the soft-boiled egg course. "It's a new program. Amy was the one who found out that I could get into it."

Jordan had chosen a mentor over a girlfriend, Camille realized. A mentor who had quietly succeeded in getting Jordan back into school had received the "honor" nod. This was interesting. This was maybe a little exasperating? Amy had succeeded where Mother had failed?

"All I did was collect the literature," Amy said. "We were both looking for classes that would really improve our skills. Some ed classes are a complete waste. They've finally started giving people credit for experience and hands-on learning, and Jordan is a natural."

In other words, Jordan was succeeding in finding her own way. Camille listened to the giggles of girls following Rosemary's instructions for handling soft-boiled eggs in old-fashioned eggcups. She watched them ooh and aah over the vintage handkerchiefs Rosemary had collected for them in her online auctions—white with a variety of purple and lavender crochet trim for the bridesmaids, all white for the bride. She watched Jordan savor the bridal spotlight and wondered at all the steps she was taking and the many women who were sharing in them.

Martha would say this was a good thing. Camille would have to agree.

From the time Jordan had taken her first step from Daddy's knee to Mom's waiting hands, Camille had urged her on to the next and the next. But Jordan had to take those steps in her own way and her own time. A mother couldn't help calling for them, and once they were taken, ever deeper into the community of women, she couldn't call them back.

But sometimes, just for an instant, she desperately wanted to.

After she'd served the fruit soup and garden salad, Camille

slipped into her bedroom to retrieve the bridesmaids' gifts. Once they'd gotten into the spirit of Grandma's hobby, she and Jordan had pulled up their chairs behind Rosemary, the expert bidder, and cheered her to victory in the final seconds of several of the auctions for vintage jewelry to suit the style of the bridesmaids' outfits. Jordan wanted four different pieces—a clip for Lauren's beautiful hair, a whimsical pair of earrings for Beth, a brooch in the shape of an inkwell and plume for Amy, and a bracelet for Kelly's slender wrist. They whooped it up when Rosemary beat a particularly persistent bidder for the brooch, but they didn't get a bracelet until the third try. They cursed those faceless, sneaky bidders who'd been hiding in the cyber brush, waiting to pounce on Grandma's bid in the very last second.

For the hundredth time in the last few weeks, Camille tasted bittersweet tears—the kind that tingled but didn't escape.

"Mom?" Jordan peeked around the door and noticed the gifts lined up on Camille's dresser. "Oh, you wrapped them. Thank you. I meant to, but I didn't get to it." She closed the door behind her. "Grandma was right about the breakfast. I'm glad we did this at home instead of going out. We can just kick back and enjoy."

"The girls are going to love these."

"We saved the description for them, too, so they know the history. Amy will love that. She's a history buff." Jordan's party cheer faded into an apologetic glance. "I was going to tell you about the college program. We *just* found out about it, and it looks like something I can stick with, you know? Because I'll be working at the same time, and it'll make more sense to me."

Camille shook off her silly feeling of being slighted somehow. "I'm just glad the opportunity came up and you're taking advantage of it."

"I know you were a good teacher, and now that I've tried it, I know I can be good, too." Jordan glanced away. "I wanted to surprise you and Dad with the news at the same time."

"He'll be happy for you."

"Bridget didn't say much, except she wanted to know where the degree would come from. I suppose it sounds more like a training program than real college."

"It sounds good. It all sounds very good, honey."

"Is it a good thing?" Jordan teased. She laid a hand on her mother's shoulder. "I didn't mean for this wedding to be so much work for you, Mom. I really appreciate all you've done."

"It's been as much work as I made it. I didn't know I was going to enjoy it so much." Camille arranged the wrapped gifts in two stacks of two. "I appreciate your putting up with all my homemade touches."

"*Hand*made," Jordan corrected as she stretched her hand out beside her mother's for comparison. "Maybe I'll try my hand at some handiwork once we get settled into a home. Do you think I have your hands or maybe Grandma's hands? If I bit my nails and soaked them until they pruned up, they'd be Grandma's hands, wouldn't they?" Jordan tilted her hand, triggering a glitter demonstration from her diamond. "She said her mother used to tell her a story about some warriors in the Philippines who bit their fingernails down to the quick as part of the preparation for going into battle. She told me she was doing battle with those seed pearls." Jordan chuckled. "Grandma says you have hands like your father, but pretty and feminine."

"She said that?" Camille smiled. It was a loving comparison, coming from Mama. "I think you have your own hands, a little like hers, a little like mine."

"I love you, Mom." Jordan's quick embrace caught Camille by

surprise. "I'm telling you now because I don't want us getting our mascara running on the big day."

"Good idea." Slow on the uptake, Camille squeezed her eyes shut, squeezed her daughter's slim waist. "I love you, and I'm very proud to be the mother of the bride." With a quick press of cheeks, Camille knocked back the tears and snatched up the gifts. "You take these. Did I tell you how much I admire the way you picked these out especially for each girl? Each woman."

"No, but . . ." Jordan smiled at her mother's furious blinking. "You know, I'm not going far away, Mom. We can save a little mush for later."

"Great idea." Camille grabbed a shopping bag off the floor and gestured for a return to the party. "Grandma has a game planned. Whatever it is, humor her."

"No problem."

The gifts were a huge hit. The bridesmaids were fascinated by the history of their jewelry, and everyone wanted to know more about Internet auctions.

"I was hoping we'd be able to style your outfits with the accessories today," Camille said. "That was part of the breakfast plan. How much work still has to be done on them?"

"The shoulders on my jacket are huge," Beth Praeger said happily. Oversized clothing was a rare worry for Beth.

"Isn't that the style?"

"It's not padded huge. It's drooping-over-my-shoulders huge. Valerie says they might not be able to take it in without taking it all apart."

"Mine's built for Dolly Parton in front," said Kelly Vaughn of the slender wrists. "Not that she isn't a beautiful woman, but I could fit both my boobs in one of Dolly's cups and still have room for my boyfriend's hand." Kelly shrugged. "If I *had* a boyfriend."

"What happened to Carl?" Amy asked.

"Carl was weeks ago," Jordan said with a laugh.

"Carl is like twentieth-century history," Kelly said. "That is so over."

"So he's not coming to the wedding?" Camille wondered.

"Oh, God, no," Kelly said. "But don't change the head count. I'll have somebody else to go with by then."

"Back to the dresses," Bridget said. "Didn't *any* of them fit right?"

"I don't think they did anything to mine after the first fitting," Lauren said in disgust as she nibbled at the corner of a raisin-toast point. "It's still shaped like a cereal box."

"But Valerie says they've never failed to pull it together by the wedding day," Jordan said, coming to her service provider's defense. "And they've been in the wedding business for nine years."

"Are you saying we don't have to worry?" Bridget asked.

"I'm not worried. Valerie has everything under control. I told her I want everyone fitted by Wednesday, and she gave me her word."

"What's the mother of the bride wearing?" Amy asked.

"Not telling. I want to make a splash, too."

"You didn't tell me you'd found something, Mom. What's it like?"

"It'll be a surprise. All you need to know is that it's in keeping with the color palette."

"Long or short?"

Camille closed her eyes and shook her head. "Not telling."

Rosemary followed Camille into the kitchen with a trayful of eggcups and toast plate covers. "You haven't found anything, have you?"

"Mama, I don't know what's going on with me. I've gained another five pounds." She took the tray. "Okay, more like seven." Rosemary was still giving her the mother's eye. "Eight, then. I bought new bras the other day. I had to buy a D-cup. Mama, I've never worn a D. I don't want to pay three hundred dollars for a dress in the size I am now."

"Pay five hundred and it'll be a smaller size."

"Five hundred!"

"Well, you're gonna have to wear something." Rosemary eyed Camille's hips as though she were trying to account for the eight pounds. "Funny. You used to *lose* weight when you were under stress."

"Don't remind me. And I don't see anything funny about it."

"You were laughing at the Dolly Parton crisis and the disposable boyfriends," Rosemary reminded her. "It's always something, you know. Every change takes some time to adjust to."

Turning to set the tray on the counter, Camille measured the wisdom of asking, of discovering indirectly, as was their current routine, what she ought to be able to discern but might not want to know.

"Will you help me find a dress?"

Rosemary laid a slight hand on her daughter's back. "I'm trying to save up my energy now, like socking away pennies in ol' Rosie the pig. Remember Rosie?"

Camille worked up a smile and turned to Rosemary with it. "I was saving up for a powder blue mohair sweater and a purse with a shoulder strap."

"But you have to have a dress, and somebody's got to go with you. Otherwise, you'll buy something just because it's on sale. Tomorrow." Rosemary wagged her bony, nail-bitten finger. "Or tomorrow night. I'll ask Jordie what she's got going."

"She's got so much on her mind. Ellie's taste is no better than mine, and Bridget doesn't look at price tags."

"How about Creed? He's always had an eye for what looks good on you."

Camille hooted. "You think I want him seeing what size I'm looking at on the racks?"

"For Pete's sake, Cammy, you look fine." Rosemary folded her arms. "That man still loves you. You do know that."

"In his way, maybe. Whatever that is."

"Well, whatever it is, you might want to bring it to bear on picking out the right dress for this occasion."

She might want to, but she definitely wasn't going to.

"I think I'll see if Ellie's free tomorrow," Camille decided. "Ellie and Bridget. Between the two of them, and you if you feel up to it . . ."

Rosemary shrugged. "Suit yourself, then."

"You're supposed to say, 'We'll get it done.' "

"We'll get it done," Rosemary recited dutifully as she plucked the shopping bag off the kitchen table. "Let's have some fun with these girls. Did you get a look at these treasures I found on eBay? We girls are going to play a game of 'What Did They Do with That?' "

"Did you find the game on eBay?"

"Heck, no. I made it up. Sort of."

Rosemary's game consisted of guessing at the uses of women's tools from days gone by. As the items were passed around the table, each woman took a guess. The correct guess earned the guesser the object as a prize. There were buttonhooks and corset lacers, a hair-curling tong, a hip pad—which evoked peals of laughter—a shoe saver, a needle case, all kinds of odd kitchen tools and laundry items, and trappings of the toilette.

Camille didn't expect to have as much fun shopping for the mother-of-the-bride dress as she had playing breakfast games, but the excursion on the following day yielded a surprising find—a chic suit that magically took off all eight new pounds and then some. As soon as she admitted that the moderately priced shops were simply not stocked for youthful mothers of the bride and allowed Bridget to show her where to shop, Camille's prospects started looking up. She chose a stunning ivory suit with gold trim.

"It's the cut that makes the difference," Bridget insisted.

"It's the price," Camille said. "It's just like in the old days, when only rich people were allowed to wear purple. Only now it's the rich who get the clothes with the flattering cut. They like to keep the common folk looking frumpy."

"Well, you get what you pay for."

"So I've heard," Camille said as she whipped out her credit card. "And for this occasion I'm paying for the queen's tailor."

· · ·

Jordan hadn't been able to get away for her mother's dress shopping, not that she'd tried very hard to rearrange her schedule. When she'd heard that Ellie and Bridget were going with Camille, Jordan decided that she would be of more use at a gas station attendants' convention than serving as the fourth wheel on that particular shopping cart. A best friend's opinion always seemed to be more valid than a daughter's, and she couldn't remember the last time her mother had made a fashion statement or sought her daughter's advice in putting one together. Her mother was an artist. She created style. She didn't have to follow it.

Jordan was certain that her father had been born with style. Trends didn't matter to him. How he looked mattered to him and he didn't care what people thought—unless it somehow affected his family's image. Jordan understood why Camille had warned her against suggesting that she wanted something that might be beyond his means. And she'd been careful, which was why it surprised her when he came looking for her on her last workday before the wedding.

At first he said he wanted to see her in action in her classroom, which was the reason he'd stopped by before the children were dismissed. She introduced him as her father and said that he was a singer. He obliged them when they asked him to perform, but he said that Jordan would have to accompany him, since he didn't have his guitar. They sang some of the songs he'd taught her, like "The Bear Went Over the Mountain," and "The Rainbow Connection," which she'd taught him.

"Jordie, I want you to help me out," he confided when Amy offered to take the children to the bus. "Grandma says your mom found a nice dress for the wedding. Have you seen it?"

"I have, Daddy. It's beautiful. Wait till you see."

"That's what she said about your dress. I have a feeling I'm gonna be one weak-in-the-knees cowboy on Saturday." He looked the part when he shoved his hands in the back pockets of his jeans. "I want to surprise her with some pretty jewelry to go with it, and I need your help picking it out. Can you spare your dad a couple of hours for a little shopping?"

"You'll have to tell me straight out what you want to spend, okay?"

"It's payday, honey. I wanna shoot the whole wad."

"Just how much is a wad?"

"It's a pocketful of green." He slipped his arm around her shoulders and ushered her down the suddenly quiet school corridor. "We're gonna turn it into something that sparkles."

He followed her in his pickup to the mall, and she met him at the appointed jewelry counter in the store she'd suggested. The store was not busy, and neither of the two clerks had much to do. But they stood back and watched while the Indian cowboy and his daughter browsed the glass cases.

"What Mom needs with her outfit is some great earrings," Jordan mused. She wished the price tags hadn't all been carefully turned under the items.

Her father pointed to a flashy pair in a velvet box. "Are those real?"

"They're real rhinestones. They're very chi-chi."

"I want something real." He moved along, perusing the displays beneath the glass. Jordan felt as though she were protecting his back while the salesclerk moved in, keeping his distance, wiping finger-prints off the glass with a gray polishing cloth.

"What do you think of these?" Creed pointed to a glittering pair of pavé-set diamond earrings.

"They're real, all right," Jordan said. "Those would be beautiful with that dress."

Wordlessly the salesman brought the earrings out on a velvet-covered stand and made a production of turning over the tiny price tag.

Creed whistled. "They're *real* real."

"You may have noticed that we're running a sale on diamonds, but these are never marked down. These are from our designer collec-tion. The combination of black and white diamonds is really very pop-ular." The salesman slipped the earrings back under glass, closed and locked the sliding door. "Maybe you'd like something a little smaller."

"I'd like something that'll show up."

"You know, you can get very flamboyant costume jewelry in, say, cubic zirconia. We don't carry it here, and we only carry rhinestones in a few estate pieces. But you can get CZs in the store just two doors down."

"I don't think that's what we're looking for," Jordan said, shooting the man a cool glance.

"What's cubic zirconia?" Creed asked.

"They're man-made and far less expensive than diamonds. But they look fine in a decent setting."

"I'm not looking for fake jewelry." He nodded toward the earrings the man had taken away. "I'll take the ones you just showed me."

"How will you be paying, sir? We'll need identification with any-thing other than—"

Creed pulled a clip of bills from his pocket. "Will cash work for you?"

"Dad, wait." Jordan pointed to a smaller pair of diamond-studded earrings. "This is Mom. They're called love knots, and those are real diamonds. Very elegant. She would get more use out of these."

"You're right, Jordie. Those designer jobs are kinda gaudy. Your mother isn't like that." He joined his daughter and asked to see the earrings she had suggested. "Love knots, huh?"

"May I see that slide?" Jordan asked. The clerk waited until Creed handed the earrings back. He put them away, and then showed Jordan the other piece. "Dad, she has an Omega necklace that would take this slide perfectly. You could get the earrings and the slide for less than half the price of that gaudy stuff."

"You're your mother's daughter, all right."

"I'm not being cheap, Dad."

"Did I say 'cheap'? You're using good financial judgment. I appreciate that, and your husband will, too." He told the clerk to wrap the jewelry, and then he smiled as though he had a surprise under his hat for Jordan. "Now there's one more thing we need to find, and that's a crown for my princess."

"Oh, Daddy. That's so sweet. But we decided to use a little floral—"

"I've already consulted with your grandma, who told me what you really want and where to get it. She says you're wearing her pearl necklace."

Jordan nodded. The pearls hadn't been her choice, but she'd made her peace with them. "They were her mother's, actually. This will be their third wedding."

"She says you need pearls and crystals to go with the pearls and beads on your dress. We want you to pick it out." He was fairly beaming with the prospect of one last round of playing Santa Claus. "You'll have the ring from your husband and the crown from your dad. Does that make you a fairytale bride?"

She put her arm around his waist and walked with him to the cash register. "It makes me feel like a very special woman."

Chapter 17

⌢

*I*t was a dreary autumn Friday. The forecast for Saturday—Wedding Day—was clear and unseasonably warm, but the drizzly Friday morning had become a dreadfully iffy afternoon. The sugar maples in the Delonga neighborhood had turned pink, and the elms and oaks were dithering between green and gold. Under a gray sky, the slick, wet colors were vibrant.

With James's help, Camille had assembled a crew to help her haul boxes of decorations to the hotel. "Keep thinking, *No rain*," she told the young men she had just met, groomsmen she'd commandeered. She'd been warned not to take on these chores herself, but she was glad she hadn't listened. What else would she be doing if someone else were in charge?

The storage room she'd been offered held most of her carefully packed and labeled boxes, full of everything she had planned. It would go up quickly Saturday morning. She'd tried everything out, and it all worked perfectly. The tiny lights and candles galore were guaranteed to make a splash. There would also be details less noticeable—birds in the cages and butterflies in the willow branches—but she would know they were there.

"What should I do with these, Mrs. Burke?" Tall, blond, bespectacled groomsman Gavin Kendal stood behind the handle on a cartload of potted mums.

For the time being, she had given up telling anyone she wasn't really Mrs. Burke. These kids knew Jordan's last name, not hers.

"Wheel them into the courtyard. They go in that big round planter in the middle."

"Just set the pots in there? I can handle that."

"I should find someone who's with the event they're having here tonight and make sure it's okay."

She approached a woman who was setting tables and explained her plan. The woman shrugged. Fine with her. As far as Camille was concerned, she had permission. On to the next item on her list.

Gavin stuck his head back inside the glass door. "There are a few pots that won't fit, Mrs. Burke. Should I just put them anywhere?"

"Use your judgment, Gavin," she said, following him outside. "Let's see, one at the end of that bench and another below, to the side. Fabulous, Gavin. What do you think?"

"It looks great. Should I do the same with these?"

"I trust your judgment." She glanced over her shoulder as she started back inside. "No, right there. That's perfect."

The table-setting woman approached, giving Camille a moment's concern that she'd changed her mind about the minor liberties she was taking with hotel policy. Camille had, after all, been told not to do any decorating until the next morning.

"Are you the florist for Saturday's wedding?"

"You might say I'm the planner." Camille suddenly felt a little awkward, adding, "It's my daughter's wedding."

"Oh. Wow. Busy day for you, then." The woman turned to the wall of glass that separated the lobby from the courtyard. "That looks nice with the flowers. The ones they put in last spring died a long time ago. I hope the weather clears up for you."

"Oh, it will."

. . .

By the time people started arriving at the church for rehearsal, there was hope for the sky's clearing. Was it too much to hope for the ground's drying as well? Camille commented about the weather as she introduced herself to Mrs. Coulton, the wedding director.

"Rainy rehearsal, sunny wedding," the short, barrel-shaped woman quipped. "Is Mom getting nervous? As Bridget will tell you, once I have everyone's full attention, I will give directions that are simple and comprehensible to every member of the wedding party. As long as we all pay attention, tomorrow's event will run smoothly. Now, Mom, you sit back here with Bridget until I call for you."

She started to move on but backed up on another thought and leaned closer to Camille to speak in confidence. "This cameraperson must be told to stay out of the way during the rehearsal. We don't like having distractions during rehearsal. Your husband asked if she could stay and I was loath to refuse him a special favor, but during the wedding we don't want photographers distracting us, and we don't need that now either."

"Did you tell Creed this when he asked?" Camille asked.

"Such a wonderful name," the woman said, glancing toward the front of the church where Creed stood next to Ellie at the piano. "And a charming man. I also didn't want to authorize the soloist's rehearsal with the pianist, and normally I wouldn't permit it, but your husband explained the circumstances, so I let them have a few minutes."

Camille wondered what "circumstances" Creed had come up with to charm the barrel woman. "But did you mention the trouble with the photography to him?" she asked.

"No," Mrs. Coulton said with a tight smile. "I'll leave that to you."

"The one bit of dirty work she's willing to pass on, no doubt," Camille muttered to Bridget as she slid into the rear pew beside her.

"I thought you weren't having a videographer."

"She's somebody Creed knows." Could she be jealous?

"Are they trading favors?" Bridget laughed at the look of disapproval Camille gave her. "You know, he sings at her wedding dance if she does this video."

"Creed doesn't *like* doing weddings," Camille grumbled as she watched the young woman—all women under forty looked young to her lately—move across the front of the church for a different angle. Then she brightened. "You know what? Maybe you're right. It didn't occur to me." Somehow the thought made her feel better.

Then she saw Mrs. Coulton barreling down the aisle toward the chattering group of wedding participants, including James and Jordan, seated in the front pews. "Were you stuck with this woman for Lauren's wedding? Was she this bossy?"

"It's her job. She's overseen lots of weddings. She knows all the pitfalls and how to avoid them."

"Does she know the risk of crossing the mother of the bride?"

"What are you going to do after this weekend when your reign as mother of the bride is all over?" Bridget grabbed Camille's hand, squeezed it, and laughed.

Camille frowned theatrically. "I'm not sure. What did you do?"

"Got a divorce."

"Well, as we know, I'm one up on you there. Guess I'll have to come up with something to take the cake back, huh? Maybe I'll get pregnant."

They exchanged looks, each mirroring the other's grimace. Then they laughed together.

"Now let's get everyone lined up," Mrs. Coulton announced. "Everyone except the groom should be lined up in the vestibule. Where are the ushers? We have to be out of here in twenty minutes."

After her stroll up the aisle on the usher's arm, Camille tried to slide down the pew and slip out, telling herself she wanted to scout out a few places for planting certain details. But Mrs. Coulton refused to allow anyone, including "Mom," to stray from her sight. Camille was forced to watch the procession.

Maybe it was because Creed was wearing jeans and Jordan was carrying a bouquet of shower-gift bows affixed to a paper plate, but watching them walk down the aisle together didn't choke her up the way she'd feared it would. She drew a deep breath and congratulated herself on her composure as he moved into the pew beside her.

"It's goin' good, huh?" he whispered.

"So far," she acknowledged.

They walked and talked through the procedure only once. While the rest of the party chatted at the front of the church, Camille tended to her details, finding places to put the baskets she'd trimmed and filled with packets of tissue for wedding tears—she thought this a particularly nice touch—little bottles of wedding bubbles, programs, and rose petals.

"You can't leave those there."

Where had the barrel lady come from? Talk about eyes in the back of someone's head.

Camille clutched her beribboned basket of programs. She felt as sheepish as a kid caught sticking gum under the chair. "But I have so many details to take care of tomorrow morning."

"Nothing must be left here. I'm sorry, but that's our policy."

"Is there something going on here between now and two o'clock tomorrow?"

"What time is your florist scheduled for setup?" Mrs. Coulton demanded. "That's when you can put that there. We can't be held responsible for items left overnight."

"But this is a church. Surely a basket of programs would be safe here overnight."

"Not from me," the church lady warned. "I made the one exception for your musicians, but they really should have arranged something off site."

"Ellie lives out of town."

"And I made the exception," Mrs. Coulton reiterated, as though profuse homage might be in order. "We average two weddings a week here, and everyone has special circumstances. Every wedding is special, and yours will be, too." She smiled as Creed walked past. "The music sounded very nice."

All the woman had heard so far was Ellie and the pianist. Wait till the old battle-ax heard Creed sing tomorrow, Camille thought. She'd probably wet her bloomers.

Camille bade the woman a pleasant good night and turned to

leave, glancing at the four baskets she'd stashed on the hat rail above the coatrack.

Hee, hee, hee.

"Mrs. Burke?"

Camille turned slowly.

Hands primly folded at her waist like the patron saint of elementary-school teachers, Mrs. Coulter glanced overhead, then at Camille.

"*All* of your baskets, please."

.   .   .

A procession of cars made its way through pockets of fog, past the shores of suburban lakes. It was a twenty-minute drive to the country club Bridget had chosen for the rehearsal dinner, which was the first official combined gathering of the wedding party and close family members.

There were many introductions to be made among people from out of town, family members seldom seen, others who gathered often. Despite all the recent tensions, conflicts were set aside, personal problems forgotten. Feelings were warm, and arms were welcoming. Bridget even found a few pleasant words for Timothy before he tactfully faded into the woodwork, assigned to sit with his mother, Ramona, and Lauren's husband, Tony. Camille's brother, Matt, had flown in from California, as had James's Uncle Ron. The dining room was abuzz with more than the exchange of pleasantries. It was not a convention or a conference or a fund-raiser. It was a gathering of families about to be joined through a marriage.

Camille was introducing Matt's wife to the bridesmaids when a warm hand closed around her shoulder. "Faith's on the phone."

"They've arrived?" She excused herself and turned to Creed. "Do you think they can find this place if we give them directions? You give them directions. I'll just get them lost."

"No, there's a problem. Come on." He took her arm, explaining as he led her to the phone in the foyer. "The hotel wants a credit card. Faith doesn't use credit cards."

"They have mine. I made it quite clear—" She put the receiver to her ear. "Faith? It's Camille. I'm so glad you got here safely. What's the problem?"

"I don't know. This guy says I have to give them a credit card before we can have the rooms you reserved for us."

"I've already taken care of the bill."

"This guy says he also needs my credit card, but I don't have any credit cards."

"Put the desk clerk on the phone."

"My sister-in-law wants to talk to you," Camille heard Faith say.

"Yes, this is Carl, the desk—"

"What's going on? I reserved four rooms for Faith Spotted Horse and her family. I spoke with you about leaving gifts in their rooms, so I know you have them in the computer." She looked at Creed. He encouraged her with a nod.

"Yes, ma'am, I have the reservation, but we need—"

"You have *my* credit card. That's all you need. It's after six o'clock, so you've already charged my card for the rooms, haven't you?"

"Well, yes, but we always take a card number from the guest in the room. What about incidentals? Do you want—"

"It's not exactly incidental that you charged my credit card for four rooms for the Spotted Horse party, and my family is standing there at the desk. This could have been settled later."

"I'm sorry. I didn't understand. You want everything to . . . I'll cut the keys immediately, Miss Delonga."

"Excellent. I hope you'll extend profuse apologies with those keys."

"Yes, ma'am. I'll put Mrs. Spotted Horse back on the phone now."

"Camille?"

"Yes, Faith, it's all straightened out. I'm sorry. Can you come over and have dinner with us? Creed will give you—"

"We're all pretty tired. We just want to get into our rooms and put our feet up. We'll see you soon."

Camille hung up the phone and turned away, fuming. "They said it was standard procedure. For incidental charges to the room? That's bullshit. They've already charged my card for the rooms." She looked up at Creed. "They'd been sitting there for God knows how long because—"

"They don't have a credit card," he finished for her.

"It's on my—"

"It's tough to go anywhere these days without a credit card or a checkbook. That's why they stay home a lot." He laid his hand on Camille's shoulder. "It's all fixed now, hon. We'll call back in a few minutes and make sure they got into their rooms."

She looked up at him, feeling angry and crappy and ashamed of the embarrassment she felt she'd caused. This was not the way this part of the plan was supposed to go.

"It's okay," he told her. "They need time to get settled in."

"This place is hard to find anyway."

"Yeah." He slipped his arm around her shoulder. "Thanks for keeping after me about calling. I'm really bad about this stuff. Especially since . . ."

"Since what?"

"Since I don't have you to make me be good."

She smiled. He'd gotten a haircut, and he looked delicious in his new sport coat and tie. She'd never been able to make him do anything, but the notion had her smiling anyway. "You have to make a toast, you know."

She started toward the dining room, but he held her fast. "I have something I want to give you tonight. Something for you to wear tomorrow."

Camille looked up at him, stunned. She'd seen the lovely tiara he'd given Jordan. Oh, God, she hadn't gotten him anything. Speechless, she touched the knot in his new tie, smoothed the strip of silk as though it needed her attention.

He smiled into her eyes. "Later. When you have a few minutes for me."

"I wish I had . . ."

He shook his head. "I know how you are when you're in the middle of something. All I need is a few minutes."

She couldn't be certain what he read in her eyes, but in her heart she had stored much more than a few minutes for Creed Burke.

. . .

James Mayfield would not see his bride again until her father escorted her down the aisle of the church. Following the groom's dinner, he and his men marched off to his mother's house, where, according to James, they planned to sip some brandy, trade a few stories, and get a good night's sleep.

The bridal suite at the Countryside Inn was reserved for the bride and her maids for the night before the wedding. Camille had another suite for herself and her "golden" girlfriends—Mama, Bridget, and

Ellie. She planned to visit up and down the hotel corridor with wedding guests and enjoy a girls' slumber party—the emphasis on slumber. Camille liked the sound of her plan.

But from the look of distress on her daughter's face when she appeared at the golden girls' door, the plan was on its way out the hotel window.

"Mom, come in here and look at these dresses."

Jordan grabbed her mother's arm and dragged her out of her room and down the hall, listing the outfits' shortcomings until they reached their destination. There, in the bridal suite living room, four young women struggled with suits in various stages of disarray.

"We picked them up this afternoon," Jordan explained, following Camille as she examined a jacket with uneven buttons, a skirt that fit like a leotard. "There wasn't time to try them on, and Valerie wasn't there, so we just signed for them."

"What else could we do?" Lauren complained. "We were supposed to have them days ago."

"Apparently the seamstress who was working on them quit," Amy said.

"Or got fired."

"Look at these shoulders," Beth whined.

"If I try to sit down, this skirt will split." Lauren unzipped her skirt and relaxed what there was of her stomach. "This isn't even the same one I had, unless they moved the zipper from the back to the side."

"What are we going to do, Mom? Can Grandma fix them?"

"We can't let her find out about this." With the rest of her head in a tizzy, the one thing Camille knew for sure was that Mama needed rest. "I hope she's gone to bed.

"Go get your Aunt Faith," Camille told Jordan as Plan B began to take shape in her mind. "Aunt Stella. I think Ellie sews. Bridget . . ." Lauren's skeptical look made Camille smile. "Yes, we can put Bridget to work, too. She and I can follow somebody else's directions. Valerie, Schmalerie. We shall overcome."

"Aunt Faith, Aunt Stella," Jordan recited as she hurried down the hall. "Don't wake Grandma, but get Ellie and Bridget . . ."

A mother's work is never done.

Forget testosterone, Camille told herself as she returned to the bridesmaids' huddle and pumped it with estrogen.

"Where are we going to find a sewing machine?"

"I have one at home," Amy volunteered. "It'll take me ten minutes to go get it."

By the time the team began to assemble, Amy had the sewing machine set up on the table. Word had leaked to Rosemary, who had run into Ramona on her way down the hall and dragged her along. Camille met her at the door.

"We came to see what all the fuss is about."

"What fuss?" Camille tried in vain to block Rosemary's view of the goings-on. "Get some rest, Mama, there's no fuss here. Mama!" Camille was easily shouldered aside, first by her wiry mother, then the stouter Ramona.

"Oh, dear." Rosemary circled each maid in turn, zeroing in on each problem immediately. "Ohhh, dear. Don't sit down in that skirt," she told Lauren. "What is going on with this jacket? Take it off and let me see, Beth."

"Mama, I thought you were asleep."

"I thought they were going to take these rags apart and make clothes out of them." She examined the lining of Beth's jacket, which was bunched and tacked in somebody's idea of a make-do fashion. "Ramona, look at this. Do you sew?"

"I used to. A little."

"Faith, I've heard you're a fellow quilter." Rosemary handed the jacket over to the Indian woman she'd never met. "What do you think is going on with this jacket to make it bunch up like this?"

"I think we'll have to take the lining out." Faith was ready with a pair of fingernail scissors.

Rosemary made a call before she dove into the project.

A few moments later there was a knock at the door, which Bridget answered. "Man on the floor," she called out merrily. "He's asking for someone named Rosie."

"Is it the chauffeur, Grandma?" With the repairs under way, Jordan was smiling again.

"It's my son-in-law. I asked him to bring some refreshments."

"Is that you, brother?" Faith called out. "I come to your party and right away you get me working."

"Why do you think we invited you? Rosie needed some help with the sewing." He handed Rosemary the bottles she'd ordered—juice, water, soft drinks, and sherry. "Keep my sister busy so she doesn't make any more trouble with the nice fellow at the front desk."

"I was ready to tell him his hotel wasn't up to my standards and then hit the road." Head bent over her seam-ripping task, Faith nodded at her niece. "But we came for Jordie's wedding."

"I'm so glad you did," Jordan said, squeezing her aunt's shoulder. "We're in serious trouble, Auntie."

"We'll fix it." Faith glanced at Camille. "Do you always have to have a credit card to stay in a hotel? Is that why they say don't leave home without it?"

"These rooms were all taken care of." Camille sighed. "They had no reason to ask you for another credit card."

"I even had to show my driver's license. Do you always have to show ID?"

"If I ever stay in one of these places again, I'll get a passport," Faith's sister Stella put in dryly.

"I thought it would be fun for everyone to stay here the night before the wedding," Camille explained as she looped a yellow measuring tape around Lauren's hips. "Next time you'll stay with me."

"This is the first time I've done this."

"Stayed in a hotel?" Camille lifted one shoulder, warning Lauren with a glance not to express her surprise. "It's usually not this complicated."

"How about your uptown weddings?" Faith wanted to know.

"We didn't mean to get too uptown," Camille said with a laugh. "You know me. I hate to spend money. But once you get started, a wedding seems to take on a life of its own."

"Is it worth it?"

"I guess we'll see." Camille gestured for Lauren to hand over her skirt. Then she turned to Faith. "I'm so glad you're here, and I'm sorry to have to ask you to help save our bacon."

"I don't know about bacon, but my relations are always worth saving." Faith plucked a thread from the jacket lining and released a gob of bunched fabric. "Eeee, look at that. Somebody ought to teach these city people to sew."

She looked up from her chair, smiling at Camille. "I think we spoiled my brother a little bit, but he's the only one we had. You're the only wife he had, and Jordie's the only child. Family is family. So here we are. I don't know what's happening tomorrow, but I know we're fixing these dresses up tonight." She pulled the lining away and examined the shoulder seam. "*Tuale!* Who did this?"

"A wedding shop."

"You should have called me before," Faith said, laughing. "I could have made these, easy."

"I wish I had. I wish you weren't so far away. I wish—"

"There's no wishing these things right, sister, so let's get to work. Jordie, get me a real seam ripper."

"Seam ripper," Jordan called out, the merry bride turned surgical assistant. "Auntie needs a seam ripper, Grandma."

"Comin' right up."

Chapter 18

*C*amille opened her eyes to a Christmas-morning feeling. A glance at the bedside clock reminded her that she hadn't planned to get up quite this early, but she knew that there was no point in trying to go back to sleep. Today was the day.

She crept out of bed, taking care not to wake her mother, washed, dressed in the T-shirt and pants she'd put in the bathroom for this morning, and tiptoed into the suite's parlor, where Bridget and Ellie were sound asleep on a Murphy bed. Bridget had offered to help with the decorations, but Camille decided that Bridget would prefer sleep to coffee, so she left all the golden girls to their rest and headed for the café.

The bridesmaids' dresses had been remade. Like Santa's elves, Camille's family and friends had worked late into the night to perform the miracle needed to make a fairy tale come true for Jordan. Ramona had pitched in on the handwork. Bridget had done most of the ironing. The slipshod tailoring job had been remedied by skilled women's hands, utterly convincing Camille that Santa's most efficient elves, not to mention God's most altruistic angels, were female.

"What time does the café open?" Camille asked the desk clerk.

"Not until eight, but there's coffee in the bar."

"There's also coffee in my room," said a voice behind her.

She turned, smiling. Hair damp, feet bare, Creed stood in front of the door to his room in rumpled T-shirt and jeans. She had to remind herself that this was where he lived.

"Good morning," she said.

"How goes the battle with the dresses?"

"They're fixed," she said happily as she followed him into his room. "Oh, Creed, it was touch and go. Thank heaven for Faith and Stella. Mama, Ellie—even Bridget got into the act. I was the least useful, but I've got my work cut out for me today." She took a seat on the little couch. "Today's the day. Can you believe it?"

"I have coffee and cinnamon rolls," he said as he poured two cups of coffee. "And a little present for you."

"I didn't forget." She was glad to get the coffee. He sat across from her on the bed and reached across rumpled sheets while she went on talking. "By the time the dresses were finished, I hoped you were asleep. You have a big job to do today. Several big jobs, but the main one is—"

"Giving our daughter away, I know. I hope I don't blow it." He retrieved a gold box from the night stand and handed it to her. "And I hope I didn't blow this. Don't feel like you have to wear them if they're not right."

"Oh, Creed," she started to admonish, but she already had the box open, and the gold and diamond jewelry was winking at her. "Creed," she whispered, "they're perfect."

"Jordie helped me pick them out."

He sipped his coffee, but she knew he hadn't taken his eyes off her. She could feel his relief in her reaction, his settling into satisfaction.

"Now I see why she made sure I was going to wear that gold necklace." She looked up at him. "Thank you. I love . . . them. They'll be perfect with my dress."

"Is it white?"

"Sort of an off-white. Ivory. Gold trim."

He nodded, glancing at the box, then back into her eyes. "This is the kind of wedding you should have had."

"Me?" She shook her head, smiling. "We did what worked for us."

"And we did things that didn't work for us." He cleared his throat needlessly, swallowed audibly, glanced away, then back again.

Something was coming. She held her breath and recklessly permitted herself to get lost in his eyes.

"But I've never loved any other woman, Camille," he said, almost inaudibly. "I know it wasn't . . . what it should have been. But what we had together was the best part of my life." He gave a diffident shrug. "Maybe it still is."

"Jordan is the best thing we did together." She swallowed, wide-eyed as an innocent child still waiting and wishing, wanting God only knew what. "Isn't she?"

"Maybe. The best so far anyway." He nodded toward the gold

box. "Well, I wanted you to have something to wear today that comes from me."

"You were always full of surprises, Creed. More thoughtful than I was most of the time."

"No," he said sadly. "I was just as likely to give you something when I'd been gone too long or I'd broken a promise as I was for 'just because.' This gift is just because the light of our lives is getting married today. And you're her mother. And for better or worse, you let me be her dad."

"Oh, Creed." She clutched the box and willed away the tears that made her whole face burn. *Always* was the song he'd chosen for her. She wanted *always,* and it had flown past her. She had missed it. Raspy now, she could only repeat, "Oh, Creed."

"It's our day, too," he said, moving from bed to sofa. "The one promise I've never broken is to love you until the day I die. I want you to know that." He waited until she looked up at him. "Believe it. It's the only truth I know."

"I . . ." He was looking for more than she dared give. Tears were too dear. Love? She'd given and given. "I don't know what to say."

"Don't say anything. I know how you feel about me. I know you wish you didn't love me, but you do. And I know . . ." His hand tightened around his coffee cup, and she realized that he was working to keep it steady. "Like I said, you let me be her dad."

"You're not alone, Creed. We had to stop trying to live with each other because . . . because we couldn't make it work." She laid her hand on his knee, rubbed the soft, worn denim. Worn soft, she thought, not out. "But we're still your family. Your family is still my family. I understand that better than ever now, and I hope you do, too."

"You know what scares me?" He leaned back, searching the ceiling as he drew a deep breath and released it slowly, shaking his head. "Looking foolish. Becoming an old man with no dignity. I've seen too much of that."

"I've watched those women in your audiences. Even now you have them mesmerized, Creed. You don't look foolish to them." She answered the question in his eyes. "Nor to me."

"Women are generous. I've learned that much. But I don't know why they're still smiling at me like that after all this time. I'm old enough to be . . ." He laughed. "I think it must be the song."

"Take my word for it—it's the singer. You're very good, Creed, not to mention sexy as all get-out. Yes, *still.*" She paused, glancing into her cup for answers. It was as good a place as any to look for answers that probably did not exist. "I've never understood why, but you and Jordan both, you underestimate yourselves. You're good enough to—" She looked up, smiling again. "You're good. A good thing."

He chuckled. They'd had this conversation a time or two. At least she'd admitted this time that she didn't understand. Maybe someday they would leave it at that.

Maybe today was the day.

"What do you need help with this morning?" he asked.

"Do you want to help me fix up some frou-frou?"

"Is that anything like getting your mojo working?"

She lifted one shoulder, the one coy bone in her body.

He took her hand. "Lead ol' Mr. Fixit down your garden path, baby."

The tables had already been arranged according to Camille's design. Score one for the hotel cleanup crew.

She'd left her box of tools, tape, fasteners, and scissors in the car. Creed took her keys and went out to the parking lot while she spoke to the woman in charge of table setting. When Creed returned, he took all her boxes out of the storage room. They had been packed according to placement, so that once the box was in place, the items could be arranged quickly.

Creed commandeered a ladder, and together they hung garlands, swags, and wreaths, all studded with lights and adorned with flowers. Pots of spray-painted curly willow were arranged according to Camille's map, along with bowls of floating candles, the festooned Victorian birdcages—one of which would be used to receive envelopes—an assortment of garden lanterns and water features, including a huge goldfish bowl with white fantails and black Moors. An ordinary hotel banquet area became a series of garden rooms.

When Bridget was able to join them, Creed took his leave. He had a band to set up and a bride to escort around town.

"Aren't you going to the salon with the rest of us?" Bridget asked Camille.

"My hair is easy to fix, and I don't have time for a facial and fingernails." Camille stuck out one hand for Bridget's consideration. "They look all right, don't they? I just did them." She looked up at the sound of retreating footsteps. "Creed, wait."

He turned as she caught up with him.

"I won't see you until we meet at the church." She threw her arms around his neck, kissed his cheek, and whispered, "I'm a little nervous, too."

He slid his arms around her waist and held her until she made the first move to back away. "Thank you," she said, and he nodded, turned quickly, and hurried to his room.

"What was that all about?" Bridget wanted to know.

"He gave me a beautiful set of earrings and a slide"—she patted her collarbone—"you know, for my necklace, to wear today. I was so surprised."

"Pleasantly?"

"It's a big day for both of us. Yes, pleasantly."

"I was pleasantly surprised that I didn't feel the urge to put my hands around Timothy's neck last night. Does that mean it's a big step for me, too?"

"It is if it keeps you out of jail," Camille said, smiling. She tapped Bridget's arm with a loose fist. "It's your son's wedding day. Isn't that a big day for his parents?"

"It is for his mother," Bridget admitted. "I still don't understand why you didn't hire . . ." She noticed the decorated doors, peeked inside, and scanned the banquet room. "Camille, this is looking very nice."

"This is only the beginning," Camille claimed as she bent over another box and removed the photo albums she'd put together. "But we have to get moving. As soon as the tables are set, I want you to put out the favors. We've got the guest book table to decorate and some things to arrange on the head table."

Bridget was not a fast worker, but she was meticulous. What she did, she did right, which meant that Camille would not have to redo. Score two for Bridget. Two good hours, and most of the work was done.

"Camille, I hate to desert you, but I've got a hair appointment."

"Ellie took Mama over to the salon with Jordan's wedding attire," Camille said, checking her watch. "Creed's going to take her from there to the church. I'm getting dressed here so that I can connect with the florist and the bakery and make sure everything is set up properly. With any luck, we'll all rendezvous at the appointed time and place."

"Why aren't you helping Jordan get dressed?"

"She has maids and Grandma for that." Arms akimbo, Camille surveyed what was momentarily her territory. "We need space right now. We'd just get on each other's nerves. These are the details I do best."

"For once I wish you'd let the professionals do their jobs," Bridget muttered quietly as she walked away.

The pastry chef was setting up the cake when two boys arrived from Your Dream Wedding. They delivered lattice panels decorated with tulle and lights, which were placed in strategic locations, including behind the cake table and the head table. Next came the six-foot floral candelabras and the mirror tiles to go under the brandy snifters and votive candles for centerpieces. Camille directed the placement of each element around the bones of her layout. It was good to have work to do. Bringing her design to life made her feel infinitely better than primping would just then.

"Oh, Belle, the cake is magnificent," Camille told the pastry chef as she arranged the pillars that would support the top two cake tiers. "Where's the topper?"

Belle glanced up at Camille. "Aren't we using flowers?"

"I brought you a porcelain topper. The doves, remember? It's an old family—"

"Omigod, that's right. I built the top layer to support a top piece, too. It's at the bakery." She touched Camille's arm to reassure her. "But don't worry. I'll send a driver back with it. You go get dressed, and I'll wait for the flowers."

"I need to make sure she puts the bouquet clips on the head table and does the punch bowl and the—"

"You have Valerie Florin, right? Her flowers are always wonderful."

"Her bridesmaids' dresses were a disaster." Camille's hands went up in unexpected dismay. "You cannot imagine—"

"Camille, take a deep breath while I give you a word of advice. I've set up lots of cakes and seen lots of mothers and heard about lots of last-minute glitches. Are the dresses presentable?"

"They are now, after we—"

"Okay." Belle signaled a cease-fire. "Then that's out of the way, and now is not the time for you to talk with Valerie. You don't even need to see her. I'll get the cake topper over here, and I'll wait for the flowers. Everything will be perfect." Hands on hips, Belle surveyed the work that had been done so far. "Seriously, I can't believe what you've done with this room." She wagged a finger. "Now you go get ready for your daughter's wedding."

"Thanks, Belle. The cake is fabulous."

"Go."

Camille had the suite all to herself. This was a good thing. She permitted herself a ten-minute bath, a few quiet moments to soak in a tub of scented water and in the knowledge that she was surrounded by good things.

But there was no more than ten minutes on the schedule for hot water and Zen meditation. Another fifty minutes for hair, makeup, wiggling into the control-top pantyhose and shaking her head over the D-cup bra. Then came the pound-shedding dress and the heart-stopping love-knot earrings. She added the slide to her necklace, arranged the mirror doors so that she could see herself coming and going, and finally declared even her own presentation to also be a good thing. Transfer a few essentials from the big purse to the small purse and she'd be set. Driver's license, lipstick, hair pick—she laughed, wondering whether a giggling group of twenty-second-century bridesmaids would someday be playing "What Did They Do with That?" with her hair pick—and car keys . . .

Car keys.

Creed had them.

How was she going to get to the church?

She could try getting a cab, but they were scarce in the suburbs. That would mean a wait. Maybe the hotel had a car. With all she was paying them for this wedding . . .

She would check at the desk.

The people setting up the bar in the banquet-room foyer distracted her from the desk. She noticed the fresh flowers on the punch-bowl and groom's-cake tables.

"Is the florist here?" she asked the bartender. Belle was right. She didn't need to run into Valerie Schmalerie at this moment.

"I think they left."

Camille wandered into the main banquet room, and there it was. *Finis. Magnifique.* She couldn't resist kissing her fingers to the results.

A man from the bakery was putting the final touch atop the cake—two crowning doves.

"Excuse me," Camille said on impulse. It was worth a try. "Are you going back to the store?"

"Yes, ma'am. How does that look?"

"Perfect. Would you mind giving me a ride to the church? It's right on your way."

"Sure, if you don't mind riding in a bakery truck. Are you here from out of town?"

"Actually, I'm the mother of the bride."

The man laughed. "Guess somebody's in for a comeuppance on that little oversight in the planning."

"Well, no. I'm the one who did the planning."

Chapter 19

$\mathcal{I}$t was a long step from passenger seat to pavement, but Camille took it gracefully, thanking the driver by name after they'd had a few good laughs over her predicament on the way to the church. She straightened her skirt and waved good-bye, making hitching a ride to her daughter's wedding on the bakery truck seem like part of her plan—just in case anyone was looking.

But the person looking wasn't just anyone. It was Creed, who was having a good laugh for himself as he pushed open the church's side door.

"I'm not even going to ask," he told her as she scooted past him. "I was about to send out a search party."

"You shouldn't have to ask. You've got my keys."

"Didn't I give them back to you?"

She heard the door click shut, turned to him, and caught her breath. "I don't think so," she managed to say, suddenly preoccupied with *his* amazing presentation. She had never seen him in formal attire.

"I thought s . . ." He took her hands in his. "I think you look fantastic. Good enough to eat."

"I just got out of a"—watching him in wonder as he lifted her hand to his lips, she couldn't think what to call the vehicle, but clearing her throat also cleared her mind—"bakery truck."

"Sweet." He tasted the heel of her palm, slid his tongue over his bottom lip, and smiled only with his eyes. "I was afraid you'd taken up with some baker man. Or maybe that guy who stole the tarts."

"That would be the knave of hearts, and I think I'm looking at him."

He stepped back, still holding her hands. He wore a silver brocade vest with a long black tie and a black jacket with satin lapels that fit as though it had been made for him. "How do you like the rented duds?"

"I like the way you look in them." She flashed a bold smile. "So wickedly handsome, just looking at you in church has to be a sin."

"Whoa, lady, you'll have the bride's ol' man blushin' to beat hell."

"It won't show." She glanced over her shoulder. "Where is she?"

He nodded toward a closed door.

"I'm dying to see her, but . . ."

"She looks so beautiful it hurts," he assured her, and she closed her eyes and remembered her first glimpse of Jordan, the beautiful baby whose birth banished her mother's hurt. "She's dying to see you, too, *but.*"

"I don't want to start crying."

"Let's start with a laugh, then." He winked at her as he slipped his arm around her shoulders. "Come on."

He ushered her into a small room furnished for waiting, where he announced, "Look who just rode into town on the bakery truck."

"Bakery truck? Mom, where have you . . . ?" Jordan turned from the window facing the front lawn, which had been her lookout station. Her demand dissolved into a soft smile. "Oh, Mom. You look fabulous."

"Oh, sweetheart." Camille took slow steps toward the backlit splendor that was her daughter, too clean and white and perfect for touching, too radiant to be real. "You look so beautiful," she managed to say, fixing the vision in the fullness of her heart.

With her dark hair and vivacious features, Jordan was the picture of a forest creature in fresh snow. Every facet of every hand-stitched bead glistened in the sunlight, and the gentle cascade of the silken fabric subtly enhanced every feminine curve that was Jordan.

"Mama, look what you made," Camille whispered as she took her daughter's cool hands in her warm ones. There were no tears. She felt the tingle, but she was smiling too hard for tears.

"I'm looking at what I made," Rosemary said quietly from her vantage point in a huge corner wingback chair. "You're looking at what you made. I'm so proud of both of you." She gestured with a flourish. "And look at these maids we remade."

"You all look wonderful," Camille said even before she could actually tell that it was true. "All the seams are holding?"

Lauren shifted her bouquet into one hand and needlessly brushed at her long, straight skirt with the other. "As long as I don't breathe, I think I'll be okay."

"And the flowers are gor—"

"Where's Mom's corsage?" Jordan remembered suddenly. Amy handed her the remaining corsage, the one designed especially for the mother of the bride, with roses, purple accent flowers, herbs from Camille's garden, and gold trim.

"Rosemary for remembrance," Jordan quoted as she pinned the flowers to her mother's jacket.

"Photo op!" Kelly said, and the photographer snapped several shots.

"Here comes another one," Amy said, handing Creed's boutonniere to Jordan, who turned it over to Camille, along with a hopeful look that would not be denied.

Camille couldn't resist smelling the rose first, touching one of the velvety sage leaves she'd grown for the occasion. "Sage for wisdom," she said as she pinned his boutonniere over his heart. It was probably the wrong side, but she didn't care.

"And for cleansing," he said. Their eyes met, full of remembrance and the wisdom of their ages.

There was a knock at the door, followed by Mrs. Coulton's inevitable appearance.

"It's time to seat the mothers."

"Guess I got here just in time," Camille said.

"What's this about a bakery truck?" Jordan wanted to know.

"I'll tell you all about it after I hear all about the pampering they gave you at the salon." Camille grabbed Jordan's hands for one more squeeze, one quick kiss on her cheek. "Oh, sweetie." With the light touch of her thumb on Jordan's cheek, Camille rubbed the lipstick off and the kiss in. "You are the princess bride."

"Mrs. Burke, you're holding up the proceedings."

"Well, I guess that's my prerogative, isn't it, Mrs. Coulton?" Camille backed away, smiling. "Okay, okay. Letting go now."

"Mr. Burke, your boutonniere is on the wrong side."

"No, it isn't, Mrs. Coulton," Creed sang out as he gave Camille that playful wink of his. "It's right where I want it."

The ushers seated Rosemary, then Bridget, and finally Camille. She felt so much like the queen mum she was tempted to offer the royal wave. Instead she recognized friends and family with as many directed smiles as her stroll down the aisle permitted.

Your Dream Wedding had nearly redeemed themselves in Camille's eyes with their glorious floral arrangements. All the altar flowers had been arranged on floor-stand candelabras, which would be quietly transported to the reception. Far be it from Camille to let an arrangement be put to less than full use, particularly when it included more candles.

Now she and Bridget were charged with lighting the candles flanking the Unity candle. Two houses about to be joined by a marriage.

Of course, Bridget's house was about to be sold.

Oh, well. There would still be one house left, and Bridget was welcome to relocate her household. Camille took her friend by the hand. Together they stepped down from the sanctuary, one comfortable ivory pump and one dyed-to-match blue brocade mule with a three-inch killer heel.

Piano music then filled the church, and the procession began.

The bridesmaids carried teardrop bouquets, overflowing with every shade of blue and purple imaginable. Their vintage jewelry complemented the chic lavender-gray suits perfectly. Behind her,

Camille heard Faith whisper something about the dresses. She turned to give her sister-in-law a thumbs-up. "Good job."

Faith returned the gesture and whispered, *"Lila waste."*

The bride appeared in the doorway on her father's arm. The congregation of witnesses came to their feet as one for the bride's slow glide down the aisle to Pachelbel's Canon in D. All eyes following each step. Women oohed. Men aahed. At the front of the church Creed unveiled his daughter's face, kissed her cheek, and gave her hand to James, whose eyes glistened with wonder.

Creed took his place beside Camille. Their hands came together instinctively. Within the next few moments Camille gave her reading from the Book of Ruth, followed by Bridget's reading from Matthew and Ellie's solo rendition of "Evergreen."

Time had no bearing on the proceedings. Camille would have been content to preserve the church and everyone in it, like a ship in a bottle, to have and to hold for all time. This was one instance she wouldn't have minded if the middle-aged minister had gone on forever, listing all the reasons people had been coming together this way generation after generation, taking the same vows this couple was about to take. This was her daughter's wedding day, and twenty-four hours were not sufficient.

Much of the sermon was happy talk, in praise of marriage, the celebration of all of its promises, the recognition that loving relationships were the cornerstone of family and community. This was the occasion for happy talk. *Keep it coming,* Camille thought, only half listening, so full was her head, so high with hope. *Make it all come true for Jordan and James. The whole beautiful fairy tale, beginning to . . .*

"What does happily ever after mean?" the minister was saying.

Camille tuned in a little closer. Was he reading her idealistic mind? He had an answer for only one rhetorical question: Would they be happy all the time?

"Not if they're human," the minister said with a wistful smile. "As beautiful as they look at this moment, I can almost believe I'm looking at two angels. But I know I'm not. I'm looking at a man and a woman, who are about to make some promises that they will find hard to keep sometimes. Cherishing her today is easy. Cherishing her when she's nine months pregnant during the dog days of summer takes a little more patience."

A few males chuckled considerately.

"And cherishing him when he wants to camp out on the sofa and watch football on the big-screen television set he overdrew the checking account to buy can be a tall order. Especially when you want him to go to your Christmas party."

The courteous laughter was distinctly female.

"You'll say these words easily today. They'll sound very romantic to you, and they are. This day is the dream," he declared with a broad gesture. "It's a beautiful dream. You'll have pictures to remind you, but a picture album won't get you through the difficult times, the for-poorer, in-sickness part. In times like that, the photographs seem to fade. They begin to look like someone else.

"That's why you must keep this dream in a place that's safer than a picture album. You must hold it in your heart. The heart believes, even when the mind forgets. Even when the eyes take in the pictures and the mind says, 'I must have loved her once, but I don't remember now,' even then the heart knows the truth. When the mind says, 'What happened to the man I married?' the heart knows the answer. Keep today's beautiful dream in your heart. Cherish it. You need your dreams to help you build your life together in the real world.

"Today is just the beginning. You have so many days ahead of you. You'll make a home for each other, with each other, in each other. Today you have brought two families together. James becomes part of Jordan's family, and she becomes part of his. In the real world this will present challenges for you, but today you have the dream. You have a wonderful blend of the people you love, a blend of traditions and personalities and cultures. Cherish the dream. Hold both families in your hearts. You bring new faces into the lives of both families today, and today is only the beginning."

Camille risked a peek at Creed, who chose the same moment to take the same risk. Their story had had its own beginning, its own ups and downs in the middle, its sad little end. *Now what?* Here they stood, side by side, dressed to the nines, holding hands, drinking in the happy talk from the knowing side of the cup. Camille smiled. Bittersweet as it might be, the knowing side suddenly tasted like a good thing.

But it was a side, not an end. Straining to hear the vows her daughter meant for her new husband's ears only, Camille flinched at the words "till death do us part." So that was it? That was the moment, the time to write "The End"?

Was that before or after the happily ever after?

Answer me that, preacher man.

Ah, the wedding rings. Camille tipped her head to watch James slide a shiny new gold band onto Jordan's hand. There was no end to a ring. Camille imagined endlessly loving words engraved inside, and she wished blessings on those words, whatever they might be.

After they used their mothers' candles to light the Unity candle, Jordan and James presented long-stemmed sterling roses to their mothers and grandmothers. Jordan looked puzzled when her father left his seat for the song that was listed on the program as a piano instrumental, followed by another of Ellie's solos. Creed had hidden his acoustical guitar in the pulpit. The surprise duet would have brought the house down had the foundation not been made of rock. The harmony Creed and Ellie had discovered in their voices—a little classic country, a little classic gospel—became "The Rose" most cherished, that tenacious autumn bloom.

Following the minister's blessing, James was finally invited to kiss his bride. The congregation of witnesses applauded, and the recessional began. There was no receiving line. James and Jordan dismissed their well-wishers with hugs and kisses, row on row. A few more photographs were taken before the couple strolled merrily through a barrage of bubbles, climbed into their stylish old limousine, and were driven away by the French-Canadian chauffeur with the lovely telephone voice.

"Jacques is definitely a looker in that uniform, Mama."

"I never could resist a man in uniform," Rosemary agreed. "Now that they're married, there's no call for a chaperon, is there?"

"I'm afraid not." Camille slipped her arm around her mother's shoulders. "But we haven't seen the last of him."

"No, we haven't, but he's going to drive them around the lake, play some music for them, give them some time alone," Rosemary informed her. This was Grandma's gift, her part of the plan. "I understand there's a scheme in the works for the groomsmen to steal the bride, but the groom gets her back."

"I should hope so," Camille said with a laugh. "Meanwhile, let's go open the bar and greet our guests."

Creed shoved his hands in his pants pockets and jangled his keys. "You need a ride, or were you going to call the bakery for your chauffeur?"

"What kind of vehicle do you have to offer?"

"Same old pickup."

Camille stopped in her tracks and stared with mock horror. "You took your daughter to her wedding in a pickup?"

"It's clean. I even covered the seats with brand-new white sheets."

"Tied down with satin ribbon," Rosemary put in.

"Let's see," Camille deliberated theatrically. "New bakery truck, young driver, or old pickup truck with . . ." She linked her arm with Creed's. "I think I'll stick with the vintage theme."

"Then let's party."

Chapter 20

$\mathcal{I}$n their cobalt blue motor carriage, the bride and groom arrived at the Countryside Inn an hour and a half later under a warm, cerulean sky. They were attended to by their dutiful chauffeur, welcomed with even warmer applause, and showered by their guests once again with breezy bubbles.

"Sorry we're late, but the car broke down," James shouted, grinning.

"Yeah, yeah."

"Likely story!"

"And we ran into bandits, but James fought them off," Jordan claimed. Camille would have attributed the fresh bloom in Jordan's cheeks to the adventure had she not added, "And exacted a tribute of champagne."

Jordan and James posed for more pictures.

She had turned her veil into a gossamer wrap, leaving the pearl and crystal ornament her father had given her to adorn her smooth, sleek coif. They got Rosemary into the act with Jacques the chauffeur and his grand old car.

The time had come to eat, drink, and be merry, with much toasting to be done and many cheeks to be pressed. Jordan and James seemed to float an inch above the floor, gliding amid twinkling lights and glowing candles. All that radiance was redoubled by the banquet room's huge windows and the mirror tiles on all the tables, which were scattered with rose petals and foil-wrapped chocolate coins. Surrounded by votives, a single rose floated in a crystal brandy snifter on each table. There were favors of bulbs that would bring purple tulips to the springtime yards of family and friends. There were traditional candy-coated Jordan almonds—an ancient symbol of fertility—serving as eggs in tiny birds' nests. There were wisps of tulle and tall bunches of curly willow, blossoms and butterflies and beauty everywhere. With the help of many hands, Camille had created an ethereal fairy garden, where guests mingled with drinks in their hands and the glow of soft light on cheerful faces.

It was a dream come true.

The wedding she'd never had? Perhaps, she thought. And since the creative aspect of dreaming was the part that appealed to Camille the most, this was the perfect way to experience the wedding she'd never had—as the mother of the bride. Like the glass surrounding myriad flickering bits of light, the happiness in Jordan's eyes magnified Camille's own joy. She hoped the wedding, in all its glorious excess, exceeded Jordan's dreams, but she suspected that it would take some time for the day and all its details to sink in.

There would be no shortage of pictures, what with the still photographer and the videographer and the single-use cameras that had been scattered about the tables for the guests to use. There would be plenty of recorded memories, along with the place in the heart to which the minister had eloquently referred. Jordan and her husband would relive the day in quiet times, and it would take on new luster. Some dreams had a way of improving with age, with retelling and remembrance.

The toasts came fast and furious, full of both playful and wistful reminiscence, followed by a lovefest of introductions, recognitions, and expressions of appreciation. The fest continued with a feast on food selected but hardly touched by the bride and groom, whose eyes were mainly content to feast on each other's faces. Seated up front and framed by garden lattice, lights, and flowers, they made a loving picture, a royal centerpiece.

"Where's Mama?" Camille asked Creed when she crossed his path in their separate rounds-making.

He had started to scan the room when Ramona spoke up from her seat at a nearby table. "She went to lie down for a few minutes," she reported on the tail end of a sip of wine. "She said she'll be back out shortly and not to worry. Of course, I'm a little worried, but it's no good telling her that. She'll just laugh it off."

"She's going to miss—"

"She'll see it on the video," Creed said. "She's had a big day."

"I'll check on her later. We'll do the cake now, and then you're on, Mr. Lonely."

"Am I allowed to change my clothes? This getup doesn't look much like Only the Lonely."

"Being the only father she has, lonely or not, you'll have your dance with the bride in this getup." She smoothed his satin lapel. "After that, maybe you can shed a layer."

The cake cutting began with the bridesmaids' charm pull. The four young women pulled ribbons tied to silver charms, which had been buried under the cake. Amy's tiny wedding bells foretold that she would be the next bride, while a ship's wheel meant travel and adventure in Beth's future. A crown forecast power for Lauren. But all the girls shrieked when Kelly found a baby carriage at the end of her ribbon.

Jordan reached for the heirloom cake knife, festooned with ribbon. Camille immediately glanced toward the door, hoping in vain for her mother's appearance. Plenty of pictures were snapped as the bride and groom fed each other from the first piece. *Worth a thousand words,* Camille thought, or one firsthand glimpse.

But this was not a night for regrets. Each sterling moment was to be savored as it ticked by. The servers made short work of the lovely wedding cake while the wedding party moved on to the groom's cake, which was decorated in honor of James's love of fishing. Because it was chocolate, the children quickly put in their bids for "fish cake" as James doled out the toy buckets full of candy worms to nieces and nephews and the children of close friends. He cut the first pieces of chocolate cake for his groomsmen after their mock charm pull garnered them an assortment of fishing lures.

With Bridget supervising at the groom's-cake table, Camille took the opportunity to slip away, hurry down the hall, and sneak into the suite. There was a light on in the living room, but the bedroom was dark. She would just take a peek.

The bed was empty, as was the bathroom. Assuming she had

failed to notice Rosemary's return to the party, Camille checked a few more places on her own way back—the ladies' room, the small anteroom they'd set up for the gift table and conversation area. She finally went outside into the small courtyard, where a few smokers were having their cigarettes and enjoying the unseasonably balmy night air. Camille exchanged pleasantries, promised someone a dance, noticed that the banquet room was just as lovely from the outside looking in. She could see Jordan and James speaking with Jordan's Uncle Matt and Creed's Aunt Patsy. Ramona's nephew was offering her one of his candy worms. Two of the groomsmen were refreshing their beer. Creed was testing the microphone.

"You've done a beautiful job, Cam."

Camille turned to find Bridget sitting at a patio table with Ellie and Stan. A glass bowl filled with floating candles illuminated her friends' faces.

"We have, haven't we?" she said happily. She perched on the front edge of a patio chair. "It's been the ultimate labor of love. How was the cake?"

"Delicious. I have to say, it was every bit as good as the one we had from Barnett's, and it was certainly elegant."

"Jordan is so lovely," Ellie said. "That dress is incredible."

"Mama outdid herself. It meant so much to her to be able to make Jordan's wedding dress. Speaking of which, have you seen her anywhere lately?"

"Rosemary?"

"Didn't she tell Ramona she needed a rest?" Bridget recalled.

"She's not in the room. I wonder whether she got someone to take her home." She touched Bridget's jewel-bedecked hand. "How's it going with Tim?"

"I'm not *with* Timothy anymore. But we've been civil, I think. Haven't we, Ellie?"

"You've been the model of civility, Bridge." Ellie peered through the windows. "It looks as though we're getting ready for the first dance."

Creed had taken center stage. His band looked a little cramped in their corner of the room, but they had surely played in tighter quarters.

"My daughter, Jordie, and my son, James," he began, deferring to the couple with a gesture. Then he grinned. "I can't believe I have a son. And he came complete with his own car."

The wedding guests–turned–audience laughed as Creed fished in his breast pocket.

"You gave me a list of choices for the first dance. 'The Way You Look Tonight,'" he ticked off first, reading from a piece of paper before glancing apologetically at his daughter. "I can't do it, honey. I tried. I even put the tux on and tried again. 'Some Enchanted Evening'? Honey, your dad's lungs just aren't that big."

"Don't disillusion me now, Daddy."

"So then I went through the band's repertoire, and I kicked out one song after another. 'We Don't Need the Booze to Get a Buzz On' just doesn't cut it. 'Easy Come, Easy Go'?" He looked at James. "Not if you value your hide, son. 'Two of a Kind, Workin' on a Full House'? We'll see. That one's a little too jaunty. We'll do that later.

"But I found this one on a Willie Nelson tape, and I figured if Willie could sing it, Creed could sing it. Let's see if that's true. 'To Each His Own,'" he told the band, "for Jordie and James."

It was better than true. The newlyweds glided across the floor in a world of their own as family and friends smiled and sighed and exchanged candlelit, dreamy-eyed glances. At the end of the first song, Creed allowed time for a kiss and applause before he tapped James on his shoulder and asked whether the ol' man might cut in. He sang "Daddy's Little Girl" while he danced with his daughter.

For the first time that day, Camille found herself dabbing at the corners of her eyes with her mother-of-the-bride lace hankie.

Creed escorted Jordan back to her new husband as he swung into the first verse of "I Just Want to Dance with You." The band kept playing while he announced, "Now Jordan's dad is gonna dance with Jordan's mom." He stretched his hand out to Camille. She took it, and he folded her in his arms. He sang to her while they danced. At the end she hugged him. He leaned close, for her ear only, and whispered, "And then some."

"Now, wait a minute, you two," Ellie said into the microphone she'd just snatched from Creed while he was concentrating on other things. "If you think that's your last dance, think again. I've been practicing this next song for weeks. This one's for the whole wedding party." She signaled the band for the introductory bars of "Someday Soon," and everyone who was "of an age" applauded. The dance floor was soon full of pump-handle "slow" dancers.

Creed put on the best show of his life. He'd assembled a playlist of country rock and old favorites, but for tonight there would be no "lyin', cheatin', hurtin', or dyin' songs." Between verses he danced with his sister, his Aunt Patsy, Bridget, even Ramona. More than once he tested Camille with a tempting glance, but she wasn't one for coming forward without a proper invitation. Besides, she had to see to her guests.

And she had to find her mother. No one had seen Rosemary leave the hotel or heard of anyone giving her a lift anywhere. Once again Camille headed for the suite. To her surprise, a man dressed completely in black was just letting himself out the door.

Camille froze right there in the corridor, watching the man pull the door shut with exaggerated care. *Scream for help,* she told herself, but she recognized the man in time and turned the scream into a shout.

"Driver!" The man turned, just as surprised as she was. She felt chagrined. *Driver,* for heaven's sake. "I mean, Jacques."

"It's really Jack. I just—" He gestured, openhanded, equally embarrassed.

"That's my room," Camille snapped. "My mother . . ."

"I just took her for a ride."

"You mean, in your car."

Of course, in his car, dummy.

"Yeah, in the Packard." He appeared to study the number on the door, as though marveling at an art form. "She's worn out, poor soul. Amazing woman, your mom. She was telling me what a fine time it's been."

"The wedding?"

"Well, that's been the cherry on top of it all, hasn't it? Lovely couple, those two. Your mom was telling me how nicely everything came together." He touched the brim of his black cap. "I'll let you go in and say good night to her now. She's very, very tired."

"Thank you," Camille said quietly. "Good night, Jam—uh, Jacques." The son-in-law was James; the chauffeur was Jacques. She felt silly, giddy, downright weird to lay claim to a son-in-law and a chauffeur. But she was reassured that the latter was there to deliver her mother, not—as she had thought for one terrifying second—to take her away.

She let herself into the dimly lit room, relieved to find her mother stretched out on the sofa, shoes off, feet up, pillows behind her back. She was sipping on something in a plastic cup.

"Mama?"

Rosemary answered with a weary smile as Camille approached.

"I was worried. You slipped away without saying a word."

"I told you Jacques offered me a drive around the lake." Smiling as though she had a secret, Rosemary smoothed her watercolor chiffon skirt over her legs.

"You didn't say you were going during the reception." Camille lifted her mother's support-hose-clad feet and sat on the sofa, placing Mama's heels in her lap. She wondered what kind of perfume Rosemary was wearing. It smelled sweet and prairie-ish. Eau de Alfalfa?

"I thought I did," Rosemary said languorously. "I thought about taking Ramona along, but I decided to keep him to myself."

"It was quite shocking, let me tell you, catching a man stealing away from my mother's bedroom." She began massaging the stiff toes, the fallen arches, the callused balls of the feet.

"Ah-ah-ah," Rosemary groaned, at once agonized and ecstatic. "Aah, foot massage. One of life's very good things."

"You missed—"

"Don't tell me." A prohibitive gesture disallowed regrets. "I'll see it when it comes out on video. There was so much excitement, so many people. This is the part I leave to you."

"How are you feeling, Mama?"

"Happy," Rosemary said, closing her eyes as she tipped her head back. Her fair fell away from her face almost naturally, but Camille could see the elastic cap that held it in place.

"Any pain?"

"You're driving all that away, Cammy." She opened her eyes, smiling. "You and the drugs."

"What drugs? Or should I say, which drugs?"

"I just smoked my very first joint."

And, oh, what a self-satisfied smile mother gave daughter. They shared that look for a long moment. Camille's head ran the gamut of responses. She was genuinely shocked, then terrified, then torn with utter sadness, then pasted back together by the peace her mother shared through her eyes just as surely as Jordan's had shared joy.

And then they laughed. They giggled like two artless girls getting into the New Year's champagne. They hooted like two teenagers paging through forbidden magazines. The laughter was stronger on one side than it was on the other, but it was merry, at least for a moment, before it bubbled down to a soft fizz.

"I finished Jordie's wedding dress," Rosemary said with swelling pleasure. "I knew I could do it."

"It's the most beautiful dress I've ever seen, Mama."

"That makes three of us," Rosemary whispered. "If it suits three generations, it must be nearly timeless."

"Oh, yes." Camille kneaded both feet furiously, trying to get something going, transfer more life, more energy. "Time stands still on a day like this. It must be a woman's version of one for all and all for one."

She would not have answered the knock on the door at that moment, but she had a feeling it was Creed. "She's here," Camille told him happily as she gestured to invite him in.

"Is she okay?"

He had shed his jacket and tie, unbuttoned the vest, rolled his white sleeves midway between wrist and elbow, and opened his collar. All he needed was his black cowboy hat and he'd be dressed to sing "The Gambler."

"She's frisky enough to be running around the lake with the chauffeur. Right, Mama?"

"Damn straight," Rosemary said, cheerfully echoing one of Creed's expressions. "But I'm going to have to renege on our dance, Creed. I'm all done for the night."

"Been rode hard and put up wet, have you?" He took a seat in the chair across from her. "Old cars and older halfbreeds, they'll do it every time."

"Is that a fact? Why am I just finding that out now?" She laughed.

"Tell him the rest, Mama." Camille couldn't wait for Rosemary to stop giggling. "Mama's been smoking grass. Can you believe it?"

Creed grinned. "I thought I smelled a private party goin' on in here."

"Not me," Camille said, hands up in all innocence. "I wasn't invited."

"You've never touched the stuff," Rosemary said.

"How would you know that, Mama?"

"I know you." She giggled again. "I beat you to it. I tried pot before my daughter did."

"I know her, too, and you're right, Rosie." Creed reached across the arm of his chair and took her hand. "Did it help?"

She nodded, still smiling. "Why aren't you out there singing?"

"The band's taking a little break."

"Cammy, you go see to your guests." She looked up at Creed and pointed to the bedroom door. "I need a little help getting from here to there."

"Do you need help getting undressed, Mama?"

"If I do, I'm way past being shy about asking."

"She's turned into a veritable hussy." Camille slid Rosemary's feet off her lap, onto the floor.

"It's wedding fever," Rosemary said, smiling as Camille pulled her upright. "Careful. I hear it's contagious."

Creed started to help her to her feet, but when she slid her arm around his neck, he whisked her into his arms. "I'll bet that Canuck couldn't do this," he teased.

"That's for me to know," Rosemary said.

Camille started toward the door, but she stopped when she heard Creed softly singing "I Just Want to Dance with You" back there in the dark bedroom. It would be a few moments before she'd be able to see her guests.

Chapter 21

"Mom, where's Grandma? I heard she was MIA," Jordan sang out.

Curses. Caught crying in the corridor. Camille drew a deep breath as she looked for the will to smile and a way to secrete her damp hankie. *Up your sleeve*, she thought. *Up yours, the old lady's way*. Ah, there was the smile.

And here was the bride, not quite fooled. She touched her mother's arm, and the damn hankie dropped to the floor.

Weepy laughter bubbled in Camille's throat as she recalled the last time she'd had a use for cloth handkerchiefs. Her La Leche League breast-feeding manual had advised stuffing them into her nursing bra to absorb leaking milk. It was impossible to fold those huge men's cotton handkerchiefs into a natural-looking breast shape. She'd had square breasts for a year, stuffed with damp hankies.

Not *damn* hankies. Precious hankies. Without hers, she was forced to use the tear-wiping side of her forefinger.

"What's wrong, Mama?" Jordan's wedding gown puddled around her feet as she stooped to recover the lacy white handkerchief. "You're not crying, are you?"

Camile shook her head quickly. "Happy tears."

"Did you find her? Is she okay?"

Another deep breath, and Camille was steady. *Steady as she goes.* "She just went to bed, a tired but very happy camper."

"Is she asleep yet? I want to say good night."

Camille nodded as she took the key card from her skirt pocket and slid it into the lock. She touched her finger to her lips and led the way far enough inside so that Jordan could hear the last few bars of Creed's song coming from the bedroom. But for a sliver of light beaming from the bathroom for navigation, the suite was dark.

Jordan turned to her mother, eyes wide, fingertips pressed to her own lips. "Dad's in there?" she mouthed, and Camille nodded, eyes welling up again.

Jordan gave Camille's arm a quick squeeze as she turned and headed for the back room, the soft swish of her dress announcing her visit. "I came to say good night, Grandma."

Camille braced her back against the wall and listened to the murmur of words like "most beautiful bride" and "most beautiful grandmother," with thanks pouring out on both sides as Jordan and Creed exchanged stations. He came to Camille in the dark, peeled her off the wall, held her tight in his arms.

"Don't let me . . ."

She didn't have to specify. He tucked her under his protective arm, swept her down the hall to his room, and scooted her through the door to privacy.

"I'll be okay in just a minute," she said unsteadily. He touched her shoulder. She turned to him, and they held each other and wept together in the dark.

"We're a fine pair," she said finally, taking his face in her hands, wiping tears with her thumbs. "Sometimes."

"We've done all right lately." His beautiful voice was tight and hoarse.

"Well, what are we going to do now? You're supposed to be singing, and I'm supposed to do whatever it is a mother of the bride does at the end of the night, which isn't supposed to be this."

"What?"

"Hiding in a dark room crying, for heaven's sake."

"Mark it on the calendar. Camille Delonga did something she wasn't supposed to do." He touched her hair. "Every once in a while someone calls you Mrs. Burke." She nodded. "You don't always correct them."

"I gave up for the time being. The time being the occasion of our daughter's wedding. We're the mother and the father of the bride. We only get to wear those titles once."

"That's right," he said, his voice soft with affection. "But I'm just wondering, how do you feel when someone calls you Mrs. Burke?"

"I know who they're talking to," she said, trying to sound matter-of-fact. But it would have been a rude tone if she could have pulled it off, and an unfair response to a fair question. "I mean . . . after all this time, it still feels natural to sort of . . ." She needed another deep breath. "Answer to that name, I guess. It's part of my life that hasn't really . . ."

"Gone away?"

"The feelings . . ." Handfuls of his sleeves at once allowed her to perch on his arms and hold a forearm's measure of space between her body and his. "Oh, Creed, this is high tide for the ocean of our . . . emotional life." She gave a quick laugh. "Did I really say that?"

"I'm gonna be singin' it next week. We've got an ocean of emotion, and baby it's hiiigh tide," he sang as he pulled her into his harbor.

"Oh, Creed." It felt so good to sink against him, just for a moment. But a moment was all she would allow. "We've got to get back to the party."

"Yes, we do. This is a hell of a party, hon. You done good."

"You, too."

She lifted her face to receive his open-mouthed kiss and to give him hers. Then, arm in arm, they returned to their daughter's wedding reception.

The band was dutifully entertaining with instrumental music as Creed made his way back to the dance floor for one more set for the young diehards. By the grace of flattering candlelight, no one seemed to notice that Camille had washed away most of her mascara. While the bride and groom strolled among their guests in the courtyard and put their feet up in the gift room for a nightcap with their wedding party, Camille bade good night to departing friends and family. Some would attend the gift opening at Bridget's house the next day. Others drifted off to their hotel rooms or their homes with yawning faces and smiling hearts. There could be no drawback, no disparagement of a celebration of love and marriage. Not this night.

Camille told herself that she didn't want to awaken her mother. Bridget had gone home to prepare for the gift-opening brunch, and Ellie had retired to a room in the hotel with her husband, Stan. Camille decided to make the short drive home. She would sleep in her own bed.

When she emerged from the bathroom in her nightgown, she found Creed standing in the bedroom doorway, backlit by the hall light. It might have been a fantasy, but real or imagined, it was unquestionably some form of Creed Burke.

"Your mother let me in," he teased.

"You let yourself in."

"You left the door open."

"I would never take that kind of a risk."

"Why make that claim when you know it isn't true?"

She proved his point by meeting him halfway, in the middle of the bedroom they'd shared years ago.

"I asked your mother about that sermon, about the meaning of happily ever after and what she thought it meant to you."

"What did she say?"

"She said she didn't think you had decided yet. Your story's not over yet, and you've never loved anyone but me. Either you're going to carry a torch for me until the grave finally puts out the fire, or you're going to give me another chance." He laid his hands on her bare shoulders. "Which sounds better to you?"

"I only get two choices?"

"That's it. It's more than a lot of people get. Me, for instance."

"How so?"

"I have to go with what you decide."

"That would be a first."

"Well, according to Indian tradition, the home and all its contents belong to the woman. All the guy can claim are his weapons and his horse."

"His guitar and his pickup," she said, laughing as she slid her arms around him. "There's been no one else, Creed. I can't keep that a secret, since even my mother has succumbed to your charms and become your ally. But what about you? How many women have you loved since me?"

"None," he said, taking her head in his hands and sliding his fingers into her hair. "None before and none since."

"I asked the wrong question."

"You asked the one that matters. You don't wanna ask whether I've had sex since we split twelve years ago, and I'm not gonna talk about it."

"What about before we split?"

"That was a long time ago. Is that what you want to talk about now?"

"No."

"I love you like crazy, Camille. I don't know what to do about it except come to you and tell you how I feel." His eyes plumbed the depth of hers. "And ask you to tell me straight out how you feel about me."

"You're the only man I've ever loved, Creed. But you know that. We had no trouble with the loving. It was the living together that caused us so many problems."

"Let's go back to the loving, then. Can we start there?" He caressed her shoulders, slipped a finger under one nightgown strap and pushed it over the edge until the gown drooped on one side.

Like her aging boob, she thought. But she was not inclined to cover it up. Not now.

"I love you like crazy, Camille. Let me love you now."

"We had a wedding today, didn't we?"

"That we did," he said, backing her toward the bed. "A fine, fine wedding."

"What comes after the wedding for the mother of the bride?"

He grinned when she started unbuttoning his shirt. They had decided to find out together.